CROSSING MAGDALEN BRIDGE

Michael Tanner was born and educated in Oxford. He was a schoolmaster for 18 years prior to becoming a critically acclaimed and award -nominated author specializing in sport and history. Besides contributing features across the print media, he has been involved with radio and television at both local and national level. *Crossing Magdalen Bridge* is the fourth novel among his 31 titles.

Other Novels by the Author

The Tinman's Farewell

The Black Bridge

Red Hand

CROSSING MAGDALEN BRIDGE

In memory of Peter Newsam who lit the way

CROSSING MAGDALEN BRIDGE

A Story of Town and Gown

Michael Tanner

Contents

PART ONE

Mounting the High Wire

One

Mick Bernard stared straight ahead as implacably as an Easter Island statue.

Much as he'd love to have shared the imposing mien of those giant megaliths, Mick considered his appearance utterly nondescript. His nose was too fleshy, his lips too full, his skin, like that of many an 18-year-old youth, too unreliable, and his brown eyes too narrow. His saving grace was a shock of wavy dark brown hair, much admired by ladies of a certain age, which paid homage to the long cavalier ringlets of infancy captured in a photograph sitting on the sideboard back home. His natural expression, though lively and alert, seldom showed itself: he had the power of making his face look dull and so disinterested that people either failed to notice him or concluded he was too aloof to bother with. However, since an extended holiday romance he'd paid more attention to his dress and personal hygiene. At last appreciating his headmaster's maxim that 'the hallmarks of a gentleman are hair, nails and shoes', he began ensuring they were shampooed and manicured and polished on a regular basis. One aspect of his appearance of which he was proud was an athletic build that served to answer his every call on the rugby pitch.

'Still time to change y'mind an' come home,' said his driver behind a half-hearted grin. The amateurish attempt to lighten the mood at a pivotal moment in the lives of both father and son failed to disguise the fact Roy Bernard meant every word. But on this dank October afternoon a sullen Mick Bernard paid no attention. His mind was made up long ago.

Mick knew their route backwards: he'd travelled down the Iffley Road and into Oxford more times than he cared to remember. Past the Oxford University rugby ground where he'd watched the Dark Blues play at every opportunity; past the running track on the other side of the hedge where Roger Bannister was the first man to run a mile in under four minutes; past Magdalen College School where the sight of its pupils sporting their black blazers with the red piping had once sparked his desire to become one of their number. Ahead lay the Plain where Oxford's three eastern arteries, St Clements, Cowley Road and Iffley Road, coalesced to pass over Magdalen Bridge.

This was frontier territory; Oxford's Khyber Pass. And although crossing the Cherwell did not invoke the finality of the Styx, Magdalen Bridge spanning it marked the border between 'Town' and 'Gown' – which, in local street-lore, made crossing it pretty close to an ancient Greek's last journey. However, in Mick's estimation this journey felt more like Caesar's crossing of the Rubicon: once done the die was cast. There was no turning back.

Town, he knew, was senior to Gown. The Saxon burgh predated the University by five centuries and frequently set about proving who was top dog. He'd read about the riots that erupted in 1355 on the Feast of St Scholastica: a tavern brawl escalated into a full-scale street fight that resulted in 63 students crossing their personal Styx; there were free-for-alls even as late as the tail end of the 19th century. By this date fortunes had changed: the University had grown rich and powerful while the town and its citizens were in decline. But once the car factories offered remunerative employment in the first quarter of the 20th century and began attracting workers from further afield to swell the suburbs a third society had emerged to stir the pot: a council estate underclass.

In consequence Magdalen Bridge had long become symbolic for residents of East Oxford's most concrete and cultural desert comprised of half a dozen council estates because it was hereabouts the fug from their chimneys and Cowley's car factories, once dubbed 'motopolis' and workplace to many of Mick's relations besides his own prescribed destiny, gave way to the pristine stone and ivy-creepered colleges of the University that they'd been raised to distrust and despise. But Mick had endured a school visit to 'motopolis'. Its message was stark: that way madness lay. A blue-collar job 'on the line' or a white-collar one in the offices amounted to life in a straightjacket. Mick was not travelling far from the nest as the crow flies but as an eaglet soaring to new heights and new experiences.

Roy Bernard seldom drove his 10-year-old green Austin Cambridge faster than 30mph but it would still take just 10 minutes at this time of a Thursday to reach the city from their house on the Hill Rise estate that held the unwanted label of Oxford's roughest. Mick could bike it in not much more, and after a night necking Harp lager in the Turf Tavern with his mates, he'd even walked it like a sozzled crab in half an hour.

'This is a first for me, you know,' said Roy. 'I haven't ever driven over Magdalen Bridge.'

Mick cringed. He could decipher exactly what his father had said but the sounds issuing from Roy's mouth were more like *Oi ent never driven over Mag'len Bridge*. Mick's 'Orks-ferd' tongue was not the one he wished his College to hear. He found Oxfordshire's rustic voice full of dropped aitches and pronouncing such as 'want' as 'wornt' and 'like' as 'loik' utterly abhorrent. He loathed it because it suggested the speaker was a simpleton, a dimwit. And he loathed it because he knew he spoke in exactly the same peculiar dialect if he didn't take the utmost care - which he'd spent the last 12 months trying to do. All the Bernard clan spoke like this: aunts, uncles, cousins, grandparents; as did his mother Edna and her family, the Jaykes. It wasn't until he started at South Oxford Grammar School and began mixing with pupils from beyond the estates that he realized the accents, diction and grammar adopted in highbrow television programmes were not confined to the aristocracy. Even his surname was an embarrassment. He knew of no famous Bernard, no politician or sportsman of renown. His was a name ordinary: suburban or rustic, it shrieked underclass. He couldn't afford to drop his guard in College otherwise he risked becoming a laughing stock. Watching the Cherwell disappearing beneath Magdalen Bridge reminded him he was about to jump without a safety net.

'You must've?' he answered eventually.

'Can't remember last time I was even in the town. Get anythin' I need from the new shops in the Cowley Centre.'

'You don't say.'

Roy rolled his Woodbine into the corner of his mouth. 'My visits to town are as rare as teddy bear crap.'

Mick stifled a chuckle. Whatever his shortcomings, his father did have the comic touch, albeit sometimes nudging coarseness. And on the rare occasions he chose to unlock it, Mick was similarly blessed. Roy's quirky taste in humour was epitomized in his love of a joke told by droll Scots comedian Chic Murray about a drunk seen repeatedly throwing himself into the gutter who, when asked what on earth was he doing, replied 'I've a bar of chocolate in my back pocket and I need to break it!'

Roy veered toward the centre of the High Street as St. Frideswide's College approached on the right. He noticed a line of gleaming parked Jaguars, Zephyrs and Zodiacs that would've done justice to one of the upmarket car showrooms on the Banbury Road but managed to bump the Austin up onto the kerb and grab a space close to the College entrance. Their arrival triggered no words. Father and son seldom conversed more than was necessary nowadays: communication was strictly functional; proffering advice was 'as rare as teddy bear crap.'

They got out of the car and went round to the boot that contained Mick's trunk, acquired second-hand for today's purpose. Roy hauled the trunk onto the pavement. The boot's interior was spotlessly clean. As was the whole car; its bodywork sparkled like an emerald on wheels. No driver of Royal Army Service Corps vintage would allow his vehicle to be anything other than spick-and-span; every Sunday, without fail, the bonnet was raised for Roy, rag in hand, to engage in five minutes of meticulous work that removed every speck of grime from the engine, leaving the rocker cover as green and shiny as the day it came off the production line. After much pestering from his son Roy had reluctantly consented to giving him a driving lesson. But 20 minutes around disused roads adjacent to the Sandy Lane home of speedway and greyhound racing with Mick behind the wheel was more than enough for Roy to stomach as his precious Austin was brutalized. After gears crunched and the car jumped along like an angry kangaroo he halted the lesson: 'Those gears ent got no teeth left! Move over! I'm drivin' now.' There would be no more lessons.

Roy proceeded to sweep back into place the errant lock of hair that had defeated its Brylcreem and slid down over his brow. He'd passed on his wavy dark brown hair, medium height and build to his son, though his muscles were waning while his son's waxed; but his swarthier skin, suggestive of his grandmother's antecedence - Gypsy Sarah they called her - he'd kept to himself. He raised the trunk into the perpendicular and leant on it, the ever-present Woodbine cupped inside the palm of one hand, while his only child went into the Porter's Lodge to discover the location of his room from the College List pinned to the notice board. He watched another son and father, and even one father, mother and son, undertaking the same chore of unloading, carrying and enquiring. They smiled sheepishly at him and he risked similar in return. 'Staircase VIII, off the Back Quad', Mick said matter-of-factly on returning. Roy took one last drag before dropping his dog-end on the ground and stubbing it out under the sole of his shoe.

The Front Quad welcoming them was everything Mick envisaged the inside of Oxford colleges looked like. He'd cycled and walked past a great many of them but St. Frideswide's was the only one he'd briefly explored and was seen to involve inhabitants; it was a living, breathing, entity and not just the stone monument it appeared from the outside. Mick felt he'd been given the password to an exclusive club, entry by invitation only and strictly off limits to hawkers, pedlars and nosey-parkers. Admittedly St. Frideswide's was a college in miniature: the Front Quad was on the small side, nowhere near the grandeur of Christ Church's for example. Currently it seemed all the smaller, the abnormal traffic converting it into a makeshift roundabout by the adoption of a one-way system that prevented incoming trunks colliding with departing parents. Yet the postage stamp of grass with its picturesque well in the centre and a magnolia tree in one corner was, he decided, a composition hard to better. The buildings defining the Quad represented an architectural history of the College. The oldest range contained the Junior Common Room and the Buttery, its bar and social heart, and its tall chimney shaft a reminder of St. Frideswide's medieval foundation. At opposite ends of the Quad were Dining Hall and Chapel of 17th century origin. Buildings of more recent age completed the rectangle. Mick admired the Chapel's façade but nursed no conviction to frequent its interior. He'd once gone into a church in search of God's guidance but left on finding God wasn't there. He was eager, however, to sample everything on offer in the Buttery.

The homeliness of the Front Quad made the lunar landscape of the Back Quad all the harder for Mick to bear. There was no Back Quad – which rendered St. Frideswide's even smaller than usual. All that met his eye was a huge crater where the Back Quad had stood. The buildings had been demolished during the summer vacation in readiness for the construction of a new block containing Dining Hall, changing rooms and modern undergraduate accommodation. Access to Mick's room on Staircase VIII involved traversing a plank bridge over a series of water-filled holes that did justice to anything the Lake District could muster.

Mick's room lay on the third floor. The Staircase reverberated to the noise of over-excited teenagers, loud radios and the thump of trunks bouncing off step after step; his own added to the hubbub amid whirling dust devils thrown up from the bare boards. He entered his new home and conducted a brief survey: a bed; a wardrobe; a desk; a bookcase; two chairs either side of a wall-mounted electric fire; and a coffee table dotted with cup rings, cigarette burns and well scuffed edges indicative of many pairs of shoes. Grey distempered walls occasionally pocked by pin holes and remnants of sticky tape that once, Mick surmised, must've secured the pin-ups of previous occupants. He went to the window; the panes had dirty corners and the sill was a graveyard to a squadron of flies; on the plus side it offered a fine view of The High and the vast Victorian edifice that was the Examination Schools. The disturbing prospect of sitting Prelims in there at the end of Hilary Term redirected his gaze toward the Eastgate Hotel next door. Some pubs were owned by colleges: Wadham owned the King's Arms on the corner of Holywell Street; Lincoln owned the Mitre in Turl Street. St. Frideswide's didn't own the Eastgate

Hotel but Mick would soon learn its students contributed mightily to its profits. Something else suddenly struck him: his room possessed neither sink nor lavatory. Ablutions were to be undertaken in the ground floor washroom.

He hoped his sigh went undetected by his father. This was not the University of *Zuleika Dobson*, the only tale of Oxford life he'd read. The reality of his new abode hit him like a slamming door. This room spoke to him of anonymity. It was soulless. Yet it had a history. It had witnessed the hurly-burly of student life despite being as impersonal as a shoddy hostel. It was ill-suited for tea and crumpets or a sherry party. It was the kind of domicile he imagined enduring had he left school for a dreary job at Cowley as his parents had envisaged. But whatever its drawbacks and imperfections it offered him the opportunity for rebirth. And it was his. His alone. That elevated the room to something special.

Just as well Mick couldn't read his father's mind at that moment because it whirled with negativity. The possibility of Roy airing an opinion on his son's new quarters, however, was as unlikely as finding a virgin in a bordello. His keen eye had detected the dead flies and the spider busy in one of the corners above the window. But as a veteran of World War II he'd spent many a night in worse billets than this while chasing the Germans out of Italy. If these grim four walls weren't exactly what he'd expected for his son, who had worked so relentlessly to earn them, he wasn't about to say so.

'Where d'you wornt this?' he confined himself to saying.

'Just leave it there. I'll sort it later.'

'I'll be orf then.'

'Okay.'

There was no handshake for good luck, no manly hug or paternal kiss on the cheek. This wasn't the Anglo-Saxon way and most definitely not the Bernard way. Mick had no memory of a hug or kiss from either Roy or Edna. But his father must've kissed him once. Mick frequently suffered from painful cold sores on his lips which, he discovered from Dr Sherry, derived from the *herpes simplex* virus that is transmitted by contact and lies dormant until activated by the body becoming run-down in some way. Roy also suffered from cold sores; but not Edna.

Roy's hand reached for the door handle. 'Just one thing,' he said with the timidity of a father who lately had felt incapable of advising his son. 'Remember. Try, try an' try again. But if it dunt work give up! No point bein' a silly bugger!'

Neither man risked so much as a grin. Stretching the emotional boundaries at this stage would cause a scene. Yet Roy Bernard admired his son for the dogged pursuit of dreams that he regretted he lacked himself. But he just couldn't tell him. Bearing the soul was as bad as hugging. And he knew he'd make a mess of it if he tried. He spoke in short, wooden sentences. Attempting to express anything complex would likely end up with him bamboozling himself and his son. And, in any case, he didn't want a lot of praise going to Mick's head: he and Edna had received enough ridicule when they'd made too much of him passing the 11-plus; and then playing for the County Schools. References to him going to Oxford University were viewed even worse, as unforgiveable bragging. Being associated with the University in any form was frowned upon; even the Bernard who worked at Merton as a 'scout' was derided behind his back. Roy freely admitted he was in awe of Mick, for his academic success and his sporting success, which, he accepted, was not necessarily a good state for either of them. He did, however, so wish Mick was a better footballer than rugby player, though his son's growing profile in local sporting circles was still useful currency in the Wellington Arms once a few pints of Morrell's finest had loosened his tongue. Roy reached for a

Woodbine as he walked briskly through the Front Quad, head down and shoulders hunched. He had no desire to stay in this foreign country one more second than necessary. He'd had enough of them during the war.

Mick set about unpacking. He opened the wardrobe. Inside he placed a new grey suit from Burton's in Queen Street. Once equipped with white bow tie, mortar board and short black gown of a 'commoner' (as opposed to the long black gown of a 'scholar') that he'd been advised to purchase second hand from his scout, the College servant who looked after his room, this comprised the undergraduate uniform known as *subfusc* to be worn on all University occasions such as examinations, matriculation and graduation. The rest of Mick's 'wardrobe' comprised his grey winter overcoat, a blue anorak, one pair of trousers and a pair of jeans; two pullovers; a couple of casual shirts and sets of underwear (in the light blue currently all the rage) and half a dozen pairs of socks - plus what he stood up in. He decided the wardrobe's sparse contents looked as lonely as he felt

Mick did possess a blue double-breasted blazer his mother had dressed him in for a family birthday party but he hated being reduced to a mannequin. Edna Bernard was displeased by her son's ingratitude but however much it got under her skin she was used to it. It would've meant little to him had he known but a few miles away his mother was presently feeling just as lonely, sitting silently in his bedroom with a shoe box on her lap. She'd retrieved it from the sideboard the minute her son and husband had departed, leaving her standing at the living room window; a cursory nod of the head her only acknowledgement to Mick embarking on a new life. She took out a handful of photographs that recalled the first decade of her son's life when they shared so many good days: there they are feeding the pigeons in Trafalgar Square; laughing aloud at the antics of Brumas the polar bear cub and Guy the gorilla at London Zoo; being left wide-eyed by the size of the preserved blue whale carcass when its nationwide tour stopped outside Oxford railway station. It made Edna think of the simple pleasures at home: making jam tarts; watching him iron handkerchiefs and use a spoon to scrape, and then gobble, the crusty skin from the rim of a rice pudding basin; making the paper chains for Christmas decorations, and the rag-rug beneath her feet at the side of his bed. And even the bad times, like the day she held his hand at the dentist while Mr Reed extracted his baby teeth. Edna's hands went to her cheeks to still her head. All these assorted memories made the big red muscle in her maternal chest bang away more ferociously. There was one test remaining. She opened the wardrobe; it was empty, but for a blue double-breasted blazer. That neglected, forsaken, garment spoke loud and clear. Her son really had deserted her.

Mick had turned his attention to the rest of his trunk which was taken up with books, writing equipment and rugby kit. From their cardboard box Mick took a shiny pair of Elmer Cotton boots, the brand he'd noticed were worn by all the top players in the University XV. To Mick there was no more intoxicating, erotic even, aroma than leather boots polished to ebony perfection. They spoke to him of passes and kicks made, tries scored, talent fulfilled and a future in the game involving the highest honours. The first step towards this goal was to don the dark blue jersey of Oxford University and ultimately win his 'Blue' by playing against Cambridge University in the Varsity Match at Twickenham on the second Tuesday in December in front of 60,000 spectators. Obtaining the Oxford degree in History that might lead to a career as a military historian was of secondary, and distinctly minor, importance.

Above all else Mick wanted to become what they called a 'sore throat player', one so brilliant that spectators roared themselves hoarse in appreciation of his talent. He reached for the tin of Dubbin wrapped in a rag inside one of the boots. Scooping some of the wax onto the cloth he massaged the leather until it felt as supple as Burlington Bertie's gloves. He treated his boots like the precious objects they were. A craftsman must look after his tools, he told himself. And when it came to playing rugby Mick fancied himself a craftsman, an artist even. He was a scrum-half, the link between the big, tougher men of the pack, the forwards who scrummaged and knocked hell out of each other trying to win the ball, and the speedier, lighter men constituting the backs, the three-quarters, who ran with the ball with pace and ingenuity. Piano shifters and piano players some called the two contrasting parts of a rugby team. And the scrum-half was the principal piano player, the band leader, strong enough to withstand the close attention of opposing forwards yet quick of guile and deed to orchestrate his three-quarters.

Rugby was Mick's means of expressing himself with an eloquence he found impossible to replicate off the field. He couldn't sing a note; couldn't paint a wall let alone a picture; couldn't act anything other than the fool; and had no time for small talk because he knew he was no good at it. He lacked the imagination to compose a poem or a story. Facts were his forte: he'd relate how many archers Henry V deployed at Agincourt but ask him to analyze *Ode to a Nightingale* and he'd throw up his hands in despair. Mick clung to the notion that every individual has something in which they are articulate: rugby was his *lingua franca;* his lines well rehearsed and honed. Crossing the whitewash galvanized him like a boxer climbing through the ropes. He adopted a new persona: he became creative, assertive and combative in word and deed, a player, and a person, respected by his peers. He aimed to earn the respect of his fellow Freshmen in the same way, by demonstrating he was more than a match for them. They might come to respect and accept him via other criteria in the long run but he felt one good performance on the rugby pitch in the coming weeks would work the oracle in the short term.

Mick picked up the books and lovingly placed them on the top shelf of the bookcase. He counted just nine: four volumes of CRL Fletcher's *Introductory History of England*; the *Cambridge Historical Atlas;* and a *Dictionary of Modern History*. He hoped these were sufficient for an Oxford undergraduate about to read for a degree in Modern History. Yet he knew what hope brought: hope can be a killer. Four paperbacks completed his library: *Roget's Thesaurus*; Hemingway's homage to bullfighting, *Death in the Afternoon;* and the novels *Tom Jones* and *Zuleika Dobson.* He picked up the last-named, the satire on undergraduate life at Edwardian Oxford by Max Beerbohm revolving around the femme fatale of its title; he flicked it open to find the signature of its owner: 'Peter Clifton', the man who'd lit the way to this room. Returning the slim volume to its companions, Mick took a step back to admire them. They looked lost. He split them up and shuffled them around the shelves in search of a more eye-catching effect. No joy. They still resembled the occasional palm tree in the Sahara. However Mick arranged them his bookcase bore no resemblance to the shelves groaning with leather-bound volumes that he was convinced would be gracing the rooms of his fellow Freshmen. Nor had he brought any photographs to fill the gaps. He'd love to put a photograph of Sam Owens in a prominent place for his scout to admire. But he didn't possess one. And if he had one to generate jealousy among any of his future chums it was bound to ignite thoughts of lustful banditry whenever Sam appeared on the staircase. Better to keep Sam to himself because in Mick's mind kissing Sam Owens was as close as he'd get to kissing Julie Christie. Neglecting to purchase a poster of Julie to stand proxy was an obvious error, but one he vowed to rectify in the next day or so.

Yes, there were many additions he could make. Other posters to keep Julie from feeling lonely; borrowing books from the College Library to bolster those empty shelves; a half-empty bottle of wine abandoned on the coffee table to suggest convivial visitors, late night imbibing and intellectual debate. But at this moment he was attacked by that nagging sense of inferiority he'd often anticipated might accompany this step into the unknown. The atmosphere was proving to be depressing when it should have been stimulating.

Mick looked at his watch. It was time for his first dinner in Hall. Afterwards there'd be registration forms to complete under the eye of the Dean. He decided to re-acquaint himself with the Junior Common Room en route. It was here he'd waited before his interview the previous September. Then the JCR was completely devoid of life since Michaelmas Term was some weeks away. Now it buzzed with an undergraduate zeal shrouded in the odour of what Mick would grow to recognize as a musty concoction of ancient leather, discarded newspapers and sweaty masculinity. Yet, he mused, the JCR still spoke of homeliness if not male hygiene. He sank into the same chair where he'd tried to compose himself prior to his grilling by the Principal and the Senior Tutor on the off chance it would help settle his nerves.

That it had failed to do so 13 months earlier was forgotten.

Two

Two others had shared Mick's ordeal that September afternoon: Nicky Bright and Bryce Anstruther. Mick's first impressions of them were twofold. Both were dressed in snazzy suits and both possessed perfect complexions. Mick had no suit; he wore his sports coat and best trousers and before leaving home a cursory examination in the mirror over the kitchen sink identified a red lump on his chin – please, he implored under his breath, don't let this volcano erupt on this of all days. The usual courtesies established that both his companions were public schoolboys applying to read Jurisprudence.

Nicky, taller of the pair, was a bundle of nerves and couldn't stop talking. Mick found his jabbering amusing and reassuring. Nicky announced his brother was already at St. Frideswide's: if that wasn't an ace in the hole, Mick couldn't imagine what was. Nicky, however, was convinced it would count against him: 'One Bright in the College at one time is enough!'

Nicky shook his head, exhaled audibly and turned toward Bryce. 'What do you play?' he asked, by way of clearing his mind. 'Everybody applying here must be a player of something!'

'Golf.'

Nicky swept a hand through his spiky crop of black hair. 'Shit! That beats my squash!'

He waited for Mick to reveal his sport. 'What about you, Mick?' he said to break rare seconds of silence.

'Rugby,' said Mick.

'Shit! Bugger!'

Mick and Bryce laughed aloud.

'Who for?'

Mick didn't wish to boast or brag because doing so was strictly avoided where he came from unless one was spoiling for a fight. But he really wanted to. Nicky's wide-eyed expression demanded an answer.

'Well…I played for Oxfordshire Schools last season…'

'Fuck!'

Mick felt the lump on his chin start to throb. Hearing the 'f' word uttered in such a posh voice within the hallowed walls of an Oxford college caused him to laugh so violently he thought snot was bound to fly from his nose.

'You're a certainty!' continued Nicky. 'You know what they say about interviews here, don't you?'

'No…' said Mick.

'When you go in they'll throw you a rugger ball. If you catch it you'll be given a place. If you drop-kick it back you'll get a scholarship!'

The loudness of Mick's laughter spoke to it being genuine rather than nervous. The irony of prowess on the rugby field being a trump card was not lost on him. Football was the game of the Bernard family: granddad Bernard had been offered a contract with Aston Villa when the club was in its pomp between the wars but turned it down because he didn't want to leave Oxford. Roy Bernard inherited his father's ability, winning a hatful of medals at Temple Cowley Secondary School before adding another hatful in the local Oxford leagues after the war. And football had been Mick's game too. He'd excelled in his primary school team and with the local Sunday club. He'd inherited Roy's leg power and shooting boots; the afternoon father decked son out in his own kit for a photograph was one of the proudest moments in Mick's infancy. He may have looked more like a clown in baggy shirt, saggin shorts and outsized boots making it difficult to stand, but he was in heaven to be considered worthy of wearing them. Rugby, on the other hand, was a game played by 'toffs' not Townies like Mick: that is until a Welsh games master transformed him into a performer far superior to his alter ego on a football pitch.

The entrance of the College Porter instantly put paid to the hysteria that had enveloped Mick and Bryce. He stood in front of them, back as straight as if he'd a broom handle stuck down his trousers and he was preparing to drill a platoon on an Aldershot parade ground. His brown bowler hat had a jaunty tilt to it and his garish green checked suit reminded Mick of the back-street bookmaker in British films usually portrayed by Sidney Tafler. A thick ginger beard and brown boots that squeaked as he moved completed the very picture of the former Army sergeant he was eventually discovered to be. 'Mr Bernard, the Principal will see you now.'

The Porter led Mick across the Front Quad to the Principal's Staircase and gestured him to ascend. Mick did as he was bid and came upon the door carrying the sign 'Principal.' Somewhat bizarrely snatches of the shipping forecast came to mind as his stomach turned choppy with the onset of a gale force nine. He ran a finger round the inside of his collar. And then he knocked.

'Come!' said a voice. Mick entered to see two gowned figures sitting either side of a coal fire like two cats warming their bones. They rose in unison to greet him with handshakes, both decidedly limp. Both men were well into their 60s, short, slight, with skin like vellum and pates as shiny as billiard balls. The immediate difference Mick spotted was one wore a dog collar instead of a red-crested tie.

'Pleath, make yourthelth comfortable,' said the one on the left, pointing to the chair positioned directly in front of the fire. He was the Reverend Joseph Reilly, Principal for the last 14 years, owner of a lisp mimicked by generations of his students, and known to all as 'Prinny'.

Prinny's companion was Randolph Tulloch, Senior Tutor and Tutor for Admissions. It was he who'd attracted sportsmen to St. Frideswide's with Reilly's active connivance. St. Frideswide's was a relatively small foundation with little money to entice elite academic students via extravagant scholarships and made little impression on the Norrington Table based on the class of degrees achieved each summer. Students at St Frideswide's who gained Firsts were rarities. But students who gained Blues were prolific. Tulloch reasoned the quickest way for the College to carve a name for itself was in the sporting sphere. Hence a stream of cricketers, golfers, rowers, footballers, rugby and hockey players had entered St Frideswide's under the stewardship of Reilly and Tulloch.

Tulloch's opening gambit didn't involve lobbing a rugby ball at Mick, although it may as well have been. 'Ah, Mr Bernard...have I pronounced that correctly?'

'Yes, sir, that's correct: Ber–nard not Ber-nud.'

'I see you play a bit of rugby?'

Mick's brain engaged his poshest voice before answering: 'Yes, sir.'

'Scrum-half, isn't it? Oxfordshire Schools 19 Group last year, aged only 16?'

'Yes, sir.'

'May we expect you to continue playing? Assisting College to another success in Cuppers? Perhaps you have aspirations to play at University level?'

'I'd like to think so,' replied Mick. He hoped he'd paid the Queen's English the respect it deserved but in his mind he heard himself saying *Oi'd loik t'think so*. Had he answered Tulloch's question truthfully he'd have confessed winning his 'Blue' was the sole reason he wanted to enter his home town university.

'What persuaded you to apply to St. Frideswide's?' continued Tulloch.

'I visited College in the summer holiday and it looked such a homely place, being so compact, that I thought it must be a friendly place, just like my school. And I've always been so happy at school.'

'I see,' said Tulloch, directing a rheumy gaze at Mick that seemed to be urging amplification.

Mick took his cue. 'I think if you're happy it's easier to work, to learn.'

'Quite so,' said Prinny. 'And you think you'd be happy here? What do you know of life at an Oxford college?'

'I've read *Zuleika Dobson*.'

Reilly and Tulloch exchanged smiles across the fire. And let drop the reference to Beerbohm's somewhat dated novel of high comedy that bore scant relation to life in modern Oxford.

'Anything elth?' said Prinny.

'I've watched a lot of games at Iffley Road,' ventured Mick, gaining confidence, 'and I noticed many of the best players come from St Frideswide's.'

'Yes, indeed,' said Tulloch. 'And we can always use another good scrum-half!'

Prinny chortled. Mick risked a smile.

Somehow Mick survived the 20 allotted minutes that passed like 20 hours in the dentist's chair. They asked him about his interests. He was careful not to mention dog racing or betting on the gee-gees. Instead, he spoke of the cinema and Shakespeare productions he'd seen. When asked to be specific, Mick referred to the recent screen adaptation of *Tom Jones* and a production of *Richard III* at the New Theatre. It helped that he'd read Fielding's novel, and Shakespeare's vilification of Richard was full of the injustice he despised and had stimulated further investigation on his part. But he didn't confess to either visit being compulsory rather than voluntary.

His inquisitors bade him farewell and directed him toward his interview with a History don. Mick stole as much time as he dare, putting his faith in the cool air of the Front Quad to revive him. He knew he must be sharp as a tack in this coming encounter. The first interview was merely the 'social' chat; the second interview would be academic and testing. Mick found the room, knocked and heard the same invitation as before: 'Come!'

The Reverend James Hammond, also the College Chaplain, proved to be a small, grey-haired gentleman whose wing-backed armchair seemed to be consuming him. He rose, shook Mick's hand and gestured toward the empty chair opposite his own. Mick had mugged-up topics for this interrogation: Bismarck; the French and Russian Revolutions. Hammond nodded at Mick's answers. The interviewee answered with due solemnity but the interviewer was too wily not to know the answers were scripted.

'What aspect of the Modern History course at Oxford, as opposed to the Ancient History course, most appeals to you, Mr Bernard?'

Mick was also ready for this question: 'Oxford is one of the few universities in the country that gives me the chance to study Military History, which is a particular interest of mine.'

He sat back proud of the fluency with which the sentence had been delivered. It seemed to him that Hammond was likewise impressed. Fifteen minutes shot by as they discussed the campaigns of the Peninsular and Crimean Wars. By the end of this discussion Mick's folded arms lay relaxed in his lap when once they'd been clutching the arms of his chair. His time with Hammond must soon be up. He'd made it without committing any major mishap.

'As you know,' Hammond began slowly, 'there's a general election imminent. How do you think the people on Rose Hill will vote?'

Mick wriggled. The voice in his head scolded him for being so naïve as to think Hammond had exhausted all his ammunition. Oxford dons were partial to throwing a hand grenade into a tutorial, or in this case an interview, to test how quickly the student or candidate thinks on his feet. Can Mr Bernard be relied upon to enliven a tutorial? Raise it from the dull to the sparkling? Make the hour go faster? And not reduce the tutor to daydreaming about the research he'd rather be doing toward his next publication?

The volcano on Mick's chin began to pulse in a manner indicative of imminent eruption. A chilly silence seemed to go on forever. Say something, implored the voice in Mick's head, anything will do.

'Well, sir,' Mick eventually said, 'they'll all vote Labour.'

'And why might that be?' Hammond shot back.

'Labour is the political party of the people, the people who do most of the labour, and the people on the estate believe they are those people.'

'I see,' said Hammond in a hushed voice suggestive of interest. 'Does any other reason occur to you?'

'They all read the *Daily Mirror* and that's a Labour party newspaper.'

'But how can you be so sure about their daily reading habits?' said Hammond, quickly and a trifle smugly.

'Because I'm the paper boy who delivers their papers!' Mick retaliated with alacrity and certainty. 'I deliver 106 papers every morning and 95 of them are the *Daily Mirror*!'

Mick astounded himself. However unintentionally he'd led Hammond into an ambush. His interrogator leaned forward, nodded and smiled – but gave no further indication as to whether Mick had defused the grenade with aplomb or had shot himself in the foot for being a smart arse.

'That will be all, Mr Bernard,' Hammond said, escaping from his chair and holding out his hand. 'I look forward to reading your entrance examination papers in December, when perhaps we'll meet again.'

Mick shook the hand and departed with fingers crossed that would not be the case. His school had told him only borderline candidates for a place were called for a second interview in December. If a candidate heard nothing he was either 'in' or, much more likely, 'out'.

Three

'Howdya get on?' asked Roy Bernard as Mick collapsed into the Rexene armchair nearest the fire, his exhaustion more mental than physical.

Usually occupied by his father, the chair offered the best view of the television on the opposite side of the fire in addition to the greatest warmth. A second armchair was positioned so close to the television it may just as well have been inside it. This belonged to Edna. When Roy and Edna were in their deputed seats Mick was reminded of the phrase describing marriage as 'the ever widening gap by the fireside.' Mick's realm, more of a Siberian outpost, lay on the far side of the room, the cold side, on an uncomfortably rigid two-seater settee he invariably shared with his cat, the tabby, white-bellied, Mister Jinks – unless he escaped to kneel in front of the fire and toast a piece of bread. From his distant perch Mick needed a telescope to make sense of the snowy, often flickering, images on the 14-inch screen of the Stella television set, which became even more obscure as he grew into an increasingly shortsighted teenager. A gate-leg table beneath the front window (only opened for Sunday dinner) and a large pine sideboard against the facing wall completed the furniture in a room measuring barely 12 feet square. The floor was covered with linoleum and a few rag-rugs; the walls with floral-patterned wallpaper of dubious taste. Above the living room was his parents' bedroom; his own miniscule bedroom sat on top of the bathroom, overlooking the back garden. The bathroom served mainly as a lavatory because the house lacked running hot water and, furthermore, as it was the coldest room in the house, removing every stitch of clothing was inadvisable; the recent acquisition of an immersion heater was turned on for exactly one hour every Sunday evening along with the paraffin heater being lit in order for Mick to enjoy a hot bath in some sort of comfort. Roy and Edna made do with a strip-wash in the kitchen.

The living room was the heart of family life in the Bernard household since the kitchen, in Edna's words, 'wasn't big enough to swing a cat.' Her heart's desire was a piano; she could only play one song, *Over The Rainbow*, which after a few port-and-lemons in the pub of a Saturday she'd hammer out on the ancient 'joanna' and croon along in her best imitation of Judy Garland. But a paucity of cash and space snuffed out that dream. Just as well, a younger Mick had decided when hearing Edna's performances from his lonely spot in the corridor outside the bar, nursing his bottle of pop and bag of crisps. To Mick's mind any resemblance the cramped Bernard living room bore to a padded cell seemed more than coincidental. It was a cold space in both Fahrenheit and charity; a monument to world-weariness.

Mick puffed out his cheeks. 'Not too bad, I think,' he said, oblivious to his father being relegated to the less desirable armchair. 'Managed to answer all the questions. Met the Principal and two dons – the tutors – and they were all very decent and friendly.'

Mick's flow of information was drowned by shrill voices from the back garden. Looking to his father for elucidation was unnecessary. It was yet another of the interminable slanging matches between Edna and Mrs Dowler. Their house was at the end of a line of four that in Edna's eyes made it semi-detached and consequently elevated herself a cut above her neighbours, particularly one like Norma Dowler who spent more time in the Wellington accepting drinks from any man who'd pay (and goodness knows for what else besides) than keeping in check her tribe of ragamuffins. Unfortunately for Edna the shrubs and small trees dividing the front garden of their large corner plot from the Dowler's eyesore were no barrier to any of the Dowler brood intent on retrieving a ball or just winding-up snooty Mrs Bernard by lobbing dirt at her front door.

Father and son heard the back door slam. 'I'll swing for 'er! So 'elp me if I dunt!' said Edna to no-one in particular as she marched into the living room, Woodbine in one hand and a duster in the other.

'Wos she bin doin' now?' asked Roy.

'That bloody dog o' theirs bin in the front garden again an' dug up all my daffs!'

'Mick's back,' said Roy, eager to change the stuck record. 'Reckons he did all roight.'

A shaky Woodbine went to Edna's mouth for a long drag. She squinted against the smoke and blew out more blue smoke. First that trollop Dowler and now her own son: always caught between the pincers of one bloody problem or another - and the menopause didn't help. She was living on her nerves nowadays and was convinced all this palaver about Mick's future would put her in the loony-bin. She'd no idea what to do next or which way to turn. She just couldn't think of a way out of this mess. Her thoughts went first one way and then another. She'd never missed an opportunity to tell anyone within earshot how well her son was doing, despite detecting an icy reaction from certain members of the family, and Mick getting a place at Oxford would be the proudest achievement of the lot. But she worried at the cost, to him as well as to her and Roy. Mick wouldn't fit in at an Oxford college; he'd be unhappy. And if he did fit in could her and Roy ever hope to fit in to the different life he'd live. They thought they'd put a stop to this fantasy last year. And if Mick found out what they'd done it would destroy all hope of them maintaining any kind of relationship.

'So you're carryin' on with this then?' she grunted in Mick's direction, hoping for an answer she knew she'd not get but not waiting for the answer she knew she would get. Instead she turned her back on him and began sweeping her duster across the top of a sideboard that needed no attention. Whatever anyone might say about Edna Bernard, including her son, no one could accuse her of presiding over a dirty house. Every surface was dusted and polished daily. She never knew who might drop in, one of Roy's sisters who lived nearby or Florrie, the acceptable neighbour in the adjoining house. They'd not be able to gossip about the dust on top of the television or the dullness of the front door's brass knocker and red step. Or, heaven forbid, her son's state of dress: he was never allowed to leave for school unless he was turned out spick and span. Cleanliness superseded Godliness in her house.

Mick watched her elbow pumping a path along the sideboard. 'Of course I am. And if I don't get into Oxford I've still got six other chances of getting a university place through my UCCA application.'

Edna continued to pummel the sideboard, making no effort to turn around. 'Uncle Gilbert says he can get you an apprent'ship in the drawin' office at Cowley…'

'Don't be daft! I did tech drawing for a year at school and hated it! Why on earth would I want to do it for a living! I'd rather shit on my hands and clap!'

'Thass 'nough of that language!' snapped his mother.

'There's plenty of bad language in this house!'

His mother cooled at the truth. 'Good money…'

'Is that all you can think about, money? Life's about more than just money!' Mick snapped back. 'I've been round the factory and there's not enough money in the world to get me in there five days a week!'

The harsh words filling Mick's mind made him look toward the window. How could two people get to their age, he pondered, and live through a world war yet retain such a narrow view of the world. What a banal life they led. All the Bernards and Jaykes were the same. None of them had demonstrated an iota of ambition. They stayed local, stayed together and were the same in middle age as were as young adults - stuck in the 1940s. And they'd probably stay in that condition until they were buried in the village churchyard. No aspirations and no advancement between the lot of them.

Edna took a long drag and swallowed her thoughts along with the smoke. She could no longer relate to her son and the life he led. She tried to imagine what he got up to with his pals, what they talked about and where they went for amusement; or what it was about playing rugby he enjoyed so much. But imagination wasn't one of Edna's strengths whereas she had a degree in nursing a grouse. Her son's ingratitude for all the sacrifices she'd made on his behalf hurt deeply. It gnawed away constantly at every grain of her being. She'd no idea how to broach the matter with her son and bring about some kind of amicable resolution; or the vocabulary to do so without running the risk of losing control and embarrassing herself by shedding tears. Even if a woman's tears were the most toxic poison known to man they could not be Edna's weapon of choice. Women like her, steeled by war, were immunized against weeping. But inside she was forever drowning in tears.

This was another of those moments when Edna wished it hadn't been raining that day 23 years ago. She'd been queuing outside the Headington cinema to see *They Drove By Night* and rain poured off the back of her umbrella onto the man behind her. Hearing a muffled complaint, she turned to see a smartly dressed young man who might've stepped from the film they were waiting to see (starring the always dapper George Raft alongside her own fashion icon, Ida Lupino) were he not so shy-looking. She invited him underneath her brolly. On striking-up a tentative conversation they discovered Edna was working alongside Roy's sister Dot in the local factory manufacturing parts for Spitfires. They watched the film side by side and Roy was cock-a-hoop when Edna agreed to meet him again later in the week. Their first date amounted to a long walk around the nearest slice of countryside – which happened to be the extensive site of the local sewage farm. Roy's pals were impressed because Edna was a quite a beauty with the finely drawn face, crimped hair, full lips and rosy complexion of Ida Lupino. What they failed to identify in Edna was her resemblance to the kind of character Ida Lupino often portrayed on screen: a calculating man-eater. The bashful and timid Roy Bernard was lamb to the slaughter. They married during Roy's last leave before he sailed for North Africa; she was just 18 and he 22. This made Edna a war bride and she maintained her *de facto* status as head of the household when her husband returned to 'civvy street' in the manner of so many other wives left to hold the fort. This ilk of wife, and mother, knew they could cope with every aspect of running house and home without recourse to any input from their husbands. They brooked no nonsense from husband, child or neighbour, and gave rise to a nationwide species of fearsome kitchen despots, living room autocrats and bedroom dictators.

'The works has got a decent football team an' all,' interjected Roy.

'I know football's your game,' said Mick, quietly. 'But rugby's my game now. And that's that.'

Mick read his father's eyebrows which he knew arched, as they did now, whenever he wanted to say something but couldn't bring himself to do so. Rugby was as foreign to Roy Bernard as American Football: he couldn't recognize a scrum-half from a fly-half; and if the Number 8 was named after the number on his jersey why weren't the other positions? Despite his own football prowess he'd never become, much to Mick's disappointment, one of the dads who regularly attended Saturday or Sunday games to watch their sons perform. Nor did he suggest walking round to the 'rec' for an educational kick-about. Mick presumed his dad loved him because that's what dads, and mums, did. But Roy was a typical Anglo-Saxon male of his era: emotions were buttoned up as tightly as his pyjama bottoms. Showing emotion was a weakness. The army had rammed home that message: you don't win a war by loving the enemy.

Roy Bernard was accustomed to his wife's invective to the point where he'd just calmly sit out the bombardment from behind the *Daily Mirror*; he was astute enough to know there was more chance of halting a forest fire with a water pistol than stopping Edna when her fuse had been lit. Roy was a true 'Townie', one of Herbert and Louise Bernard's seven children, his father an odd-job man at the car factory whose remit included pushing the tea trolley and his mother a wizen little creature whose single defining feature was the absence of a finger she'd accidentally sliced off with a bread knife. He was born at home in the village adjacent to the Hill Rise estate, and left school at 14 to join his elder brother Albert delivering coal. He didn't forsake Oxford until answering his country's call. Not that he accounted for any Germans himself. His experience driving a coal lorry ensured basic training was the only time he fired a rifle or wielded a bayonet. Upon its completion Private 14591800 was immediately attached to the Royal Military Service Corps as a truck driver. Although packed off to North Africa he disembarked to learn that particular theatre of war had ended and within a fortnight he'd re-embarked for Italy. Mick reasoned this brief acquaintance with Tunisia probably accounted for the annual appearance of dates and figs on the Bernard sideboard at Christmas because Roy was the only one who showed any interest in eating them. After three years and 123 days active service, followed by tours of duty in the Mediterranean and Austria, Roy Bernard was finally 'demobbed' as an 'exemplary soldier, hardworking, reliable, trustworthy, sober, honest and loyal', the single tiny blot on his record being the loss of three days pay following a 'disturbance' during an ENSA concert in the NAAFI.

That 'blot' fascinated Mick because it was safe to say Roy Bernard seldom gave offence to anyone: Mick appreciated very early in their relationship that humility was a word coined for individuals like his father. At forty-four years of age Roy remained as meek as ever. He was still wedded to lorries: driving a trailer laden with car bodies from the Cowley plant to Birmingham. Although regularly awarded certificates by British Road Services for his competence, he did come home one Saturday as white as an altar cloth. It transpired that as he turned left at the roundabout coming into Banbury his trailer went dead straight and crashed through the window of a sweet shop. Fortunately the shop was empty and no bystanders were hurt. Securing the trailer was one of the jobs Roy's cab-mate was meant to undertake and he'd obviously been negligent but, as the senior man aboard, it was Roy's responsibility to check all was in order. Roy was let off with a warning.

At home Roy didn't so much relax as loaf. His interests were few. He didn't read beyond the *Daily Mirror* and *News of the World* and had no inclination to listen to music. He liked watching Westerns and laughed aloud at Tommy Cooper, Chic Murray, Al Read and WC Fields. Televised sport would be watched studiously and anything similar on radio, such as a big fight, would see his ear bent to the loudspeaker. But live sport he could largely do without, even his beloved football. The odd outing to watch a First Division match involving his team, Aston Villa, and the even rarer outing to a racecourse were his limit. He was, however, a compulsive collector of oddities - coins, broken watches, fountain pens - that he was convinced would one day fetch 'good money.' The fate of his biggest find rankled. While turning over the soil of the tiny vegetable patch he'd created in the back garden he unearthed a rust-caked blade which he put to work as a spade cleaner. Mick thought it a relic of some vintage and took it to the Ashmolean Museum where it was identified as mid 17th century dagger, most likely lost by one of the Parliamentarian troops that occupied their hill during the siege of Royalist Oxford in the Civil War. Roy was not best pleased to be told the most valuable item he'd ever found had been donated gratis to the Ashmolean.

Thus did Roy find it easy to shun the limelight. He was a listener not a talker. He never drew attention to himself. Anything remotely praiseworthy made him blush; scant praise never seemed to come from his wife but Mick increasingly noticed how his father's general diffidence broken-up by the occasional quip drew giggling acknowledgement from other women. Mick decided the cliché stating a man might laugh a woman into bed may have some truth to it. It was one gift he'd acquired from his father, albeit by study rather than instruction. And it was a gift he longed to test.

Friday was the one day in the week Roy could not avoid being centre stage for it was pay day. Mick would watch him deposit his £20 wage packet on the table whereupon Edna extracted the notes; after putting a £1 note in each of three pots, that Mick grew to know were for the rates, gas and electricity (the last two notes ultimately exchanged for one shilling coins to feed the respective meters), she passed a few back to Roy – which he'd spend on Woodbines, pints of mild of a weekend and the upkeep of the latest jalopy decorating the front garden. Edna folded the remaining notes into her purse for the week's housekeeping. Then came Friday's twin high spots. Around seven o'clock the clanging of a bell in the street denoted the arrival of Carlos's mobile fish-and-chip van that drew up outside the Bernard's front gate. Often Mick would already be out there to be first in the queue for a monster serving of crisply battered cod and a mound of thick, salted-and-vinegared chips that he'd wolf down as if supper was last year. 'Dunt eat s'fast! You'll hurt y'bells!' Edna would implore, pronouncing 'bowels' in her own idiosyncratic fashion. But an empty stomach had no ears as far as Mick was concerned. Afterwards Mick would, with any luck, see Roy reach into his jacket pocket and bring out a bag of toffees for him to divide into three piles for consumption in front of the television.

Edna was left to rule the Bernard household. Mick knew no other regime. She ruled with an iron fist inside a steel glove and a tongue so sharp that at times Mick hoped she would cut her own throat with it. Yet Mick never heard his father object or complain, let alone raise a threatening fist toward his domineering wife, who could fire one broadside after another faster than Nelson's gunners at Trafalgar. Mick always sensed a whiff of cordite in the air whenever Edna marched into the living room to halt in front of her husband hunched over his *Daily Mirror* crossword in a vain effort to avoid her gaze. For someone who'd left school at 14 with no qualifications her body language was of degree level. Mick could translate every gesture: the drags on her Woodbine grew longer, her cheeks sinking into her skull; her hands first fiddling and then tugging at the headscarf she always wore around the house. Edna Bernard may not have possessed the stare of Medusa that turned a man to stone but she would come close once the artillery opened up. Cries of 'I'll swing fer you!' or 'Yull find me with me 'ead in the oven!' would greet any dissention. When directed at Mick he more than once prayed these allusions to the death penalty or the lethal quality of town gas might one day come to his aid. He hoped, and expected, his father to feel likewise. But if Roy did share Mick's feelings he never gave any indication. One weightier consideration preyed on Mick's mind: if ever Roy and Edna did come to blows it would be his duty to intervene and to arbitrate. And he wasn't sure he'd be prepared to take that responsibility.

Every summer, for example, Edna launched a litany of hints, then specific details and finally an outright ultimatum of the consequences should Roy not comply with her suggestion for home improvements. Drip by drip this version of the Chinese water torture forced Roy into redecorating one of house's five rooms (two bedrooms; kitchen; bathroom and living room). Alas, Roy was no paperhanger: studying him trying to match the patterns on strips of flowered wallpaper provided Mick with many an amusing half-hour. Roy preferred tending his vegetable patch: after all it was in his genes because his grandfather had been a market gardener; and rows of potatoes, onions, carrots, cabbages and sprouts were laid out as smartly as any regiment of foot. The sprouts caused the one occasion Mick caught his father crying: he'd slipped a disc while pulling up the stalks. Thc pain must've been excruciating. Yet Mick was sure men weren't supposed to cry.

As adolescence took hold and Mick grew into the traditionally rebellious, and frequently obnoxious, teenager, he couldn't fathom why the man of the house, his very own 'war hero' and masculine role model, hadn't the gumption to rebel against the female who dominated him with the persistent bark of next door's Alsatian dog and far less intelligence. Despite constant badgering and hectoring Roy never retaliated. Mick reasoned his father's acquiescence could only be his way of keeping Edna sweet in the marriage bed. Roy knew differently: sexual relations with his wife had long since joined everything else in the ration book. And, he had to admit, she looked different to the object of lust he'd married: the wavy hair once natural now relied on the nightly application of curlers; the thicker ankles ruined that once attractive curve to her legs; the hint of a baby-belly and a bosom succumbing to gravity that made girdle and brassiere essential undergarments were equally effective passion-killers. Yet, he conceded, if she no longer resembled one of George Raft's gangster molls neither had he retained the toned body of a hoodlum. Roy wasn't overly bothered: sex had never struck him to be all it was cracked up to be according to bar-room bravado – which was probably just made up so the speaker sounded the greatest stud in Oxford. Not that he ignored any handsome woman sending him messages with a pout or fluttering eyelashes. Thelma, a petite peroxide blonde who'd worked with Edna at the dry cleaners on Carfax, really did set his mind to wandering – that is until Edna caught her sitting on his lap and cooing in his ear. The few sharp words that followed ensured Thelma was never encountered again. But Roy usually restricted himself to making women laugh: getting the desired reaction gave him as much pleasure nowadays as any roll in the sack with Edna. His view on life was simple enough: he reckoned he worked hard five days a week (and occasionally a Saturday) and deserved peace of mind even if he couldn't count on a quiet life in the strictest sense of the term. Ambition was never something that exercised him and, unlike his wife, he'd no trust in the sureness of social mobility. He knew he lived under his wife's ubiquitous thumb and his son's burgeoning arrogance. But a weekly shy at the football pools, a Saturday flutter on the gee-gees and a ready supply of fags and beer would see him get by.

Mick was forced to conclude that if Roy was prepared to put up with Edna's constant sniping he must love her, faults and all. Love was a subject that Mick found confusing. He loved his pet rabbits and cats, but he could never seem to transfer that feeling to humans, even his parents. The only human who gave him a feeling that he decided must be close to love was Granny Jaykes, who virtually brought-up her infant grandson while Edna worked in the local sweet shop. And Mick only came to recognize that emotion when Granny Jaykes died. Suddenly, at the age of nine, he'd known what grief was and furthermore the emotion that had invoked it. He began wondering whether that's how Roy and Edna felt about him. But if they did they never said so. And Granny Jaykes used to cuddle him, give him affectionate hugs. His parents didn't. Mick never recognized a look of love in their eyes; only bafflement, exasperation and anger did he register. They neither expressed nor displayed any positive emotions toward him and in time he reciprocated in kind. Communication was relegated to a need-to-know basis. Parents and son began living in solitary while confined within the same prison.

Eventually the flame ignited by Norma Dowler died away sufficiently for Edna to concentrate on the subject in hand. 'How are we goin' to pay for you t'go to college?'

'I've told you more than once,' Mick replied, his voice rising. 'All the tuition fees are paid by the local authority and it gives me a grant each term to live on. If I buy anything in College it goes on "Battels", an account that I settle from my grant each term.'

'You pos'tive we dunt pay nothin''?'

'You are means tested…'

'Wos that again?'

'You fill in a form with your income and if it falls below a certain level I get the maximum grant but if it exceeds the set level some money is knocked off, which you are supposed to contribute.'

Edna lifted the vase of flowers from the table and swept her duster over a surface that really had no need of it. 'So you get the lot then?'

'Probably not, but with your joint income being so low the amount you'll be expected to contribute will be pretty small.'

'Knew there'd be a catch!' said his mother, malice lining her tongue, before she took another long drag on her Woodbine.

Mick drew breath. 'I'll not ask you for a penny! I'll live on what they give me every term.'

'So we pay nothin'?'

'Your contribution will be to give me bed and board during the vacations…'

'Toldya there'd be a catch, dint I?' said his mother, looking to her husband.

Mick raised his palms. 'If I get a Vac job I'll give you some money toward house-keeping. Okay?'

His parents looked at each other without saying a word. They'd no more cards to play.

'You wornt some tea, then?' said his mother in the act of flicking her dog-end into the fire.

To Mick the very thought of Edna's cooking brought to mind how Tony Hancock addressed Hattie Jacques when faced with her Sunday lunch in a priceless episode of radio's *Hancock's Half Hour*: 'I thought my mother was a bad cook but at least her gravy used to move!' Edna's gravy 'moved' because it was tantamount to brown water; her roast potatoes seldom crunched; her cabbage was boiled lifeless. Listening to Hancock on his transistor radio in the quiet of his bedroom constituted one of Mick's secret pleasures. The comic tribulations of a self deluded and pretentious 'everyman' whose aspirations are continually thwarted struck a chord in someone with similar hopes of advancement. However, unlike the fictional resident of 23 Railway Cuttings, East Cheam, Mick recognized the pitfalls - and planned to avoid them.

Thankfully, for Mick's appetite, Edna was a magician with pastry and a demon with the frying pan. And she knew enough about her son's eating habits to answer her question for him. 'S'pose it's chips you wornt,' she announced, the last word pronounced in the purest southern Oxfordshire tongue. 'What y'wornt with'um?'

'Sausages?'

'Ent got any sossidges. I'll fry some eggs…'

'Great!'

'Beans? Rhubarb pie an' custard for afters?'

Edna didn't wait for confirmation but made for the kitchen where she spent most of her day until the television sprang into life at seven o'clock in the evening. It amounted to no more than a box room: the gas stove beside the living-room door; one small formica-topped table on which she prepared the meals and could seat one person was wedged between the Hoovermatic twin-tub washing machine and the stove; and a walk-in pantry in the far corner next to the back door. But small and suffocating though it was this was her safe haven.

Passing the gilt-framed mirror that was a wedding present from her Aunt Amy, she glanced at the features daring to confront her. She didn't want to look because she knew the message it sent. But she couldn't help it. This was her daily penance, her daily nod to the ravages of time. The sight she beheld was what 21 years of marriage and 17 years of motherhood had reduced her to. The luxurious waves, sharp cheekbones, peachy complexion and kissable cherry lips of her wedding day had been replaced by a bleak canvas of matted hair, puffy jowls and the cat's arse of a smoker's mouth.

Like her husband Edna had six siblings, one of whom, Sydney, died aged six after cutting his hand on broken glass and contracting tetanus. Her parents, Edward and Joan Jaykes, came from the same social stratum as the Bernards: traditional Oxford working class. When not wielding a sledgehammer as a blacksmith's striker at the John Allen plant manufacturing agricultural machinery in Hockmore Street, Edward seldom vacated his armchair other than to frequent the Corner House pub on the other side of the fence to their tiny semi-detached cottage at the top of Hollow Way, opposite the gate to the Slade Camp. Edna's mother, a heavy-set but warm-featured woman, had warned Edna marriage and motherhood might turn out more challenging than rewarding. But even when Mick was born Edna told herself married bliss was still possible.

Now Edna knew differently. She felt cheated. She often wished she'd never married; never had a child; never had a son. This was not how being a wife and mother was meant to be. The unity in her marriage existed only on paper: the marital obligations in the bedroom had become increasingly unwelcome. She and Roy were two ships on separate voyages that occasionally docked in the same port; days, sometimes even weeks, would pass without them enquiring about something as fundamental as each other's state of mind. They were feeling old, notably older in mind than body. They both realized they only had each other; and if that was not enough Edna was petrified of the future.

Now their son had become the third ship in that anchorage. Mick was meant to be an extension of them but once he'd developed these delusions of getting into Oxford University, Edna began to realize he was intent on the exact opposite: he was a walking contradiction of the kind of lives she and Roy lived; their teenager had become a stranger to them. Though they'd tried to keep pace with his aspirations they'd no experience to draw on and no imagination to take its place. And no amount of cajoling and bullying had managed to change his mind. She was forced to admit her son was as stubborn as she was; and she was invisible as far as he was concerned.

This was reality, her reality at least, and not the fantasy stories of wives and mothers she read in *Woman's Weekly*. Her husband lit no fires in her breast anymore and her son no longer towed the line. She knew she was a drudge and a nag, frequently got herself in a muddle and acknowledged her quarrelsome disposition was unattractive. But she had a duty to her husband and her son; her mother had instilled her with a deep sense of responsibility, the need to fulfill her duties; and Edna trusted the Bible's words 'by their deeds you shall know them.' She kept the home spotless. She couldn't name the Chancellor of the Exchequer and had never written a cheque but she treated pennies like rubies, managing the strings of a purse often half empty so adeptly the Bernards never went hungry and her son never suffered from a hole in his shoe or the backside hanging out of his trousers. She made rag-rugs out of cast-offs; and at Christmas sat for hours looping chains from slips of glossy paper cut out of magazines to act as decorations. No one who treated their domestic duties flippantly could ever win respect; and Edna Bernard craved respect above anything else, even love or admiration. It would be nice, she often contemplated, to be young again with a head full of dreams and a heart full of hope. But, for now, as long as Roy, Mick, her siblings and friends paid her respect, life could just about pass as bearable.

In any case, what could she do? Divorce was frowned upon in her circles; and she'd no opportunities to start an affair even if she could summon the nerve and the suitor to try one; besides, knowing everyone would call her a 'scarlet woman' was mortifying. And what man would give her a second glance. She longed for the days when young men gazed at her in admiration.

When she knew they were mentally undressing her; when she felt as though dynamite had exploded in those parts of her body about which polite young girls were not expected to speak. Nowadays her body was more of an encumbrance than an object of desire. Her back ached constantly from household chores: sweeping, washing and carrying heavy shopping bags. Her once elegant fingers were calloused; and at least two of her molars needed urgent repair. The feeling she was somehow falling apart was omnipresent. Nor was there any beacon of hope on the employment front: any part-time job open to her was menial and a harsh reminder of her position on society's bottom rung. She felt trapped in quicksand of her own making from which escape was as unlikely as winning big on the football pools. Her life had descended into a ritual of tiresome reactions to irritating situations. Life had ceased to sparkle.

So Edna trudged through life with monotony for her cross. The routine was incessant: make the beds; do the shopping; cook the meals; washing on Monday, ironing on Tuesday; the pub Saturday evening if she was lucky and not too tired or 'livin' on her nerves'; a drive into the country on a Sunday if she could nag Roy out of his armchair. The endless trivia; the constant bickering with her husband that finished with his silent surrender because he'd either no fight in him or saw no sense in re-fighting an old fight; the slanging matches with Norma Dowler who hadn't an apporth of 'class' about her. How Edna longed for one of the elegant semi-detached houses in nearby Westbury Crescent where people behaved properly. That the only way she could express this inner rage was to lash out verbally or physically often reduced her to sitting on the toilet, weeping lonely tears of bitter salt. But once that engine inside her was switched on she began driving downhill with her foot hard on the accelerator - and she couldn't stop. There were days, and many of them, when the gas oven seemed a preferable option. Then she would be visible again.

But for Edna there was neither reprieve nor remission. More and more she felt like the dazed boxer who often hits the canvas but always drags himself upright again. It was her duty to get up. No one could ever criticize her tenacity and industry. But she was getting old and, more significantly, felt years older than her birth certificate testified. She knew she'd lost her vim, her vigour, her vivacity. It was as if someone had ripped out her heart and put a block of ice in its place. Worse yet, lately she'd begun to feel a loss of respect; and with it self-respect. Edna Bernard couldn't abide disrespect. She never forgot a slight or what she perceived an insult. She bore grudges longer than a jilted bride. Any miscreants would be made to pay – especially if they were in direct line of fire like her husband and son.

Edna closed the kitchen door, leaving father and son divided as usual by a silence that spoke of two people from different galaxies.

Four

All Mick could discern was the word 'Disraeli'. For the umpteenth time he stared at the second question on the examination paper. There was nothing for it but to admit he hadn't a clue how to answer it. Fellow pupils who'd been re-sitting O-levels had all departed. The only occupants of the gymnasium were him and the invigilator, who happened to be Wyn James, the man who'd converted him into a rugby player. Mick slowly raised his hand to attract James's attention.

'I'm finished, sir,' he said meekly as the invigilator approached brandishing the sheets of file paper he presumed Mick was requesting.

'Really? You've plenty of time left,' urged James. 'There must be something more you can do?'

Other masters at South Oxford had contributed mightily to opening the door of St. Frideswide's for Mick. But it was the rugby coaching of Wyn James that had enabled Mick to actually get his foot in the door of the University's premier rugby academy. Not completing this paper was an admission of defeat, of failure. Mick had blown his chance. A heavy silence enveloped coach and player. Mick knew how cruel it was that James of all people was being made to witness his unconditional surrender. And James registered the guilt in Mick's face for letting him down by waving that white flag.

This paper was the fourth and final paper comprising the Oxford Entrance Examination for applicants wishing to read for the Honour School of History. Mick felt the first two papers, English History and European History, had gone smoothly. But the last pair was his twin bugbears: Latin and a modern language, which in his case was German. Both languages were conditions of entry to the Modern History course which contained set texts in them. These two papers would plumb deeper waters than his interviews: he'd needed two attempts to pass O-level German and no fewer than three to pass Latin. This latest Latin tester had turned out reasonably palatable, tricky but Mick managed to complete the questions. However, the German paper he'd been wrestling with for 90 minutes was proving the mother of all linguistic disasters. He could make sense of only one of the two pieces he'd to translate into English.

'Sorry, sir,' he lamented. 'It's no good. I could sit here till midnight an' I'd get no further.'

James nodded in commiseration and accepted the single sheet of paper Mick held up. 'Okay, then.' He watched Mick drag himself to his feet. 'Don't dwell on it. There's always a chance.' James knew he was spouting nonsense but his heart bled for his protégé. 'It's not over till the fat lady sings!'

'I think she's already back in 'er dressing room!' replied Mick, raising a grin as he nudged his chair beneath his desk.

This linguistic shambles wasn't the first he'd endured in the school gym cum examination room. His mind cast back six months to his third attempt at securing a pass in O-level Latin that was obligatory for candidates wishing to read History at Oxford. He'd received no teaching time but by now knew the set book, *The Aeneid*, back to front so that paper held no fears for him. Paper One, grammar and unseen translations, was the stumbling block but it surprised him by turning out fine and dandy. Bill Lander, South Oxford's deputy head, always distributed the GCE papers and started the clock but when he told Mick and the fifth formers to turn over their question papers and commence Paper Two a ghostly pallor came over Mick. He did not recognize one sentence of *The Aeneid* staring up at him. A glance at the precise book it had been taken from, listed at the top of the page, wasn't the book he'd studied. He looked around him at the fifth-formers having their first stab at the exam but none of them appeared perplexed as him, not even Sam Owens. Perhaps they hadn't noticed, he reasoned, or else they didn't know the difference. But there was too much at stake for Mick to keep quiet. He raised his hand to attract Lander's attention: he marched across to Mick's desk, his rubber-soled brogues squeaking on the wooden gym floor.

'What is it, Bernard?'

'Sir, this isn't our paper…'

'Don't be silly!'

'We didn't study this book of *The Aeneid.*'

Lander's screwed-up eyes gave Mick the impression he'd sensed what may have happened.

'Carry on the best you can,' said Lander.

When Lander was relieved from invigilating duties 20 minutes later Mick noticed him and the incoming master exchanging words behind serious expressions. The following morning the affected examinees were brought together and given an explanation as to what had happened. The set book stayed the same for autumn re-sits but changed every summer: the new Latin teacher, Neale, hadn't noticed or had not bothered to consult the syllabus correctly, thereby ensuring everyone was going to fail the exam. This was catastrophic for Mick because if he re-sat Latin once again, which he must, a fourth time in the autumn, he must learn a new set book. The cock-up was the school's responsibility but, by some miracle or other, headmaster Jack Masterson persuaded the Examination Board to set an alternative paper just for South

Oxford, unheard of benevolence on its part. Lander was obliged to go to London to have the copies placed directly into his hands and return with the completed papers immediately they were finished. This was a monumental stroke of luck for Mick. And the two-month wait for the result seemed like two years. But he passed. As for Neale…he left.

Consequently, for the second occasion, Mick pushed through the gym's double doors like a gunslinger leaving a saloon. But inside he was feeling his goose wasn't so much cooked as carved and plated.

As December's decision day neared Mick was released from school to work as a temp on the Christmas post and was not at home when Masterson, telephoned to say that St. Frideswide's had confirmed he'd not be required for further interview. Mick accepted that, as Masterson put it, 'a brave long shot had failed to come off.' Three days later, the Saturday before Christmas, Mick left his job early in order to play for Oxfordshire Schools in the afternoon. When he came into the house to collect his kit Roy Bernard pointed to the mantelpiece: 'There's a letter for you. Says St. Frideswide's College on the en'vlope.'

Edna came in to the living room drying her hands on a tea towel. She stood alongside her husband. Their expectancy was as great as their son's – but for the opposite reason. They'd done their utmost to undermine this silly fantasy of his from the outset.

Mick took the envelope and opened it as slowly as possible, delaying the inevitable for as long as possible. Here in his hand was the *coup de grace*, the black spot, the black cap – whatever symbol of condemnation he cared to think of. He extricated the letter and began to read. He only got as far as 'On the strength of your performance in the recent Scholarship/Entrance Examination, I am pleased to offer you a place at this College to read for the

Honour School of History' before releasing a yell that could've been heard at St. Frideswide's.

Roy and Edna puffed on their cigarettes, immobilized by shock and despair: the shock of this unusual show of emotion from their son and their despair at its implication.

'Y'got in?' said his mother.

'And y'gunna go?' said his father.

'Do you have to ask?' spluttered Mick. 'Course I am!'

He waited for some words of congratulation, a simple 'Well done'. But he knew none would come. He'd no recollection of praise for passing the 11-plus or playing for the County Schools. Why should this achievement be received any differently? Praise begat big-headedness and bragging. These were cardinal sins in the eyes of the Bernard clan.

'But what if I dunt wornt you t'go,' said Edna. 'I'm your mother an' I love you, an' I dunt want to see you un'appy which you will be in one o'them colleges.'

'Well, I can assure you, sons don't necessarily love their mothers!' Mick said quickly and spitefully, without thinking.

Edna turned away, praying the taste of salt in the corner of her mouth came from a trickle of nervous sweat rather than a tear of anguish. What little air there was circulating in her living room had suddenly become as thick as a London pea-souper. No mother deserves to be spoken to like this. 'You wash y'mouth out!' she exclaimed with venom. 'Speakin' to me loik that!'

Mick knew he'd gone too far. But an apology was not in him. Apologizing was a sign of weakness.

'Are you gunna let him speak to me loik that?' Edna asked Roy.

Roy shuffled his feet and dodged the question. 'Well,' he said at length, 'yer uncles dunt think it's a good idea…'

'Those busybodies can stay out of my life! An' you can tell them that if I don't get the chance to tell them!'

'Yer Uncle Alec knows what he's talkin' 'bout!' said Edna. 'He worked as a servant at one of them colleges…'

'Yes, a scout…'

'An' he reck'ns you wunt fit in with them toffs!'

'Well,' said Mick, defiantly. 'He can sod off!'

His mother's mouth hardened into a red slit. 'Neh then,' she said, adopting the phrase Mick knew to be the germ of a scolding, 'dunt use that languidge 'bout your uncles when they ent 'ere to d'fend themselves!'

Edna advanced toward him with right arm raised and got close enough for Mick to see the spidery red veins wandering over the whites of her eyes. But Mick's glacial expression caused her to freeze. She looked to her husband for support. Yet she knew there'd be none.

Mick retreated to his outpost on the settee. He was unable to understand his mother. Although most of his mates were also only sons they never compared notes or pooled their experiences in order to find some way of solving the mother-son mystery. As a result Mick continued to see the negatives magnified and the positives moderated to the point of extinction. On rare occasions this attitude, however, did provoke a smidgeon of guilt. He'd recall his first day at South Oxford when his homework was to discover how glass was made: he hadn't a clue but Edna looked it up in his dictionary and stopped the imminent flow of anxious tears. Seeing that panic in her son's eyes caused Edna to purchase a four-volume set of *Childrens Encyclopedia* on the 'never-never' - hire purchase - from a travelling salesman who happened to knock on the door the following week. Yet any feeling of gratitude didn't manifest itself in a conscious improvement in Mick's attitude toward his mother during the ensuing six years. Mick's problem was that whatever Edna gave him, material or emotional, had to be repaid. But he viewed his repayment as slaving hard at school and bringing no shame to her house: he'd not thieved, brawled, vandalized or put a girl in the family way. It seemed whatever he did wasn't enough for his mother. Edna concurred. She wasn't conversant with the works of Shakespeare but had she read King Lear that troubled monarch's observation on one of his daughters would've had her nodding in agreement: how sharper than a serpent's tooth it is to have a thankless child.

Edna wouldn't confess as much to any living soul but she was baffled by her son's Jekyll and Hyde personality. At school his conduct was irreproachable whereas his behaviour at home was openly disrespectful, frequently impertinent and often crossed the line into dumb insolence. She'd scrimped and saved through years of postwar austerity to feed and clothe him; she'd gone out to skivvy in order to subsidize his grammar school education; to buy him the bike he wanted; the transistor radio and record player he craved – she'd even been pestered into buying him a rugby ball. She and Roy would've been happy with a quarter of such luxuries when they were his age. But her son seemed to regard them as bare essentials: his birthright. Edna had long resigned herself to her husband's innate indolence: he was her intellectual superior but she was industrious and his temperamental superior. This had always given her an edge. The same formula was not working with her son. Perhaps his departure was for the best. Let him fly solo. He'll soon come to his senses and come crawling back, regretful and remorseful and thankful.

Roy Bernard detected defeat in his wife's slumped shoulders. He, too, knew they'd lost. Their son was on his way. Their son no longer belonged to them. He had beaten the odds. Mick Bernard, a boy from a disadvantaged background, had overcome all obstacles to fight his way into Oxford University. Pride ought to have triumphed over despondency. But for Edna and Roy Bernard it didn't. Roy might've given Edna a consoling hug. But he didn't. As courting couples they'd sought to be alone and struggled. Now being alone came naturally. Even at this pivotal moment they'd nothing of significance to say to each other. A tut-tut and a sigh was all they could muster as their watch standing sentry on their son's life came to an end. Roy hunkered down with his crossword. Edna went into the kitchen to peel some potatoes to slice into chips. By such small deeds did Roy and Edna resume normalcy.

The letter in Mick's hand went on to inform him he must pass two A-levels and Use of English before coming into residence (in a later telephone conversation between Tulloch and Masterson it was made clear Mick's German 'required some attention'). It was signed by the Principal and ended: 'I shall be grateful to have confirmation of your acceptance of this offer as soon as possible.' Mick grabbed a pen and signed the stamped/addressed postcard. It went into the pillar-box on the corner before he biked to his rugby match – in which he was instrumental in the County Schools drubbing the County Colts.

As Mick cycled back to Hill Rise the sense that another dream was about to become reality fuelled every turn of the wheels. He decided to treat himself with an early Christmas present from his earnings on the Post and purchased a salmon-pink shirt with trendy button-down collar by Ben Sherman. With what little remained he bought Roy a box of dates and a cigar for Christmas and Edna a cheap battery powered egg whisk - into which he neglected to insert batteries. Roy smoked the cigar and ate the dates. Edna threw the whisk into the dustbin on Boxing Day.

The incomprehension on Edna's face and the hint of a tear in the eye that Mick detected that Christmas Day did get to him: that morning he discovered that the most toxic poison known to man was indeed a woman's tears. Although guilt did not suddenly overwhelm him it did find a path to, and a home in, his subconscious.

Five

That euphoric day of academic and sporting triumph was nearly 11 months ago. The requisite examination qualifications were met. Only the coming weeks would tell whether Mick Bernard could cope with the upheaval in every aspect of his life: academic, sporting and, especially, the social side.

Mick's first dinner in Hall was memorable for having insufficient room to wield a knife and fork. He and a hundred other garrulous Freshmen were squashed together on benches either side of a dozen long oak tables positioned at right angles to a central aisle. White-jacketed scouts - all male - ferried bowls of oxtail soup to each table, followed by the main course of lamb; tureens of vegetables were placed at each end of the table for diners to help themselves. Deciding how many roast potatoes to shovel onto one's plate posed a dilemma for Mick but less so, he surmised, for the public schoolboys who had learned all too well the lessons of the refectory that first come first served because few remained by the time the tureen was passed to him. Certainly he'd no need to worry about his table manners: this lot, he decided, behaved like a troop of baboons.

Mick spotted his fellow interviewees of the previous autumn, Bright and Anstruther, at the end of his table. He tried but failed to catch their attention – either that or they deliberately chose to ignore him. Apart from requesting the salt and pepper to be passed, Mick kept quiet. He listened. All around him were loud voices speaking like Bright and Anstruther: public schoolboys confident in their surroundings. It seemed to Mick as if they were establishing the pecking order. The loudest were intent on gaining recognition as the alpha males in this intake; around them hovered drones who laughed, shook their heads on cue and emitted a braying 'Yah!' at the end of almost every sentence. It seemed the 'better' educated one was the more one was expected, or had the right, to act obnoxiously. He did exchange courtesies with the Freshman opposite, named Colin, who appeared just as overawed by his surroundings as he. Turned out Colin was also a grammar school boy, which explained his timidity. Mick would only speak to him once more, a few days later, when Colin informed him he'd changed courses from Politics, Philosophy and Economics to Medicine. A staggering sea-change, yet one which made Mick wonder if he might make the less radical switch from his beloved History to Geography should the demands of Latin and German prove insurmountable.

After tables had been cleared, the Dean of St. Frideswide's took centre stage. 'To those unaware, my name is Gerard Townley and as Dean of College it is my responsibility to ensure you adhere to College Regulations,' said the black-gowned and capped figure prowling the aisle. 'I am more "stick" than "carrot", as it were!'

A polite titter greeted Townley's little jest from some of the drones. Playing the game, reckoned Mick: teacher's pets eager to announce themselves and earn a gold star. Reprehensible as this look-at-me attitude struck Mick, it provided food for thought. He'd better learn how to play this game pretty damn quick.

Townley's collar denoted another cleric. His stentorian delivery was at odds with his pipe-cleaner build. But it demonstrated clearly some love of the stage his position gifted.

'Gentlemen, first, would you please complete the registration form being passed to you. Once completed, pass it back down your table to the aisle where I shall collect them.'

Mick studied the form pushed in front of him. He sought inspiration by allowing his eyes a tour of their surroundings. It was the first time Mick had been inside the Dining Hall. It was not the grandest of its kind among Oxford's colleges, rather poky, in need of some loving care and not lavishly furnished. 'Top Table', where the dons would dine at the more formal second sitting, when gowns had to be worn, was on a low dais at one end with the kitchen at the other. Above the kitchen was a gallery. St. Frideswide may have been the patron saint of Oxford and its University but her miracles did not extend to endowing the College bearing her name with much wealth. The walls looked to Mick as if they were in desperate need of a lick of paint. In an effort to brighten the room, or conceal the odd crack, they carried portraits in oil of past College worthies. Perhaps they detected Mick's reservations because suddenly he imagined their piercing eyes looking down on him, like so many twinkling stars on a cloudless night, trying to judge whether he was fit to be a member of their firmament.

No, perhaps not at him exactly but the form that lay in front of him, this confession and potential suicide note. They were waiting to see what he was about to write on it. And so were his fellow Freshmen. They, he was convinced, were waiting to pounce. His pen hovered above the space reserved for 'School' and 'Father's Occupation.'

'Make haste!' the Dean intoned in a voice now bordering on the camp. 'We've much more to discuss! I must acquaint you with College Regulations.'

Mick glanced at the diminutive auburn-haired figure to his right. Mick was instantly transfixed: he was sporting a cravat. He'd never before seen anyone wearing a cravat outside of the ancient films shown on Sunday afternoon television. He forced his glance downwards and saw 'Radley College' and 'Surgeon' in the appropriate spaces on the registration form of someone called Philip Cook. Then a second peek, to his left. The fresh-faced youth hunched over his paper caught Mick's intrusion and returned it with a smile rather than the threatening glare such nosiness would've provoked back on the estate. This friendly soul swept the floppy hair from his eye-line and resumed his form-filling. Mick's attention was drawn to the name: Coutts. That he had also written 'Harrow' and 'Banker' came as no surprise. Mick inhaled surreptitiously and pondered. The pair looked like they belong here. Surely, he thought, they'll sense I don't. They've only got to look at me, in jacket, collar and tie as if it's interview day all over again and here they are confidently dressed in jeans and sweaters as if lounging before the television in their own drawing room.

Writing down 'South Oxford Grammar School' on his own form momentarily lifted his spirits for Mick was immensely proud of his achievement. His small grammar school on the south-eastern outskirts of the city had only been open for seven years and he was its first pupil to win a place at Oxford. Mick assured himself he'd probably worked harder to get here than these sons of privilege to whom it was a rite of passage. But his self-esteem was punctured as quickly as it had inflated once he came to the space reserved for 'Father's Occupation.' Now he knew why it's said beware of getting what you wish for. Once passed back down the line every pair of eyes would see what he'd written on his form. They'd think he was an oik, a country bumpkin, or a 'Townie' who'd struck lucky, a fraud who'd fiddled his way out of the jungle of suburban Oxford's council houses and factories into the cloistered groves of academe. Mick dallied as long as he could. His conscience would be outraged but he felt compelled to lie. Quickly he scrawled 'Teacher' in the hope its illegibility might conceal its lie. If guilt had an expression it now plagued Mick's face from ear to ear.

Copies of *College Regulations* were distributed. 'Read these thoroughly at your leisure,' said the Dean. 'But may I draw your attention to Section 3, Conduct and Discipline, which states "The College gate is closed at 9.05pm. The Porter will open the gate to undergraduates coming into College between 9.05pm and midnight, and a record of the times of entry will be kept and submitted weekly to the Dean. To be out of College after midnight is a very serious offence." I cannot emphasize that strongly enough.'

Townley waited for the message to sink in before resuming. 'I'd also advise you all to pay particular attention to that paragraph of Section 7 stating "Women may only be received into or entertained in rooms in College between the hours of 1pm and 10pm." I do hope that sentence is abundantly clear?'

He paused, undoubtedly for effect. 'I must warn you that undergraduates have been "sent down" for breaching this Regulation.' His message triggered a murmur of testosterone-generated disappointment that rippled from bench to bench.

A face just as quickly materialized in Mick's subconscious. The face came with a name. That face and delectable body belonged to Samantha Owens.

Sam was in the year below Mick at South Oxford and she occupied his thoughts almost as much as rugby: winning her affections was as vital to him as winning his Blue. He'd been besotted with her ever since the day he first laid eyes on her, properly laid eyes on her, when Sam emerged from her chrysalis at 16. It was as though someone had crept up behind him in a dark alley and mugged him. To Mick she epitomized the perfect blend of mind and body. She had a face fit for De Vinci: perfectly symmetrical either side of a short, straight nose with a pert tip that crinkled coquettishly when she giggled – which was often. Her figure was made for tight sweaters and mini-skirts and could detonate a trouser malfunction at 20 paces; she was such a dish that even a confirmed bachelor like Prinny might be driven to kicking a hole in the Chapel's Burne-Jones stain-glass window. Then there was a brain as sharp as a scalpel and a personality with the crack of a bullwhip. Why, she didn't even speak with an Oxfordshire accent! Her voice chimed with laughter which, along with eyes like chips of blue ice similarly disposed, Mick wished he could bottle and keep in his pocket.

In the opinion of Mick Bernard no girl looked like Sam, walked like Sam, talked like Sam. And her unique appeal was Mick's greatest obstacle because she was the spark and tinder for every red-blooded boy in the Sixth Form and countless studs chasing her in the world beyond the school gates. Mick's mates assured him Sam was out of his league. And he could see their point: a creature of her exotic plumage was never likely to be caged by one as dull and socially awkward as he. Mick knew Sam could play the field. He was happy just to be in that field, and resolved to follow to the letter his father's maxim to 'try, try and try again' for no other girl came close to having this extraordinary effect on him. Eventually he had plucked up the courage to ask her out to the cinema, and her acceptance of further dates suggested she didn't find his attentions repellent. Yet he could never find the gumption to tell her how gorgeous she was. He'd rehearse the words and hear himself articulating them but when it came to the crunch he was, in another of his father's phrases, 'backward in coming forward'. He had no option but to hope the kudos of being an Oxford student with private love nest might work some magic because he knew she had him tight on the end of her line. Thus was the 'give up' part of Roy Bernard's advice some way off in Mick's estimation.

'One last thing before you go,' said Townley. 'Using pins or sticky tape on the walls of your room is frowned upon. Please desist!' A faint chuckle denoting that particular boat had sailed swept the Dining Hall.

Induction process completed, the St. Frideswide's Freshmen tumbled out of the Dining Hall's tiny double doors into the Front Quad and an October evening heavy with the threat of rain. The Fresher pressed against Mick exhaled audibly and casually asked: 'What do you think of the place?'

'It's okay, I s'pose.'

'Bit grander than school, eh?' ventured this new acquaintance. 'The name's Killip by the way. And you are?'

'Bernard, Mick Bernard.'

'This place is miles better than my *Alma Mater*, I can assure you!'

'Where's that?'

'Ratcliffe College, near Leicester. Ruled by priests. The Black Death we called them!' Killip cocked his pomaded head and said: 'Where did you go to school?'

'South Oxford Grammar School,' answered Mick. Emboldened by this hand of friendship Mick carried on: 'But I passed the 11-plus and could of went to a public school on the Iffley Road...'

'I think you mean "could have gone", old chap...' said Killip, nostrils flaring like a snorting thoroughbred.

Mick's effort to think of a way out of this grammatical gaffe got lost in the haze of Killip's pomposity. One quality, one sin, he'd inherited from his mother was pride and he knew instantly what her reaction would be to such an insult – and it was gripping him at this moment. He felt red heat spread through his face like mercury rising. Killip had the sort of kisser Mick felt instinctively compelled to punch: 95% of him wanted to smack his tormentor right there and then but, thankfully, the other 5% told him it wasn't worth bruising his knuckles. *Typical Townie! Thinks with his fists, not his brain!* he could hear them protesting. And his personal introduction to the Dean would be to receive a dressing down and hefty fine for gross misconduct.

But he might have known once he opened his mouth he'd be rumbled. 'They might live close to us but it's a diff'rent world they in'abit on the other side of Mag'len Bridge, behind those college walls,' warned his Uncle Ben, the avuncular Bernard uncle, one afternoon over a cup of tea and a jam tart in his kitchen. 'They keeps to their side, an' we keeps to ours. They eats roast dinners three days a week. We 'ave one of a Sunday. They 'ave lunch an' dinner. We 'ave dinner an' tea. They drinks a glass o'sherry in he Randolph Hotel. We down pints o'bitter in the Wellington. They plays chess. We plays darts an' Aunt Sally. They rows an' punts on the river. We throws our dog-ends in it when we're walkin' 'ome from the Isis of a summer night.'

Such was Uncle Ben's take on the traditional conflict between Town and Gown for Oxford's soul. His wisdom had always impressed Mick. As did his 'class'. To Mick 'class' wasn't restricted to social status. It was how a person conducted themselves: how they measured up in terms of critical qualities like dignity, integrity, loyalty, humility, generosity. Mick had quickly discovered some of his College peers boasting higher social status lacked 'class' – unlike Uncle Ben. He was a classic example of an exceptionally classy individual in spite of his apparent lack of suitable credentials. He worked in the car plant, lived in a council house and had next to no experience of the outside world: apart from two years National Service he'd not moved further than half-a-mile from the house in which he was born. The moral of the story according to Uncle Ben was plain: you can take the boy out of Hill Rise, but you can't take Hill Rise out of the boy.

Splitting infinitives in his distinctive accent peppered with an 'oi' or an 'ent' would see to that. Most members of his extended family made no bones about his predicament. Uncle Reg, his mother's grumpy elder brother, was their spokesman. Though never exactly saying so, he clearly regarded Mick as a traitor to his class, the working class. Reg looked and played the part: burly of build with a ruddy face dominated by a large nose bending this way and that after being broken a few times during scuffles at chucking-out time down the pub, he never wasted the few words in his lexicon. 'Whadya wornt to be mixin' with that funny lot?' he challenged Mick one day. 'Those grads think they owns the town, roiding bikes loik nutters with those daft black gowns flyin' 'bout! S'pose it's them snooty teachers o'yours at gramma school thass put daft ideas in your head!'

Mick was well aware Uncle Reg nursed a grudge against grammar schools. His younger daughter Jean had attended Oxford's most prestigious grammar school for girls, Milham Ford. He believed she was so miserably taught about the 'facts of life' that she fell pregnant after allowing a spot of slap-and-tickle in the garden of the Wellington to go too far. Mick waited for Reg to add *Ent yer ashamed o'yerself!* But Uncle Reg was a wise enough old owl to know that words unsaid inflicted a wound whose blemish dug deeper and whose bruise lingered longer.

Killip's barefaced snobbery left Mick wretched and confused. He'd always accepted the transition from a small school to a grand college wasn't going to be easy and that it might leave him feeling miserably lost in the short term. He'd never any trouble making friends at South Oxford. There he'd been a big fish in a small pond. Here it seemed he was a minnow who'd strayed into open water and swum straight into a shark's mouth. The antipathy between himself and the Killips of St Frideswide's, he reasoned, was clearly going to be mutual. He could envisage Killip, for example, being welcomed into one or more of the various College sets, a dining club, an essay or a debating society. Oxford colleges harboured fewer loafers nowadays, 'heavies' as those of a sporting variety were labelled. Mick wanted to be accepted by his fellows. He wanted to be one of them but he didn't want to be like them because that meant abandoning his convictions. The contradiction was too obvious not to be lost on him and only served to deepen the depression starting to build inside his head. The only means of keeping afloat and demonstrating his right to be here was to excel on the rugby pitch. No sporting duffers in St Frideswide's dare denigrate one of its sportsmen who brought more distinction to the College than they did. But a thought worth clinging onto quickly subsided under the weight of others. Although Uncle Reg might be the biggest bastard in creation, thought Mick, he was probably right: I'm not going to fit-in here. In an instant he appreciated how Pip felt in *Great Expectations* on swapping the forge for London society: it is a miserable thing to be ashamed of home. Mick Bernard may never have left the house for school with holes in his socks but once sent out into the wider world beyond Hill Rise he had plenty of holes in his mind.

The rain starting to dampen Mick's face matched his mood. The heavy burden of guilt lowered his head as he negotiated the plank bridge across the puddles that were now threatening to engulf it. Guilt enveloped him like the clouds of dust he kicked up on the stairs to his room. He felt guilt for finding comfort in books and museums rather than throwing a dart or holding a fishing rod; for passing the 11-plus and broadening his horizons beyond the car factory; for abandoning the game at which his father excelled for another that Roy Bernard had no knowledge or appreciation.

All that accumulated guilt should've been enough. But now he was guilty of the ultimate treason: betraying his family and working class heritage. He was a class traitor. There was no mercy for that. He would be made to pay. The means were in place. They hurtled through his mind as he closed the door of the room he'd chosen for his dungeon. He numbered them off. Should he fail Prelims and be 'sent down'. Should Sam Owens be caught in his room after hours. Should he fail to win his Blue. Those three would do for starters. They'd cause the whole pack of cards to collapse. Then the sacrifices he'd made would all amount to nothing; be for nothing. Every Uncle Reg would crow, long and loud. Making sure he heard them. All that would stay with him was the guilt sewn into the seams of his soul.

His world was in danger of spinning off its axis like the rain he shook from his hair. He even felt guilt for feeling guilty. And it served him right because it was his fault for having ideas above his station. He stared at the teardrops of rain dribbling down the window pane and wanted to howl. But he couldn't bring himself to do it and heap more guilt on his shoulders for being a wimp. For Mick Bernard never cried. He'd decided long ago that, like apologizing, crying was a sign of weakness. He just mouthed a few crude expletives instead.

Guilt. One short, five-letter word. Yet an emotion that clung to Mick Bernard as tightly and destructively as if he was drowning in cobwebs. Other emotions came and went: happiness; loneliness; sadness. But guilt never left him. It was always there. He carried it as Atlas shouldered the heavens.

Ever since the day played out years earlier in the woods of Slade Camp that was his first memory of life.

PART TWO

Pushing the Boundaries

One

'Where are you? Yer little bleeder!' shrieked a voice laden with malice. 'Jus' wait till I gets 'old of ya!'

The sound was not the calm and comforting voice of Granny Jaykes that he loved so much. These words spat out by his mother ensured four-year-old Mick Bernard had the taste of fear in his mouth at the prospect of feeling the hand of guilt slap his cheek for the first time. The guilt that dragged over his young skin like Sweeny Todd's razor left a scar, faint now yet still discernible to those at St. Frideswide's and beyond who cared to investigate. Perhaps the past is 'another country' as LW Hartley insisted. But childhood's as much a state of mind as a period in the past. It never leaves us. It just lies doggo. So Mick Bernard decided. And he'd given an awful lot of thought to that hypthesis before reaching his conclusion.

The incident triggering Mick's lifelong malaise would seem trivial to most Oxford undergraduates but it was the first of many traumatic events that piled up into his mountain of guilt. The setting was Slade Camp, the entrance to which lay across the lane from the cottage of Ernest and Jane Jaykes. Wedged between Magdalen Wood and Brasenose Wood, testimony to the two Oxford colleges that once owned the land, part of the camp held PoWs put to work on the local farms during World War II while the rest acted as a training ground for the British Army: though watchtowers were absent, perimeter fence and guardhouse remained. Roy and Edna Bernard counted themselves lucky to have a place of their own but despite 26 Magdalen Fields sounding a rather bijou address its surroindings bore closer resemblance to its former role than anything Elysian. Mick's home was a Nissen hut fashioned from sheets of corrugated iron bent into a half-moon with each end planked. Plasterboard created rooms. There was an indoor lavatory but no bath; a tin tub sufficed. The old iron stove remained at the hut's heart. It was an object of mirth to an old soldier such as his father. Whenever Edna fantasized about central heating Roy would point to the stove and jauntily reply: 'Heatin' dunt come more central than that.'

The huts were painted black, moated by rock-strewn undergrowth and linked by rock-marked paths. Such was the landscape of Mick's infancy; his playground. It was here that fear first gripped him while playing in the woods with his best friend Nancy Greene, she of freckled face and black hair neatly parted on the left and held in place by a pink plastic slide. Mick was throwing sticks into the branches of a horse chestnut tree trying to harvest its conkers when one missile struck Nancy's head, sending blood gushing down her face. While she skedaddled, screaming, in search of her mother, he clambered up the tree in search of sanctuary, snivelling as he went. Pretty soon the mothers were on the scene.

Mick's bawling intensified and betrayed his hiding place in the crook of the tree, barely six feet off the ground. Edna grabbed him by his pullover and yanked him to the ground. Maintaining her grip with one hand she sent him reeling with a cuff round the head with the other before switching targets and drumming the back of his knees. It was the beat of a mantra that came to symbolize Mick's childhood.

'Dunt you ever do that again!' she shouted. Wallop! 'Showin' me up in front of Mrs Greene!' Wallop! 'Jus' wait till y'father gets home! If he dunt give you 'nother good hidin', I will!'

Justice had to be seen to be done. That was the code families like his and Nancy's lived by. Nancy's mum had to be mollified. His mother had to uphold family honour; otherwise she risked being labelled shameless. The symbiosis of action and reaction stayed with Mick. Crime led to punishment. Taking risks, taking a chance, had to be resisted. He could come unstuck. Retribution would surely follow. Attempting to evade such retribution high in the boughs of a tree became its epitome. He never climbed another tree. Heights terrified him. They brought it all back. The fear and the guilt at doing wrong, committing a sin. Playing safe was, well, safer.

Thus was Mick Bernard introduced to fear and its cousins, guilt and justice; but not a form of justice ratified by law. No judge; no jury; certainly no lawyer for the defence. Guilty as charged. His mother made the laws and enforced them rigorously. There was no right of appeal. Punishment was swift and merciless; always physical. Any sense of injustice had to be swallowed along with the tears.

But when the initial terror and pain had departed he was left feeling something new and strange. It was something that followed him around like an unwelcome smell. He couldn't talk about it because he had no idea what it was; and in any case he'd not yet the vocabulary to describe it. All he knew was it hid somewhere in his head waiting to emerge whenever he got into a scrape. This knowledge blotted out the sunshine in his young life as sure as any rain cloud. He grew to know this awful feeling as guilt. The events that triggered this unwelcome visitor tainted Mick's childhood to the detriment of anything more positive or enjoyable.

Attending school introduced Mick to more authority figures to stand parity with his mother. His initial experience in Headington was brief. His parents rose to the top of the council's housing list and received a semi-detached house on the new Northway estate.

With the new house came a new school: all glass and brick. But it also brought his first brush with authority beyond the home, albeit minor authority. If Mick's emotional skin had been grazed by his mother it was now to be cut open by an officious dinner lady. That the clash could only have one outcome made its impact on Mick's psyche all the more incisive. He was always going to lose the argument. But he refused to concede. It wasn't just. And it wasn't fair.

'Come along, Michael! Eat your dinner,' the white-coated woman demanded, pointing to a plate of food clearly untouched by Mick's cutlery.

Mick made no reply but merely continued staring at the gloop on his plate. It was cauliflower cheese. He hated both ingredients.

'Your mother has paid for this meal,' continued his tormentor, slightly louder. 'Do as you're told!'

Mick remained as silent and motionless as Rodin's thinker.

'You'll not have any pudding until you've cleaned the plate! This is perfectly good food!'

Tears welled in his eyes. He was looking forward to the lemon tart.

'Snivelling like as baby won't help you!'

Mick sniffed and suppressed the urge to cry.

She bent down over him. 'You'll stay here for the entire dinner hour!'

Mick's head stayed low and didn't budge an inch. See if I care, he muttered to himself.

'Your mother will be informed how you've deliberately wasted her money. You're nothing but a wilful, naughty boy!'

This threat did find a home. Mick knew he would be in his mother's cross hairs a few hours later. He could see the red mark developing on the backs of his knees and feel the sting already.

And waiting for the punishment was more painful that the actuality. Even the afternoon treat of *Listening with Mother* on the school wireless failed to lighten his mood. But, he reasoned, unlike the retribution exacted after the accident in Slade Camp, his actions on this occasion were not accidental. He could appreciate the crime did warrant some form of punishment. Alas, that punishment could only take one form: a whack.

Mick's schooling thrived after a house swap to Hill Rise. The move came about because Roy's work as a long-distance lorry driver for BRS was based nearby, quite a trek from Northway: he'd no car; refused to use a bike; and reaching the depot necessitated two buses. Furthermore, his entire family lived within hailing distance of Hill Rise. Fortuitously, the *Oxford Mail* ran a daily column advertising house swaps among council tenants: Roy and Edna responded to one from a couple living on the Hill Rise estate and the swap was speedily completed.

No sooner had they settled into the new house than there was a knock on the front door. The visitor introduced himself as a representative from Hill Rise FC: the arrival of a local football celebrity on the estate such as Roy Bernard had not gone unheralded. Roy was an inside forward (an attacking midfielder in modern parlance) who modelled himself on the likes of Len Shackleton, though his idol was Preston and England's Tom Finney with whom he'd played while in the army. Roy's strengths were the ability to spray passes with either foot and unleash a cannonball of a shot from distance. He seldom broke sweat, preferring to let the ball do the work, not his legs, and refused to head the ball ('the game's called football not 'eadball,' reasoned Roy), which struck Mick as eminently sensible since catching the laces on the ball full in the kisser left a vivid imprint and the sting of a dozen wasps. Roy Bernard listened politely to the stranger's entreaties and agreed to turn out that coming Saturday.

It was a home match on the recreation ground just a couple of minutes walk from their new home. Mick only saw his father play a few times. This would be the final occasion. And he'd never forget it. Edna walked him round and when they arrived the match was already in progress. A healthy crowd lined all four touchlines but, as was the custom, Mick was allowed to squeeze in at the front.

'Wos the score, mista?'

'One nil.'

'Who to?'

'Us – Hill Rise.'

'Who scored?'

'That bloke stood there in the centre circle, with his 'ands on his 'ips,' said the spectator, pointing a finger. 'Done bugger-all 'cept smash a 30-yarder in top corner!'

Mick's eyes followed the finger to spy his father standing in splendid isolation, slick black locks falling over his eyes. His puny chest swelled: to his six-year-old son Roy looked like a Greek god that afternoon; his pedestal could get no higher. But it transpired he was a god with feet of clay. When that clay crumbled a decade later the god fell from his pedestal and smashed into pieces that could never be reassembled.

Mick thoroughly enjoyed his six months at the local Infants school, his father's first school, before transferring to its Junior branch occupying Upton Green, a splendid Victorain house with grounds, 100 yards up the road next to the parish church. His love of school and his academic progress continued. This he attributed to two teachers: Martha Gibson and Joss Walker.

Miss Gibson taught Mick in his second year at Upton Green. She had vivid red hair cut in a 'bob', an upturned nose and her skin the colour of Carrara marble was heightened by her choice of a crimson lipstick. She was the school 'sweetheart': young, far younger than Upton Green's other female teachers, and very approachable. Every day she caught the Number 3 bus at the bottom of Mick's estate and he soon began carrying her briefcase on the five-minute walk: in short he became teacher's pet. And Mick had his own pet by now, a grey rabbit he'd named Bugs after his favourite cartoon character. One afternoon a plan was hatched.

'Michael...'

'You can call me Mick, miss, if you wornt. All me friends do.'

'I think we should stick with your full name, like we do in class.'

'Okay, miss. If you wornt.'

'Well, do you remember that composition you wrote about your pet rabbit?' said Miss Gibson, looking down to assure herself of Mick's undivided attention.

'Yes, miss. He's called Bugs.'

'Is he a boy or a girl?'

'He's a boy, miss. A buck.'

'I thought so,' said Miss Gibson. 'I wonder if the Class might borrow him?'

'Woffor?'

'Well,' she said, slowly and seriously, 'the headmaster has granted me permission to purchase a small animal, a hamster or a guinea pig or a gerbil or a rabbit, to be the Class pet...'

'An' you want to buy Bugsy?' Mick cried, looking up at Miss Gibson with horror in his eyes.

'Not exactly.'

'Phew! I'd never sell 'im anyway.'

'And quite right, too,' said Miss Gibson. 'I was thinking of buying a female rabbit...'

'A doe!'

'Yes, a doe,' she continued. 'The Class would look after her. We'd draw-up a list of people interested in feeding her and cleaning her cage...'

'Hutch,' interjected Mick, with the aitch carefully pronounced. 'It's called a hutch.'

'Yes, her hutch. I stand corrected,' said Miss Gibson, softly. Said more nicely, thought Mick, than mum if I'd told her she was in the wrong; would've got a clout, no bother.

'I could build her a hutch,' said Mick, eager to please. 'I made Bugs one. It's easy-peasy. I'll get an ole fruit box from the greengrocer's on our shops, a bit o'wire is all we need for the front of 'er run at one end of the box, an' some small bits o'wood for the latch an' to block orf 'er sleepin' end.'

'Thank you, Mick. That would be very helpful of you.'

'Thass okay, miss,' he said, moving near enough to pick-up her scent.

'Well, the idea is to teach the Class about being responsible for others.'

'Roight.'

Miss Gibson paused, not at the damage to her sensibilities arising from Mick's mangling of the English tongue, but to find the right words. 'How can I put this,' she said, her white skin beginning to flush. 'I thought it would be wonderful if she were to have babies...'

'Kittens, miss!'

'Yes, kittens,' Miss Gibson acknowledged sharply, having had her train of thought interrupted. 'Then we'd be responsible for a family. We'd raise them and sell them...'

'To the pet shop in the Covered Market, miss!'

'Exactly,' agreed Miss Gibson. 'Perhaps some of the Class might wish to buy one. But I shall certainly follow your suggestion and ask the pet shop about purchasing any kittens because that's where I shall obtain the doe. But then there's the matter of...'

'A buck t'be the dad!' yelled Mick. 'I got it now! You wornt Bugs t'be the dad!'

'Quite so,' said Miss Gibson. 'Would you agree to lend him to us?'

'You bet, miss!'

'Do you think Bugs would be agreeable,' she said, with a knowing smile.

'Corse he would, miss!' said Mick, enthusiastically, before frowning. 'So, miss, when does the magic 'appen?'

Miss Gibson felt the heat in her cheeks again. 'During the night we'll let them have the run of the stock room. That's when they get to know each other.'

'But 'ow does the...'

'I think we should leave it there,' Miss Gibson said, pointing toward the bus stop. 'Look, my bus is coming!'

With hutch constructed and doe purchased, a white the Class decided to call Snow White, Mick brought Bugs to school in a zip-up bag. The floor of the small stock room dividing Miss Gibson's classroom from Mr Walker's was protected with copious layers of old newspaper and a bed of straw in one corner to make Bugs feel at home; in fact it was better than home because he had more room to gambol about. He stayed three days and at the end of school each afternoon the doe was put in with him. If rabbits could grin with satisfaction Bugs would've sported one from ear to floppy ear when Mick took him home: space to run about; as many tit-bits as he could eat; willing playmates during the day – and a female at night. A month later Mick burst into the classroom after giving

Snow White her breakfast to announce excitedly: 'She's 'adum, miss! Seven of 'um! They're black an' white!' The choice of names was obvious. The Class named them after Snow White's seven dwarves.

Martha Gibson only stayed one year at Upton Green so Mick was fortunate to come into contact with a type of women he didn't know existed: her dress, her speech, her manners and her fragrance were totally at odds with his aunts or the women in his street. She didn't smell of cigarette smoke, a smell to which he'd already taken an ardent dislike. There was always a shroud of smoke at home: Roy and Edna even smoked while washing in the kitchen sink and between mouthfuls while eating; the sight of dog-ends being stubbed out on empty plates or dropped into tea cups Mick found revolting. And, he felt Miss Gibson liked him. This meant an awful lot to him: because Martha Gibson wasn't family. Edna, Granny Jaykes and his aunts were obliged to like him, or give the impression they liked him, because he was a blood relation and it would be rude not to. Mick was sad not to be able to continue their walks to the bus stop but this loss was countered by his teacher in Year Three.

Joss Walker was a big man with a florid face, centred on a prominent nose, a teacher who'd no need to instil discipline in his pupils since his natural manner exuded quiet control. He made a habit of calling each of his charges to his desk once a day to go over some element of their work. This was the kind of one-to-one instruction that appealed to Mick; its outcome was always put into practise and never forgotten. One morning, during the writing of a composition about a storm, Walker seized the opportunity to go through Mick's effort with him. Walker picked out one sentence: 'I like staying in bed in the winter'. He asked Mick to explain why: 'Because I loik to hear the rain bashing on the winda panes, an' the cold makes me snuggle under the blankets an' makes me feel nice an' safe.' Walker smiled and said: 'Then that's what you should have written, isn't it? Always ask yourself why something has happened, how it makes you feel. Don't be afraid to use your thoughts and your imagination. Use plenty of adjectives, the words that describe. Read as many books and stories as you can because you'll learn from them. They'll inspire your writing.'

To this end Walker promoted silent reading for an hour one afternoon a week where his pupils could bring in their own choice of book if the school library had nothing that fired their imagination. Mick became a voracious reader, having progressed from the *Classics Illustrated* series of comic-strip versions of the great works of fiction to the genuine article. He discovered the *Regency Classic* series of hardbacks that could be purchased for one shilling and nine pence from Woolworth. By his tenth birthday he'd devoured *Jane Eyre, Wuthering Heights, A Tale of Two Cities* and *Moby Dick* besides more standard boyhood fare such as *Robin Hood, King Arthur, Robinson Crusoe, Treasure Island* and *Ivanhoe*. When his books weren't offering him escapism the cinema did. Westerns starring Randolph Scott or Rory Calhoun were magnetic; Burt Lancaster in *The Crimson Pirate* hypnotic. Walker also opened Mick's eyes, or to be more accurate, his ears, to classical music. Every Thursday morning he'd bring out an old wind-up gramophone to play records for 30 minutes: Beethoven, Handel, Tchaikovsky, Mozart. The *1812 Overture* was Mick's favourite owing to its stirring backcloth of bells ringing and cannons blasting.

But Walker offered Mick much more than the academic or the aesthetic: he awarded the ultimate school prize if you were a boy for it was Walker who ran Upton Green's renowned football team. Wearing the black-and-gold shirt of Upton Green was the dream of every boy who transformed the far end of the playground into a football pitch at play time, rain or shine, whenever someone produced a tennis ball. Walker recognized a precocious talent when he saw one and put Mick into the school team while he was still in the third year. Mick's debut was watched by Roy. His performance, in a Number 10 shirt worn elsewhere with distinction by his father, was lacklustre: he wasn't physically mature enough to compete against older boys.

'How'd I do, dad?' Mick asked on the walk home. 'Well,' said Roy, trying desperately to think of something nice to say. 'Your passin' could be better an' your tacklin'...was a bit weak...an' you never had a shot, so can't say anythin' 'bout that.' Mick's eyes began to water. Roy searched for something to cheer up his visibly crestfallen son. 'But at least you dunt 'ead the ball. Thass good, cuz the game's called football not 'eadball!'

Walker's gamble had failed and he was forced to drop Mick from the team. The following season saw Mick's fortunes rise like Lazarus. It started, however, with a setback. When the first team sheet went up on the notice board Mick's name did not feature in his favoured position, number 10, among the goal-scoring forwards – he was picked at number 4, right-half, one of the all-purpose, passing and tackling players in midfield who were obliged to run up and down the pitch non-stop. His disappointment vanished once Walker took him for individual practice during dinner-time play. Walker began by telling him how important he was to the team: he was the engine that would make it work effectively. Then he told him how he'd grown bigger and stronger since last season, especially in the legs: he had the power to hit long passes like nobody else in the team, said Walker, muscle opponents off the ball in a tackle, and if anyone could score a goal from long-range it was him. Suddenly Mick had visions of his father doing just that in the Hill Rise colours. Walker may or may not have known something of Roy Bernard's football career but either by luck or judgement he'd pressed the right button to convince Mick he was going to be a carbon copy of his father. Then, collared, tied and jacketed with trousers tucked into his socks and football boots gleaming, Walker led Mick to the centre circle.

‘Now, I’m going to roll a ball across to you and tell you to hit a pass immediately toward a corner flag. If it’s to the right corner flag you hit the ball with your left foot, and if it’s to the left corner flag you hit it with your right foot. Got that?’

Walker beckoned the Davies twins, who were watching them and happened to be the team’s two wingers, to stand in either corner and retrieve the balls. ‘Find the twins here and you’ll find them in a match,’ he told Mick.

For 10 minutes Walker rolled balls; Mick smacked them; the twins returned them. With each pass Mick’s accuracy improved and Walker’s judgement went from advice to praise. ‘And one more thing,’ he said, after calling a halt. ‘If the wingers cross the ball and it’s kicked out by a defender toward you don’t think twice about shooting for goal. You’ve got a howitzer in each boot! Use it!’

Weekly repetition of these passing drills further developed the power in Mick’s legs already blessed thanks to Roy’s genes. He fired a few rockets into the top corners that season as Upton Green won their league to contest the inter-league final. The game was held on Oxford City’s White House ground on the Abingdon Road. Upton Green lost. Mick found it a tough proposition to cover the ground on a full-sized adult pitch, to make the long passes reach his wingers, and hadn’t a single opportunity to shoot at goal. On returning home he discovered his father had been in the crowd. That did it: Roy had watched Mick play twice and both were disasters. Edna pronounced Roy to be bad luck; he was a Jonah whose presence jinxed their son. Roy was banished from any of Mick’s future sporting fixtures. There was no right of appeal. That’s how it was in the court of Edna Bernard.

However, Roy was unable to jinx his son's attempt at the 11-plus examination that determined Mick's immediate academic future. Mick felt he'd done okay in the tests and was confident of the outcome. When he found the letter bearing the Education Authority stamp lying on the doormat he rushed it to Edna.

'Come on, mum! Open it!' he begged.

'Steady down an' hold your 'orses!' said Edna. 'Neh then, let's see what it says.'

She stuck a finger into the envelope, pulled out the letter and unfolded it. 'Dear Mr and Mrs Bernard,' she read aloud before mumbling through the next sentence or two.

'What's it say, mum?' shrieked Mick.

'You passed...'

'Yahooo!'

'And it says you've bin all'cated a place at South Oxford Gramma School...'

'What!' said Mick, face crumbling toward tears. 'I dunt wornt to go there!'

'It says if you wornt to be considered for 'nother school...'

'Yes! Yes!'

'...you muss write a letter to the 'eadmaster o'that school.'

'Please write one, mum!' Mick said, tugging at his mother's pinafore. 'I wornt to go to Mag'len College School! You knows that! Please write to the 'eadmaster loik they say.'

Edna studied his crumpled expression. 'I'll see what I can do,' she said at length. 'Any'ow, you better get orf to school or yull be late.'

The playground was already alive with chatter when Mick arrived: groups of boys and groups of girls swapping news of their fate. Susan Abbott, the class swot, wasn't lowering herself by attending this new grammar school: she was going to Milham Ford.

'Didya pass?' Mick yelled at his best pal, Pete Livermore. 'Where y'goin' to go?'

'This new South Oxford Gramma School, I s'pose, thass bein' built down the road.'

'I'm gunna go to Mag'len College School.'

'What you wornt t'go there for?' said Pete, scewing up his face until it looked to Mick like one of the dates he watched his dad eat at Christmas.

'I've bin past it on the bus an' it looks good. Woppin' great playground it's got. And the blazer's smashin' an'all. Lovely black thing with red round the pockets.'

'Well,' said Pete, 'all roight if you wornt t'play rugby...'

'What?' said Mick in a voice suddenly conveying panic.

'They dunt play football at all,' said Pete. 'They all plays rugby.'

'But me mum is goin' to write a letter to'um, askin' for a place.'

No school morning lasted longer than this one as far as an agitated Mick was concerned. He'd never raced home for his dinner faster than this day. He burst into the kitchen and breathlessly asked Edna whether she'd written the letter. 'Yes,' she got as far as saying before Mick started to cry. 'What y'cryin' for? It's in there on the mant'piece waitin' to be posted.'

Mick proceeded to explain between gulps that he'd changed his mind. When he told Edna his reasons she just chuckled: 'Yer a funny one an' no mistake! D'you wornt to chuck it on the fire or shall I do it?' Mick grabbed the letter and hurled it into the grate in one movement. And he stood watching until it was burnt to a cinder.

Two

'Your dinner's spoilt!' snapped Edna. 'Dried up proper! Your own fault! Bein' s'late!'

Roy Bernard adopted his customary sheepish grin in these circumstances. They weren't new; and the cause wasn't novel. 'Bin stuck in the pub, I'll be bound!' said Edna en route to the oven. 'There! Hope it chokes you!' she said, placing a plate of congealed roast brisket on the table with enough force to knock Roy's knife onto the floor.

Mick grew to learn that Sunday was the day of the week in the Bernard household for a row – albeit one-sided row, more of a tirade. Roy committed some misdemeanour and Edna pronounced sentence: a spell in the stocks to face a fusillade of verbal rotten tomatoes. Mick had witnessed his first paternal humiliation when they'd lived on the Northway estate. It had started before he'd come in from playing in the street so he'd no idea what had caused it but Edna's harangue brought about one of the rare occasions he came to be on an intimate level with his father. Roy grabbed his jacket and Mick's hand and, without so much as a word or a whisper, father and son marched out of the house in a show of masculine solidarity.

'There's a good picture on at the cinema,' Roy said, as their new concrete estate gave way to the old thatched dwellings of Headington village. 'It's a WC Fields picture. Bloody funny, he is. Mark my words, yull be in fits!'

Mick had never heard of Fields. But he took his father's word. Roy adored Tommy Cooper as did Mick whenever he saw him on television. So if Roy thought Fields was funny he must be right. And he was eager to share any of his father's passions.

'Is he as funny as Abbott an' Costello?'

'All depends what you loik, what you think is funny. Ev'ryone's a bit diff'rent when it comes to what they loiks in life. You think they're funny?'

'They're my fav'rites!'

'See what I mean?' said Roy. 'You thinks they're funny. But I dunt!'

Mick tried again. 'Is there a cowboy picture on with it?' he enquired more in hope than expectation. 'One with Randolph Scott? He's always good!'

'No, jus' the one picture of a Sunday...'

'A cartoon?' asked Mick. 'A Bugs Bunny...'

'No, 'fraid not.'

'Is the picture in colour?'

'No, 'fraid not.'

Mick began to wonder what kind of treat this outing was going to be. His downcast look vanished, however, once they entered the cinema foyer and Roy gave him sixpence to spend at the confectionary counter. He returned with a bag of Sharps assorted toffees. The cinema was already pitch dark when they chose their seats but it was clear they were among a tiny minority prepared to swap a Sunday afternoon by the fireside for the privilege of watching an ancient black-and-white film starring WC Fields. Roy instantly lit up the first of many Woodbines while Mick unwrapped a mint-flavoured toffee. By the end of the 'Pearl & Dean' advertisements Mick was on his third toffee, the one with nuts, and as the last trailer for Monday's forthcoming show slipped from the screen he'd also consumed both he caramel and the treacle options. The picture was called *It's a Gift*; Fields played the hapless businessman Harold Bissonette, harassed by his shrewish wife, his obnoxious children and his bumbling employees. Mick struggled to find much to laugh at but the sound of his father laughing fit to drop was something that stuck with him all the way home. Once inside the house Roy Bernard reverted to type: he picked up the *News of the World* and sank back into the quiet anonymity of his armchair.

The initial years at Hill Rise brought the high water mark in Mick's relationship with his parents, especially his father. Yet fear and guilt were never far away. For his first day at Roy's *Alma Mater* Mick was accompanied, there and back, by his father. They encountered a grisly scene when school finished. The school was located right next to the main Oxford to Henley road where it rose to go over the railway line. Vehicles coming from the direction of Henley would breast the rise to be quickly confronted by the 'Lollipop Man' shepherding children from one side of the road to the other. Some came over the bridge without due care and attention. On this day one of the stragglers in the crocodile of youngsters crossing the road was mown down. Roy and Mick were lucky to miss the collision itself but saw the stricken boy stretched out on the ground, his head lying on the 'lollipop'. The next morning the school was informed he'd died in hospital. They were warned, yet again, to be very careful crossing the road. They were also warned about the dangers of building sand castles in the exposed sand of the nearby railway cutting: burrowing into the sides of the cutting to collect sand was highly dangerous because the sand easily slipped and could be a death trap. A fortnight later an avalanche of sand brought down the roof of one such tunnel with just that outcome: the boy was buried alive. Edna Bernard reckoned warnings couldn't prevent children like Mick from placing themselves in danger; only putting the fear of God into them stood a chance of influencing their behaviour. She saw to it that her son would do as he was told; he'd avoid danger; and would survive.

An early Sunday at Hill Rise again saw one pint too many heap ignominy on Roy Bernard. He ignored Edna's invective in silence as usual and made great sport of consuming every dried morsel of food she'd put in front of him. Then, pushing away the empty plate, he told Mick, then aged 10, to fetch his new fishing line and they'd go down the river to see how successfully it worked. The Thames was a short walk away, over the hill and through Iffley village. The pair crossed the river at the lock and walked downstream toward Sandford until the Black Bridge, that carried the branch line from Oxford to Princess Risborough came into view.

'See that par'pet, up there?' said Roy, pointing to the iron ledge black with soot and smoke that ran along the tops of the pillars supporting the bridge. 'Thass where we used to jump into the river in the summer if it wuz hot 'nough.'

'Jump in the river from up there!' said an incredulous Mick. 'You mus' be mad to do that! There's all sorts of junk in that river! I've seen people throwin' old bikes an' cans in there jus' t'see who could make the biggest splash! You land on one o'them an' yull break yer ankle or cut yer foot orf!'

'It wuz a test o'courage, you see,' Roy explained. 'Showed you wuz a man.'

'Wuz you froightened?'

'Bet your life I wuz! 'Lookin' down at that black swirlin' water! Wondrin' what it would feel loik droppin' 20 feet!'

'Woulda stung ev'ry inch of your body till it throbbed, I bet,' said Mick.

'Too bloody roight! Thought I was sure to shit me pants standin' up there! So I 'ad t'jump…'

Mick whistled. 'What would 'appen if you dunt jump?' he added, after a pause.

'Well,' said Roy, 'you wuz a coward if you wuz too scared to jump. And ev'ryone would call you chicken.'

Mick looked toward the Black Bridge and then at the Thames beneath. 'But what if you knew it was daft to jump, knowin' you might end up cuttin' orf your foot on some bit o'junk hidden in the water,' he said, rattling off the words like bullets from a machine gun, 'and you refused to jump no matter what anyone wuz goin' to call you? You'd have to be jus' as brave to do that, wunt you dad?'

Roy looked into his son's eyes: the boy, he thought, might have a point. Perhaps he'd jumped because he was too scared not to, lacking the mental courage to stand against the crowd.

'Dad,' continued Mick behind screwed-up eyes stating the truth of what he was about to impart, 'I reck'n you mus' have courage to come down, an' not be loik ev'ryone else, an' then put up with all the name-callin', wunt you?'

Well I never, Roy decided, the boy is a clever little bugger to think that one up. 'I reck'n we should start fishin', dunt you?'

Roy pointed to a spot where a small inlet had formed, probably from generations of other anglers. Mick's new equipment was rudimentary, simply a hook on the end of a line that wound onto a small rectangular wooden frame: the angler just unwound a length of twine, baited the hook and cast into the water as far as he could – which was never going to be far because the line had no weights on it. It was, if Roy chose to admit, intended for crab fishing off the end of a pier at the seaside and totally unsuitable for coarse fishing on a river.

'Now, watch what I do, so you can do it after. Okay?' Mick watched him unwind most of the twine and begin to whirl it at arm's length into a loop. 'Now, after I've got up a bit o'speed I let go an' out she goes!'

Mick followed the flimsy length of twine as it travelled no more than two feet and fluttered into the reeds. 'Dunt you dare laugh!' father warned son. 'I'll 'ave 'nother go.'

Try as he might Roy couldn't get the line farther than the reeds: it was just too flimsy to fly through the air. After the fifth failure he threw the whole contraption into the river: 'Fuckin' piece o'shit! We're goin' home!'

The outburst caused some of the Friesians grazing nearby to lift their heads momentarily. 'But, dad,' blurted Mick. 'We only jus' got 'ere!'

Roy noticed the tears welling-up in his son's eyes. 'Do yer know 'ow to skim stones? No? I'll teach you,' he said by way of making amends. He kicked up some stones from the sand and mud at his feet and selected the flattest. Dropping into a crouch, he flicked one across the surface of the water. Mick watched it bounce once, twice and three times before it sank. 'Cor! Thass loik one o'them bouncin' bombs in *The Dam Busters*!' said a suitably impressed Mick.

'Yes, s'pose it is. Same idea,' said Roy. 'You 'ave a go.'

Roy handed Mick the flattest pebble he had left and, placing a hand on his son's shoulders, nudged him into the right position. 'Neh, then. Let fly!'

Mick pursed his lips and trusted his right arm to replicate the same arc parallel to the surface of the water as his father. With a final flick of the wrist the pebble was dispatched. Mick saw it skim once, twice, three times. And to growing excitement, he watched it skim a fourth time before disappearing. 'I beat yer! Dad, I beat yer!'

'So you did,' said Roy, to his grinning son. 'Yer a quick learner! I'll 'ave to keep an eye on you, thass for sure! Now we really are goin' home.'

All the way home Mick fell to wondering whether he'd heard his father correctly. Salty language was endemic to the Bernard household: sod, bloody, shit and bugger inhabited every other sentence as a variant of noun, adjective, verb or adverb. But having been commanded by Edna never to utter the 'f' or 'c' word and to have nothing whatsoever to do with anyone he heard using those taboo words, provoked Mick to instinctively blurt out his father's indiscretion as soon as they'd got through the back door. Roy was instantly on the receiving end of a second ear-bashing. Mick felt his father's eyes boring a hole into his skull and, realizing he'd let the side down, he slunk away to avoid witnessing the entirety of his father's humiliation. It needed some weeks for him to forget the guilt he'd felt for landing his father in the soup.

Years would pass before Mick caught his father losing his temper with a second inanimate object. It came on a frosty morning as Mick was leaving the house to do his paper round. Roy was trying without success to crank the car prior to leaving for work when there came a loud cry of 'fuckin' piece o'crap' as he slammed the starting handle into the ground, sending slivers of ice into the freezing air like so much grapeshot. On this occasion Mick merely smiled and kept his father's profanity to himself.

These early winter mornings when the labours of lorry driver and paper boy coincided amounted to a priceless opportunity for father and son to interact. Mick would rise at 5.45 in a blissfully still house to find Roy in the kitchen, all the gas rings hissing with welcoming heat, having tea and toast – which guaranteed Mick would be similarly energized before he started his round. Those snatched moments sipping tea and munching toast before braving the elements provided the nearest to male bonding Roy and Mick ever achieved.

The most telling, and most recent, occasion that Roy Bernard lost all self-control was more personal and far more instructive: it involved Mick himself. Roy was playing with Mister Jinks and, to Mick's eyes, doing so in a tormenting fashion. He shouted at his father to stop. In a flash Roy had grabbed Mick by the collar, lifting him onto his toes: 'Watch your soddin' tongue or else I'll knock y'block off!' In an instant Edna was at his shoulder: 'No, you wunt! Leave 'im alone!' Roy Bernard did as he was told and relaxed his grip.

Many a day thereafter Mick wished his father had tried to knock 'his soddin' block off': it would have demonstrated he had it in him to be the kind of alpha male his son desperately needed – and desired. If Roy Bernard was too inarticulate to censure his grammar school son with words he might at least show him who the boss was physically. But his father seldom made his presence felt. For Roy Bernard to act as an enforcer he had to lose his temper. Acting in cold blood just wasn't in his nature.

Three

The corridor leading from the front door of the Wellington Arms to the back was about the length of a cricket pitch. At one end was a heavy oak door to the public bar; at the far end was another to the saloon bar. On the opposite side of the corridor were the two doors signifying the gents and ladies toilets. Whenever any of these four doors opened a smell testifying to the room beyond drifted into the corridor: a faint whiff of pungent disinfectant and urine from one side and acrid cigarette smoke mixed with spilt beer from the other. The floor of the corridor comprised tiles, cold even in this month of September. Sitting on the floor outside each bar, like Toby Jugs on a mantelpiece, were two boys in short trousers. The boy outside the saloon bar was chuckling over a copy of the *Dandy*; beside him a half-full bottle of orangeade with a straw and a packet of Smith's crisps. The boy outside the public bar was reading *Classics Illustrated Number 98: The Red Badge of Courage.* The bottle of pop beside him was empty. He'd not eaten since a raspberry jam sandwich at tea-time. It was now 7.45 on a Saturday. The hungry boy was 11-year-old Mick Bernard.

Every time the public bar door swung open Mick tried to peep inside. He could hear the cackling laugh of his mother and was eager to get her attention or, failing that, his father's. 'Mum, can I 'ave a packet o'crisps! I'm starvin'. Please!' His doppelganger at the other end of the corridor heard this frantic entreaty and called to him: 'Here, have one of these.'

Mick walked down the corridor, sat down beside his new chum and watched him extricate the small blue bag that contained the salt and then sprinkle its contents evenly over the crisps. After giving the bag a good shake to circulate the salt, he offered the bag to Mick. 'Help yourself to some,' he said. Mick picked up a couple and happily munched them to a pulp. 'Ta,' he said, 'Wos y'name?' The boy's name was Jeremy. That's a posh name, thought Mick, who'd never met a 'Jeremy' before. Then he resumed sentry duty outside the other bar. He read *The Red Badge of Courage* for the second time until his belly started rumbling. His 'Hopalong Cassidy' wristwatch told him it was 9.45. They won't be out for at least another hour or so, he decided.

Then the door opened and he saw his father holding out a bag of crisps. At last, some food. He looked toward his corridor companion and beckoned him to come down so that he might return the favour and give him some crisps. Mick opened the bag and hunted for the precious blue bag. How Mick hated crisps without any salt: if anything it was the taste of the salt that he loved most. He unwrapped the twist of salt and was in the act of tipping the contents onto the crisps when his new pal knocked the bag out of his hand, spraying salt all over his copy of *The Red Badge of Courage*. 'You did that delib'rate, didn't ya?' he shouted, only to be met by a burst of laughter. 'Yes, course I did!' said Jeremy. 'Just a bit of fun!'

In that instant, upon hearing that last word, the hunger and the isolation and the boredom that had been building in Mick bubbled to the surface like a geyser. He'd no comprehension of his next act, which was to swing a clenched fist at Jeremy that caught him flush on the chin. Mick jumped on him and landed another blow to his nose and then another haymaker pummelled his left ear. Jeremy squealed with pain, so loud that Mick thought he must've been dying. The commotion brought Jeremy's parents from the saloon, by which time Mick had fled to the other end of the corridor. 'Mum! Dad!' he yelled, pushing open the door. 'Come quick!'

Roy and Edna emerged just as their counterparts made to grab Mick. 'Dunt you touch him!' roared Edna, like some angry lioness guarding a wayward cub, 'Or I'll put one on yer!' Edna's blue eyes must've embodied the touch-paper to her powder-keg temper now on the verge of ignition for they persuaded Jeremy's parents to back away. 'Jeremy's only just recovered from an operation on that ear,' explained the father. 'And he has to run into a thug like your boy!' added his wife, wrapping a protective arm around her son.

Mick stood against the wall, head on his chest, a study in sadness. Edna sent Roy inside to get their coats while she took Mick outside. He knew what was coming; but he steeled himself and wasn't going to cry. Edna was fuming: an evening out curtailed; an evening that saw her son shame the family name. Roy kept his opinions to himself: inwardly he smiled at the realization his son had fought and won. Mick wasn't so cocksure. This was his first fight. He'd never have a second.

***

'Get in the kitchen an' strip orf for y'wash,' said Edna as the clock struck six the following evening to signal the occasion Mick loathed. 'Ev'ry stitch orf! Wash prop'ly! Or I'll come in there an' do it meself!' The next day Mick was to start at South Oxford Grammar School. He had to be especially clean for that: what if there was an accident and he was taken to hospital and found to be filthy? There'd be no shame brought down on Edna Bernard's house. They'd find him as bonny as a new born babe.

Mick took the boiling kettle off the stove and emptied its contents into the tin bowl sitting in the kitchen sink. He looked round twice at the kitchen door before dropping his trousers and underpants. He picked up the Lux soap from its dish and, after rubbing it quickly in his hands, smeared the resultant lather over, under and round his private parts. Just as quickly, he reached for his flannel to wipe away the soap; and then the towel to dry himself and, more importantly, protect his modesty. Suddenly the door opened and in strode his mother. She pulled the towel from Mick's clutches and bent forward to inspect his handiwork. She pronounced herself satisfied at what she saw: 'Now the rest. Feet an' legs.' Then she left Mick to it, a smile playing with the corners of her mouth at the glimpse of Mick's embryonic pubic hair.

Having to run twice through the showers after games was stressful enough for Mick owing to some of his peer group being more advanced physically than him. But this deliberate humiliation at the hands of his mother hit him harder. It was on this Sunday that Mick became truly aware of his adolescent body and his need to protect it from prurient eyes. He never forgot the embarrassment his mother had needlessly and ruthlessly subjected him to - or ever forgave.

Mick, resplendent in cherry-red school blazer and cap, and carrying a bright new satchel, had a task to perform before reaching his new school. His Uncle Bob, not the genuine article but a friend of Roy's accorded the term on an honorary basis, lived in the street next to the school and his coal shed had a new occupant: a greyhound called Eddy. Uncle Bob was rarely without a greyhound. He'd take a cast-off from the nearby Cowley Stadium and house it in his makeshift kennel. The intention was to run Eddy on the local 'flapping' tracks, such as Swindon and High Wycombe, which were not run under the auspices of the National Greyhound Racing Club - and in time pull-off a nice betting coup. Uncle Bob needed a car to get Eddy to these tracks: Roy and his newly acquired 1937 Hillman got the job. Someone was also needed to walk Eddy round the estate every morning to shake the stiffness out of the dog's legs and harden his pads for running; and to sit with him in the back of the car to keep him happy to and from the track. Thus was Mick engaged as Eddy's kennel boy, walker and travelling companion at a wage of half-a-crown a week - plus a present whenever he was victorious.

'Now, Michael, watch carefully what I'm gunna do,' Uncle Bob had said on the day of Mick's tutorial in the art of attaching Eddy's collar and leash. 'Hold one end of his collar in yer left hand, unlock the door with yer roight, an' as he pokes his head out, slip the collar underneath it an' grab tother end with yer roight, an' then fasten it at the back of 'is head.'

Mick watched the drill perfectly executed on the black-and-white canine who duly presented himself. 'Think you can manage that?' Uncle Bob was scarcely bigger than Mick. If he could do it, thought Mick, it must be a piece of cake.

As soon as Mick put the key in the lock on this first morning a noise like a combine harvester started up from inside the coal shed: all swirling straw and assorted bangs. Mick edged the door open and bent low, right hand poised to grab the end of the dangling collar and lasoo Eddy's white head as it appeared. But Eddy exited the coal-hole as if the traps had just clanged open on his last stab at greyhound immortality. His head and chest struck Mick like a wrecking ball and before Mick could move the dog was up on his hind legs, front paws on Mick's shoulders and his warm, wet tongue all over Mick's face. Mick looked down at what a few seconds ago was a pristine school blazer but was now daubed with whatever Eddy had deposited overnight. Company not escape had been Eddy's priority. But the affection Eddy had shown toward his new dog-walker resulted in Mick undertaking much scrubbing in the boys' toilet at school to ward-off the attention of his new teachers. His efforts, however, failed to disguise the state of his blazer from Edna – with the inevitable outcome. But he refused to cry.

***

Mick was among 70 boys and girls gathered from the south-east fringe of the city and nearby villages who comprised the initial intake of South Oxford Grammar School. They had to make do with five members of staff. The Headmaster was Jack Masterson, a Cambridge graduate. His pupils only encountered him at morning assembly. His entry was suitably terrifying. He walked with a forward lean, as if striding into a stiff breeze, his gown trailing in his slipstream and hymn book clutched under his arm like a machine gun. This threatening gait was accentuated by a pronounced jaw that jutted forward like a trireme's battering ram and which, allied to wispy, thinning fair hair on the edge of whitening and teeth solidly clenched when he spoke, gave him the air of someone not to be trifled with. But as many of his pupils would discover, and none more so than Mick Bernard, Jack Masterson had heart and soul in abundance.

Masterson's deputy and teacher of Mathematics was another Cambridge man, Bill Lander. His superficial calmness, gimlet-eyed and habitually sporting a half-smile, camouflaged a firecracker that was liable to explode whenever a stupid answer to a mental arithmetic problem was proffered in class. He was more likeable, however, than a third Cantabrian, John Simmonds, the Linguist. Puny and sapling thin, he tried hard to ingratiate himself with his pupils but failed miserably, particularly with boys like Mick who soon grew to loathe his German lessons. The spectacles he wore hinted at cruelty and gave him a mean expression which turned to florid rage when riled – which proved often. With no specialist teacher of Physical Education available Simmonds drew that short straw, and he did manage to organize some school football matches. Mick made the team in his now accepted position of right-half to play alongside a number of new and talented team-mates. To Mick's relief there was no mention of rugby being introduced. The two women who made up Masterson's team were polar opposites. Gillian Whitmore was an Amazonian creature boasting flaxen hair and a heaving bosom, who might've starred in a Wagnerian opera, but was obliged to teach sciences. Patricia Lamb, by contrast, was small, dark, curly-haired and demure, a stereotypical daughter of Wales; she handled the Humanities.

Like most grammar schools South Oxford was modelled on the English public school. There was a school motto, *Intro Inspice* ('Look Within') and a school crest depicting three diamonds above a cross, the origins of which Mick could never fathom and never bothered to ask; and pupils were allocated to one of four houses for sporting contests and other competitions. Mick and his mates were thrilled with the vast gymnasium, which proved perfect for five-a-side football and the chance to learn basketball. Beyond the gym was a playground marked out with tennis courts and netball pitches; and beyond that were the newly seeded football pitches. The Humanities subjects were taught in standard class-rooms, with single desks laid out in rows. Art, woodwork and science gloried in their own fit-for-purpose areas; Mick adopted a low profile in the latter for slicing worms and conducting experiments to produce some gas or other was not his idea of fun. All answers and questions had to be prefaced with a raised hand; talking or turning round was frowned upon, in Lander's classes reinforced by the prompt delivery of a well-aimed piece of chalk or a board duster. Gross ill-conduct was punished with the cane, the victim's name being pinned to the notice board much like a notice of execution on the gates of Pentonville. And, once Edna took up a part-time job, Mick began having school dinners; how he relished the shepherd's pie instead of Edna's runny mince, crispy roast potatoes instead of her soggy ones and the novelty of chocolate tart instead of fruit pies.

Mick was slow to come to terms with the workload his new school imposed on him. Testing was rigorous and he wasn't enamoured with homework (two subjects per night and three on Friday) because much of it involved knowledge untouched in class and there was nowhere at home for him to sit quietly and complete it: the living room was invariably too noisy and its table frequently dominated by ash trays full of dog-ends. Matters improved after Edna bought him a writing desk and table lamp for his bedroom and the set of Cassell's *Children's Encyclopedia*, but it was so cold upstairs during the winter that he took to finishing homework in the school library during the lunch hour. Consequently, it was often rushed, and if below par a detention awaited; excellent work was rewarded with a star and ten of those were rewarded with a night free of homework. Mick struggled to achieve that goal but he soon received a detention for an inability to recall the words of Tennyson's *Charge of the Light Brigade*. Nevertheless he enjoyed his new school in the main and never once considered it an imposition to attend.

***

If his academic life at South Oxford progressed happily Mick couldn't say the same about his home life which seemed to lurch from one disaster to another. Eddy the greyhound was not finished toying with him. Yes, Mick had mastered the art of collaring him first thing; and he'd helped Uncle Bob train him down on the school field of a Saturday morning. Mick's job was to hold Eddy while Uncle Bob put some distance between them before waving a white handkerchief that was the signal for Mick to slip the collar. Off Eddy would shoot like a quarrel from a crossbow. A few sprints like this and Eddy will be ready to win, thought Mick, and I'll receive a present. But things didn't go smoothly.

As Mick eventually came to appreciate, Uncle Bob plotted Eddy's campaigns with the military precision of Napoleon. It commenced with a trip to High Wycombe on a dank, overcast Saturday in October, cold enough for Edna to insist he was wrapped up in his school kit of gabardene mackintosh, scarf and peaked cap. After being welcomed with a more exuberant reception than usual he managed to get Eddy into his dog-jacket and brought him out of his kennel.

'Eddy's full o'beans this mornin', Uncle Bob,' said Mick. 'Shall I give 'im some more water? His bowl's empty.'

'No, leave 'im, Michael.'

'But he's pantin' an' puffin' loik a steam engine!' Mick exclaimed as Eddy sniffed and licked his hand. 'And he seems awful hungry. Shall I give 'im handful o'biscuits?'

'No, Michael. He'll be all roight.'

'You pos'tive, Uncle Bob?'

Uncle Bob's lips thought about moving but didn't. Perhaps the boy should know what's going on, he decided.

'Listen carefully to what I'm gunna say,' said Uncle Bob, fixing Mick with an expression that would've done credit to an undertaker. 'If Eddy's gunna win a race he has to be runnin' in the roight grade. You know what I mean by grade?'

'Think so,' said Mick, mirroring Uncle Bob's expression. 'Dad told me. It's the way dogs are divided up into races so the dogs in each grade are 'bout the same ability an' 'ave same chance of winnin'.'

'Thass roight. Well, we have to get Eddy into a grade where he can win. And the way to do that is to get 'im into a grade lower than his true ability.'

'I get it,' said Mick, brightly. 'You have to trick the man who does the gradin'. So 'ow is that done?'

'The trick is to run 'im to lose...'

'Never!' said Mick, who thought for a while and then added: 'But Eddy wunt know that, will he?'

'Thass true. We have to make up his mind for 'im. You're roight to say he's 'ungry this mornin'. Thass because he's had no breakfast and jus' a sip o' water. But when we get near Wycombe we'll stop the car an' give 'im a whoppin' breakfast o'mince an' biscuits an' as much water to drink as he loiks.'

'And that'll make 'im so full-up he wunt run fast.'

'Thass it! He'll feel loik an el'phant tryin' to run up Ev'rest!'

'And then he'll be dropped down a grade?'

'Thass it exactly!' said Uncle Bob. 'We'll do this for a race or two until Eddy's downgraded into a race we know he's bound to win if he's tryin'...'

'An' thass when you an' dad will back 'im to win!'

'Michael, yer a fast learner!' said Uncle Bob, in the process of producing a large handkerchief from his pocket. 'If he gets thirsty in the car jus' drop a bit o'water on this an' squeeze it over his tongue.'

'Gotcha!' said Mick, pleased to be able to play a minor role in the plot.

Roy duly stopped the car at the top of Stokenchurch Hill and Eddy proceeded to gorge himself on the substantial picnic put before him by Uncle Bob. Mick watched the dog enjoying his delayed breakfast and laughed: 'He'll wornt 'nother dog t'give him a piggy-back in the race now!' The bloated dog fell asleep as soon as he touched his blanket on the back seat and dropped his head into Mick's lap. When they reached their destination Mick had to shake him to wake him up; and in his race he ambled across the line fifth of six. This same ploy was repeated the following Saturday and the Saturday after that. Only then was Uncle Bob ready to activate the final, and critical, phase of the campaign: the betting coup.

High Wycombe was the perfect venue for a coup because it was as far removed as could be from a track governed by the NGRC. The meeting was run by a farmer in one of his fields; and, crucially, it was he who 'graded' the races. Mick could hardly believe his eyes when he saw the track: it was dead straight, up a slope and demarcated by nothing more than a length of baler twine stretched from one end of the field to the other. And sighting the hare made him giggle: it was a rugby ball painted white onto which a powder puff had been glued to act as an enticing tail. To make it 'run' this excuse for a lure was attached to another length of twine and reeled up the track onto a bicycle wheel positioned at the top of the field by furious hand-pedalling on the part of the farmer. There was no weighing machine to pinpoint those dogs that were overweight and deliberately turned into tortoises for the day. As long as the farmer got the nod from the owner of a dog primed and ready to fire like Randolph Scott's Winchester rifle so he might have a flutter himself nothing was ever said; probably, Mick worked out, because every dog-owner pulled the same stroke at some time or another.

Another refinement of NGRC tracks missing from Wycombe were kennels to house the dogs prior to their race. Instead there was a holding pen, again demarcated by the ubiquitous baler twine, where dogs were to be accompanied by a handler. Mick got the job: Uncle Bob had spotted that someone with an astute eye for a profit was selling bottles of beer out of his van parked near the winning post. He and Roy departed, leaving Mick in charge of Eddy.

Mick was always wary being entrusted with Eddy when other greyhounds were in close proximity. All was silent bar some panting and yawning, until the first race approached. Then every dog seemed to sniff the call of battle and become increasingly agitated. Mick took a tighter grip of Eddy. But the instant the lids slammed open and the first six dogs left the traps the atmosphere in the holding pen changed to an alarming cacophony of howling, yelping and prancing. Eddy tugged at his leash; and Mick made the error of tightening his hold instead of giving him slightly more leash to play with. As the rugby ball zig-zagged up the field, bouncing from one tuft of grass to another past the holding pen, Eddy rose onto his hind legs and with a serpentine wiggle of his neck, slipped his head out of the taut noose Mick had so misguidedly provided. All of a sudden Mick was staring at an empty collar and the race now had seven dogs in it instead of six because Eddy had sped off to join in the fun. Mick was too far away from Uncle Bob and Roy to hear their expletives as a familiar black-and-white shape crossed the line in playful pursuit of his new pals.

Fortunately for Eddy's distraught handler both Uncle Bob and his father were cast from the same easy-going mould. 'Dunt worry,' said Uncle Bob to a tearful Mick. 'There'll be 'nother day. Jus' you wait.' Uncle Bob was right. Eddy gave him and Mick quite a few lucrative days over the ensuing three years before he was pensioned off. And when he won at Swindon's prestigious Easter Monday meeting the winner's tankard was presented to Mick.

***

Mick's eyesight was another embarrassment, and a more persistent one than any inflicted by Eddy. He'd grown short-sighted. When he hid in the back row of desks for classes he disliked he was unable to read the blackboard. This was vital in Maths because many exercises and their workings were chalked up. Mick was constantly nudging Hislop, who sat in front of him, for information – which got them both into trouble on several occasions for talking when they should've been working silently. The school's visiting nurse soon arranged for an appointment at the Radcliffe Infirmary's Eye Clinic. To Mick the outcome was painfully and shamefully obvious: he'd be sentenced to wearing spectacles. He could already hear the jeers of *Speccy Four-Eyes!* every break-time. He begged his mother to cancel the appointment as the date drew closer and closer. Answered in the negative, he asked if he might see the doctor on his own. But was told by his mother she'd not realized until now how stupid he was.

The chart confronting Mick might as well have been miles away rather than a few feet because he couldn't make out any letters bar the three on the top two lines.

'Is that all you can manage?' said the optometrist. Mick nodded.

'Tell doctor what you can see,' said Edna, prodding his forearm.

Mick stammered: 'Can only see top two loins. Nuthin' else.'

'Stop playin' the fool! Yer wastin' doctor's time.'

Mick tried again but got only as far as repeating the same prominent letters.

The doctor smiled benevolently. Edna's glare did not speak of benevolence.

'Well, Mrs Bernard,' said the doctor, producing a tube from a drawer, 'apply this ointment daily to each eye and bring Michael back in a week. That should give us a better idea of the scale of his problem.'

The bus journey home was as painful as Mick envisaged. 'You're jus' lazy!' said his mother. 'Showin' me up! Thass what it is! You does it on purpose!' Mick thanked his lucky stars because he knew only being in a very public place prevented him receiving a clout.

His ordeal worsened. The thick yellow ointment rendered him virtually blind. He could barely identify anything more than a foot from his face. He was moved to the front row in class but was still unable to read what was on the blackboard. On the Saturday afternoon, unable to read or watch the television, he went out for a walk in the hope some fresh air and a cool breeze might alleviate the discomfort. Unfortunately, the smog enveloping him also hid Uncle Reg – who passed by on the other side of the road unnoticed and unacknowledged. Mick got home to find Uncle Reg in the living room with his mother. He couldn't really make out the looks on their faces in any detail but he guessed by the deafening silence that something was up – and he might be the cause.

His mother's voice broke the stillness: 'I got summut to say t'you. Why dint you say 'ello to yer Uncle Reg this arternoon?'

'I dint see 'im.'

'You must've,' grunted Uncle Reg, a gruff and crusty bugger at best. 'You wuz starin' straight at me!'

'But I 'ad the yella...'

'He's never bin the same since he went to that posh school! Bloody gramma schools! I tellya, Edna, it puts ideas in their bloomin' heads, dunnit?'

That did it. The verdict had been returned. Edna's right hand arced through the air and smacked into the side of Mick's head with enough force to make it wobble. 'There, yer little bleeder! Yer bin told!'

Mick chewed the inside of his lip to stop himself giving Uncle Reg the satisfaction of seeing him cry. He retreated to his bedroom where the mental wound began to fester. No credence was given to the mitigating circumstances. The case was not even made. Mick discovered the hard way that the innocent might be punished as ruthlessly as the guilty. The injustice of it all struck him harder than the clout. Injustice, he decided, was intolerable, unforgiveable. He told himself not to care. But his gut would not stomach such a miscarriage of justice. And it never would.

Mick's second visit to the eye clinic resulted in the news he'd dreaded: spectacles were prescribed to correct his long sight. He wore them under duress in class. But not elsewhere. To him they were as evil as the mark of Cain.

***

Mick's childhood wasn't about to let go without screaming and kicking: it became synonymous with several forms of deprivation although it took some years for Mick to recognize them. The scales of innocence fell away once the domestic arrangements of his school-mates revealed themselves. Butter on toast instead of margarine; Corona instead of tap water; toilet roll not newspaper; visits to castles and museums not pubs. His escape came through films: how he wanted to inhabit the buckskins of Alan Ladd in *Shane* or his suit of armour in *The Black Knight.* Above all, however, his escape came through books.

Books that were items of curiosity in the Bernard household Mick discovered were actually ubiquitous and prolific. Suitably enlightened he took to planting his head in a book at every opportunity, even in the pub garden of a summer's evening and the pub corridor in harsh winter. His literary appetite was gargantuan. School libraries failed to satisfy his appetite for historical knowledge in particular: Upton Green's, for instance, could only provide *Our Island Story* which told such tales as Alfred burning the cakes, Charles I facing execution bravely and Nelson drubbing the French; but it was only an outline of British history that had been written some 50 years ago. South Oxford's was better but not by much. It possessed works with a more academic bent but Mick wanted more specific historical titles: biographies of key figures and details of battles and military campaigns; preferably newer works incorporating the very latest research. Consequently, he began taking the 25-minute walk to the Temple Cowley Library on a Saturday morning to capitalize on its superior range of titles: he was shocked to be told, however, he must read them on the premises because he wasn't allowed a member's card since he lived outside the catchment area.

If Saturdays brought Mick the certainty of enlightenment Sundays brought the possibility of Stygian gloom. Sunday afternoon threatened regular visits from uncles and aunts for tea (and sometimes a game of cards before settling down to watch the Sunday play on television) and amounted to Mick's worst nightmare. Once he heard the front gate click he'd retire upstairs to his bedroom and his books. Like every room in the house Mick's bedroom was a room in miniature: if the living room was a cell, his bedroom, in prison parlance, was solitary aka 'the hole'. His bed lay under the window with just enough space at its foot for a chair and a bookcase; his writing bureau filled the gap between the bed-head and interior wall, against which was a small wardrobe. When the bedroom door was opened it just cleared the wardrobe but struck the bottom of the bed if Mick wasn't careful - or if Edna was in a fury. The fanlight was always open in summer to grant Mister Jinks entry: he'd jump onto the bathroom roof and then spring across to Mick's window ledge and clamber inside to curl up on the bed; in winter Mick would open it when he went to bed knowing he'd soon have feline company under the sheets. There he'd hide on painful Sundays too many to count, shutting out the incessant babble from below, resisting every attempt to prise him from his sanctuary. 'Airs an' graces, that boy's got,' he'd hear Uncle Gilbert pronouncing in a deliberately loud voice aimed to carry upstairs. 'I tell you, Edna, you need to sort 'im out a'fore it's too bloody late!'

Unfortunately for Mick, his mother needed little persuasion to act accordingly because she'd watched him change since going to South Oxford: whether this turn for the worse was deliberate or just a bi-product of puberty she didn't know. But whatever the cause, she was growing tired of it. Thus Mick would hear the sound of feet ascending the stairs with the ominous tread of the hangman approaching the condemned cell and wait for the inevitable incursion, no knocking and no courtesies. 'Put that bloody book down!' his mother would demand. 'Get downstairs an' speak to yer Uncle Gilbert.' If he failed to move fast enough one hand would slap the book from his grasp while the other clipped him round the ear. All that was missing was the noose to fix round his neck.

Mick accepted his physical punishment without a qualm; any scars were now on the inside. He wasn't the only boy in his gang so punished; it was the working class way of chastising disobedient or impertinent adolescent boys. But some of his pals spoke of other methods: the stick wasn't the only weapon in the parental arsenal. He heard about reasoning and the loss of privileges. These measures sounded more civilized. But he knew they'd never make themselves felt in the Bernard household. That realization annoyed him; he became an 'angry young man', though neither he nor his mother recognized the phrase and its implications. And so he came to live in the condemned cell of his own mind.

But the teenage boy's breast can only absorb so much pressure before it explodes. Mick's emotional epiphany announced itself on a night suitably riven by Thor's hammer. And it stemmed, as so many minor catastrophes, from something innocuous: in this instance a new blue blazer Edna had bought for him to wear at a forthcoming family 'do'. Mick thought its double-breasted style made him look as fuddy-duddy as his uncles and refused to wear it: the embarrassment would kill him, he argued. Edna didn't try to reason with him. Up went her right hand. But instead of striking his head the attempted blow exposed Mick's backbone. He raised an angry hand to prevent the blow reaching its target by gripping Edna's wrist. Then he told her, calmly, he'd never allow her to hit him again. He was fifteen-years-old.

Edna feared thunderstorms and had passed on that fear to her son by always hiding with him under the stairs as soon as the first rumble was heard. The best way to overcome fear, Mick told himself upon reaching the sanctuary of his bedroom, was to confront it head on. Be that fear of his mother or fear of being struck dead by lightning. Mister Jinks, already in residence on the bed, greeted him with a roll and a stretch and offered up his white belly for a tickle. Mick opened one of the larger casements, the better to hear the rolling thunder and watch the lightning fork, daring a bolt to come down upon this house, to shatter the bars of his prison. He took no notice of the rain with which the strengthening wind began lashing his face. The cumulo-nimbus clouds bringing the storm across the river and over the hill grew larger and seemed to assume the sinister outline of a coiled black mamba – and just as dangerous. The gap between the thunder clap and the lightning bolts grew shorter: 'Count the seconds between 'em an' divide by four,' was Uncle Ben's formula. 'An' that tells you 'ow many miles away it is.' Mick's mental arithmetic told him the eye of the storm was directly above the house now. He watched the jagged flashes of yellow illuminate the back garden, the spotlight first picking out the shed housing his bike and then turning rows of cabbages into the most garish of greens. He saw the rabbit hutch wobble as a terrified Bugs raced around seeking refuge. Then it was gone. No lightning struck the house. And there would be no more whacks.

With each clap of thunder and bolt of lightning that stormy night Mick felt freer and freer. The day he was totally free of this place, free of his parents and their backbiting families couldn't come soon enough. He'd three years to wait. They were the longest three years of his life because coming to terms with a profound sense of isolation and the turmoil of adolescence at the same time began to wear him down.

His sanity was preserved during this traumatic phase of his life by the arrival of a saviour who'd light up his desolate universe like a comet.

Four

Mick's first year at South Oxford went as smoothly as might be expected in a school where not all the new buildings were ready for purpose and its staff were obliged to teach subjects that weren't their specialism. Patricia Lamb, for instance, was an English graduate pressed into teaching History. But as the summer term wound to a close she let slip that a new teacher would be taking over History in the autumn. Mick and his mates wondered what this new teacher would be like. They didn't even know whether it was a man or a woman.

The new teacher turned out to be a man who'd teach them History, English and Latin. Mick, like his 12-year-old chums, was at an impressionable age, on the cusp of adolescence. His need for someone in his life who understood his yearning for knowledge, his preference for castles and museums over pubs, and his love of books was verging on the desperate. When his new teacher proved to be father, elder brother, mentor, guru and role model rolled into one he was over the moon with joy. Peter Clifton entered Mick's young life and changed it forever.

The married father of two children had completed national service in the Army, a degree in Politics, Philosophy and Economics at Queen's College, Oxford, been a civil servant and taught in two prep schools before being head-hunted by Jack Masterson. Compared to the rest of his colleagues at South Oxford, Clifton was not so much unorthodox as heretical. He was never a joke-cracking master, leaving that to his pupils. He was not a physically imposing figure, being wiry and of a pale complexion accentuated by jet black hair, a lock of which invariably flopped over his left brow. Yet no one took liberties in his classes: intelligent pupils recognize instinctively when they are playing headstrong Alexander to wise Aristotle.

The basis of Clifton's teaching was conversation, discussion, argument - reasoned and civilized, not a shouting match - which might take place anywhere at any time. He told stories from history, sometimes acting them out to vocal approval; and stopped every lesson minutes before the bell so that written work might be checked for errors. Nor did he dress to impress for his wardrobe was limited and clearly had little bearing on his self-esteem; yet he patrolled the corridors with the swagger of a man totally comfortable in his own skin, a man reluctant to compromise – just the kind of charismatic personality to whom teenage boys deferred.

When, for example, Mick's phrase 'dishing out' in a piece of homework was ringed in bold red pen and 'distributed' was inserted in its stead Mick began paying more attention to selecting the correct words of written English rather than the spoken slang of his estate. And when he lazily wrote 'a lot' in answer to a question demanding reasoned assessment it opened his eyes and mind to the application of comparatives, the need to consider the implications and ramifications of the facts he found so easy to assimilate. Mick wouldn't have taken notice of such seemingly minor correction from any other teacher: but Clifton was different. What enables one teacher to inspire where others fail is a knotty question to rank alongside its Gordian counterpart. To Mick it was a mixture of admiration and respect; and the desire to become such an individual in adulthood.

Clifton was also a mean sportsman for Mick to admire, cutting a splendid dash with a rugby ball or a cricket bat in his hands. Slight he may have been, but if he scythed you down, his bony shoulder impaling soft belly, you knew you'd been tackled; and any return catch off his bat in the nets resulted in stinging hands for the bowler. Mick once felt that power during an impromptu game of hockey: Clifton stuck him in goal and began firing shots at him. Unfortunately he didn't equip Mick with the usual padding and one pile-driver struck Mick's shinbone with excruciatingly painful results. Finally, there was that intriguing squiggle of a scar on his left cheekbone, the so-called 'duelling scar' according to classroom gossip. That it turned out to be the result of the infant Clifton running into the corner of a table was never allowed to ruin the man's mystique in Mick's eyes. It quickly dawned on Mick that here was someone entirely at ease discussing poetry with lasses, sport with lads or Mozart with either. Whoever he was speaking to, and whatever the subject, Clifton spoke with authority and always convinced the listener he was listening to everything offered in reply.

Clifton gained his own devoted set as rapidly as Miss Jean Brodie. Mick soon found himself in the select few along with fellow history buffs Pete Livermore and Colin Walkinshaw. Clifton offered to introduce them one Saturday morning to the murky world of Oxford's second-hand bookshops in the Turl and the Broad where the kind of histories they craved might be acquired at a price suiting their pockets. After meeting at the Queen's Lane bus stop Clifton led them up the High and into Turl Street.

'Here we are,' said Clifton, pointing to a shop front that looked in dire need of some care and attention: the black paint was peeling from the door frame and the windows were coated with grime; if the premises had a name it was lost in time. Despite the unappealing frontage, however, the money from Mick's paper round was now in danger of burning a hole in his pocket.

'Looks closed,' said Livermore.

'Yeh,' added Walkinshaw, 'it's really dark inside, can't see a loight on.'

'Looks straight out o'Dickens,' added Mick. 'Are you sure it opens on a Sat'day, sir?'

Clifton smiled knowingly and pushed the door. It opened to the sound of a tinkling bell. A voice emerged from the gloom, closely followed by a hunched figure who gave every indication of stepping out of a Dickens novel, dressed as he was in black three-piece suit and bow tie with *pince nez* perched on the end of an aquiline nose overhung by a cloud of white hair. 'Ah, Mr Clifton, good to see again,' said the figure. 'And I see you've brought some new customers with you.'

'Good morning, Mr Dalrymple,' said Clifton. 'Yes, the boys are avid historians in search of some bargains.'

'History you say,' said the stooped bookseller casting a sly glance toward his new clientele. 'On the second floor. First room on the right. That's the repository for volumes of history. But I'm afraid there's no order to the shelves, you must search for yourselves.' Then he added with a chuckle: 'Dewey doesn't work here, I'm afraid!'

Dalrymple's little joke was explained by Clifton as they creaked their way up the winding staircase. 'Can you see where we're goin'?' said Mick to no-one in particular. 'It's loik a coal mine! Look at this dust!'

Clifton advised him to be guided by the banister and take one step at a time. As they reached the first landing Mick's foot thumped into something hard and a tower of books collapsed like a detonated factory chimney. 'Bugger!' said Mick. 'Sorry for swearin', sir. Jus' didn't see'um.'

Their penny-conscious host took this as his cue to switch on the lights, which showed books dotting the landing like spent landmines and walls bearing grubby prints of Oxford colleges. Mick rebuilt the pile and their ascent was completed without disturbing any more literary obstacles.

Mick's senses were struck by smell rather than sights. There was plenty of dust rising from the disturbed floorboards; but there was something else, rather like dirt but vaguely more exotic. It was the smell of damp paper, the musty smell of old books. That Mick's favourite objects bar his rugby boots possessed a distinctive smell as well as appearance made him happy beyond words. It was a smell with which he instantly fell in love and to which he rapidly grew addicted.

'Boys,' said Clifton, 'I suggest you try to find the *Introductory History of England* by CRL Fletcher. There are several volumes. They'll give you the kind of coverage and detail you're after. I'll leave you to it while I conduct a search of my own for some Keats for my nephew's birthday.'

The walls hiding the treasure they sought were floor to ceiling with shelves; they took a wall each. There was a short step ladder necessary to peruse the higher shelves that they took turns in using. Apart from a repetitive 'Nothin' up 'ere' the room fell silent as the volumes it contained for nigh on 15 minutes.

'Got 'um!' Livermore shouted gleefully. 'A whole bloody row of 'um!'

'Pass 'um down!' said Mick, eager to handle these prized objects.

'There must be a dozen of 'um!' said Livermore. He handed them to Mick and Walkinshaw, two at a time.

Walkinshaw opened one of the red-boarded volumes. 'Only half-a-crown!' he cried, unable to curb his enthusiasm.

'I've got five bob!' said Mick. 'That's two fer starters!'

'Hold on!' said Livermore, running an eye over the row of books that now lay on the floor in front of them. 'There's not one Volume II 'ere.'

'Never moind,' said Mick. 'Bound to be some 'ere if we come back in a week or so.'

Walkinshaw had been doing some counting. 'There's at least three copies of ev'ry other volume so we can buy what we wornt.'

Mick decided on Volumes I and III. He selected those with the shiniest boards and the most prominent titles stamped in black on the front. He couldn't descend the stairs fast enough and pay Dalrymple so that they now belonged to him and him alone. He, Pete and Colin felt like Oxford undergraduates as they retraced their steps to the Queen's Lane bus stop with their precious cargo tucked under their arms. For the remainder of that Saturday Mick's nose never left the musty pages of his new acquisitions.

'Bargains!' he informed his mother. 'Two more to get!' Edna picked one up and immediately put it down again. 'What 'orrible smell! They'll stink the place out!' Mick shot her an impertinent glance and took the two books up to his bedroom where he placed them on the bookcase at the foot of his bed as if they were holy artifacts – which in his eyes they were.

The following Saturday Mick returned to Dalrymple's shop on his own, armed with that week's paper-round money: if the scarce Volume II appeared he wanted no argument over its purchaser. He had to be content with purchasing Volume IV. 'No sign of Volume II,' Mick said to Dalrymple as he passed him half-a-crown. 'I'll try again nex' week.'

'Best to wait a while, young man,' said Dalrymple. 'I won't get any fresh stock to speak of in the immediate future. Come back in July when Trinity Term has finished. All the gentlemen going down after Finals will have sold most of their books back to me by then. That's when you might be lucky enough to obtain Volume II.'

Mick thanked Dalrymple for the tip and duly returned in July. 'Hello, again, Master…' said Dalrymple, as Mick made straight for the stairs while calling back 'Bernard, sir!'

'There are lots of new acquisitions in piles on the floor,' Dalrymple replied to Mick's fast disappearing back.

The hunter studied the spines of the books for red ones and flushed out his prey. He removed a Volume IV and two pristine copies of Volume I. And then there it was: Volume II: *1485 to 1660; From Henry VII to The Restoration.*

'Yeess!' cried Mick. A quieter voice drifted up the stairs: 'Ah, I take it you've found the volume you seek?'

Dalrymple took Mick's half-a-crown, and gave him back a shilling. 'A discount', he explained. 'Regular customers are always rewarded with a discount.'

'Ta, very much, sir,' said Mick.

The bus ride home was a gloriously happy one. He'd completed his quest, discovering in so doing how the joy of the hunt and the expectancy of finding one's quarry was, if anything, often more satisfying and exhilarating than actually possessing the book. Furthermore, he'd gained valuable insight into how the second-hand book trade worked when it came to prices – and the haggling of them. Mick and Dalrymple's dusty and musty Victorian lookalike bookshop became regular acquaintances. But he never did realize that his set was incomplete because Fletcher had written a Volume V covering the years 1815 to 1880. And Dalrymple, at a loss to explain how this volume was so hard to come by, hadn't the heart to tell him.

Some of these book-buying sprees might end with a visit to the Ashmolean where Clifton mesmerized his 'History Boys' with stories of the museum's relics that no ordinary guide would relate: Guy Fawkes's lantern led to the goriest tales of the Gunpowder Plotter's torture and execution; King Alfred's jewel elicited the recipe for Saxon oat-cakes. Topping even this were the holiday jaunts when Clifton's car would ferry the trio to Minster Lovell's ruined manor house wherein, he told them, Francis Lovell hid in a secret chamber from Henry VII only to expire of starvation when the only servant knowing his whereabouts died. Or they might visit castles, such as Kenilworth and Warwick; or properties that weren't open to the general public, like Studley Priory and Boarstall Tower, yet opened their doors for Peter Clifton - and even provided tea and cake.

This vibrant blend of education and socialization knocked Mick for six. It was a spring of knowledge from which he wished to drink copiously. He began to accept that acquiring knowledge was to be praised and not reviled. Only the ignorant, he concluded, refer to knowledge as a dirty word.

***

Clifton lit one further flame in Mick's breast. He introduced him to rugby: a few harum-scarum games on muddy afternoons that Mick began to enjoy more than the usual football. More specifically Clifton introduced Mick to rugby at Oxford University.

A few weeks before the Varsity Match at Twickenham the University played Major Stanley's XV, a star-studded invitation side comprised of internationals, as a stiff test of its state of readiness for the game against Cambridge. Clifton escorted 13-year-old Mick and pals by bus to the University's ground on the Iffley Road. Rain fell in biblical torrents throughout the match watched by the South Oxford group from beneath the hedge at the running track one end of the ground. Mick couldn't make out a great deal through the sheeting rain but this was compensated by the sound of collisions and the spontaneous outbursts of cheering when some dazzling piece of play ignited the crowd. Clifton subsequently initiated the first School Magazine, installed Mick as editor and showed him how to compile a match report of the Stanley's game.

Clifton brought Mick out of his shell in other ways. He suggested Mick and pals might do a 'turn' at the Christmas Concert. Usually a staid affair comprising recitations and instrumental solos, Clifton taught them the words of the Devon folksong *Widecombe Fair*, with its singalong chorus of 'Uncle Tom Cobley and All!' The curtains opened to reveal Mick, as Uncle Tom, guzzling from a beer bottle (empty, of course) before the rest trooped on as suitably dressed yokels in various stages of mock inebriation to strike up the song with each of them, Bill Brewer, Jan Stewer, Peter Gurney, Peter Davy, Dan'l Whiddon, Harry Hawke and Uncle Tom shouting their individual name during the chorus. The audience, including parents though not Mick's, went wild.

Mick basked in the satisfaction of having made people laugh: whether by deed or word made no difference to him. Like the afternoon spent sweating over Latin grammar when Clifton asked the class what case should Pompey be in if Caesar killed him: instead of answering 'Accusative, sir' Mick had volunteered 'Coffin, sir!' which reduced his classmates to hysterics and put a smile on Clifton's face. The laughter left Mick beaming like Bob Hope on television's *Sunday Night at the Palladium*.

If those events pandered to schoolboy humour, the *soiree* Clifton arranged at his cottage in Iffley was an introduction to polite social intercourse. Mick and his Widecombe carousers were obliged to make small talk with a select group of South Oxford's young ladies to low background music with nothing more than orange squash or lemonade for fuel. The girls baited them like hissing, she-cats; but to no effect.

Mick's toes weren't dipped deeply enough in these social waters for him to come away feeling any less socially inept than when he'd arrived at Clifton's home. However, he'd not left entirely empty-handed. They'd discussed his future and the prospect of a university education. Mick confessed his desire to study History at college. Clifton asked where. Mick shrugged. Where better than Oxford suggested Clifton: aim for the stars, he advised, because even if you miss them and only reach the clouds you'll be higher than the ground. If Clifton thinks Oxford might be a possibility, thought Mick, who am I to disagree. And then memories of that rugby match came flooding back: wouldn't it be fantastic to wear that dark blue jersey in a match like that in front of a large and vociferous and appreciative crowd.

Mick was 15 when Clifton left South Oxford to take up a post in educational administration. In his relatively brief career at the 'chalk-face' Clifton had inspired many pupils; none more so than Mick Bernard. But although Peter Clifton had fired his imagination about attaining the academic heights of Oxford University, Mick needed something with which to scale its walls. The man who came to South Oxford just as Mick's sporting career stalled was to provide him with the weaponry needed to storm the citadel.

Five

The wind was raw enough to persuade Mick his cheeks were being scraped with a blunt razor; he looked up at the rain-bearing skies above South Oxford's rugby pitch and shivered. Where was Wyn James?

Mick had gobbled his lunch in double-quick time to get changed and make the most of every minute of the one-to-one coaching James had arranged for his young scrum-half. But James was never one to regard punctuality as paramount. Mick stamped his feet and blew hard into blue-cupped fingers through numbed lips. He would've swapped most things for a track suit as the first drops of rain wet his hair. And the thought of heading back inside crossed his mind. But he'd no choice. Stay he must.

Mick's sporting career had come to a fork in the road. Football had lost its attraction. Teenage boys with sporting talent have high ambitions; if his sport is a team game he'll have no truck with just making up the numbers. Although Mick had represented the Oxford Sunday League he'd grown frustrated by a lack of recognition, especially missing out on selection for the Holy Grail that was Oxford Boys when some of his peers had succeeded. He could still spot and execute a long pass and unleash a cannon-ball shot but he was growing lazier and frequently prone to taking a back seat; it even cost him his place in the Hill Rise team that won the Sunday Cup. The arrival of Wyn James presented Mick with an option. Although maintaining South Oxford's football heritage, James favoured his national game and wanted to introduce organized rugby where once there'd only been the occasional free-for-all on wet winter days when the football pitches were too muddy for meaningful games.

James got down to business as soon as was prudent. He wasn't going to rush matters immediately his initial autumn term started as it was bound to antagonize the footballers whom he needed to convince that playing rugby wouldn't jeopardize their football careers: they comprised the most athletic and skilful performers among just 30 or so seniors and he needed them to fill the critical ball-playing roles within the team. When October and its softer pitches came round so did his opportunity to act. He lined all the boys along a touchline in height order to assess their potential for the game of rugby and hoped he'd find enough to fill the variety of specialized positions. One glance at the puny quartet standing nervously at one end of the line told him they were too immature for the hurly-burly of rugby. The two tallest boys at the opposite end, unfortunately, could also be eliminated from his plans: one was twiddling his thumbs between his knees and staring at the ground, demonstrating he'd no inclination to knock the skin off a rice pudding while his red-haired neighbour had a face covered in white pustules that were sufficient to put anyone off playing a contact sport. After some chin-rubbing he thought he'd identified five more fearsome prospects for his pack of eight forwards.

Then he reached Mick. He eyed him up and down, his gaze coming to rest on Mick's socks and boots. Mick wasn't wearing regulation school red and grey football socks; he was sporting red socks with white tops, the colours of the Welsh national team. An individual, thought James; wants to stand out from the crowd; and his boots are clean and bright, the mark of someone who takes pride in their kit. James pondered for a second: strong kick in either foot; his basketball shows good handling skills; bit of a cheeky blighter who won't be shy of commanding a set of forwards bigger than him and standing up to opposing forwards intent of murdering him.

'Righto!' he said, having made up his mind. 'Bernard, you'll be the scrum-half.' From that day forth James saw it as his rugby mission at South Oxford to make Mick Bernard into a top-flight scrum-half whether he liked it or not. And time had shown Mick did like it. This new game, a game he once hated, could be the game at which he might excel.

'Bernard! You can take those off!' barked the bandy figure marching across the pitch toward him with a string bag full of rugby balls slung over his shoulder. James was pointing to Mick's spanking new pair of Elmer Cotton rugby boots that had taken weeks of accumulated paper-round money to purchase and were meant to distinguish him from his peers.

'What?' said Mick, with an expression stating he must have mis-heard. 'Take my boots orf?'

'You need to feel the ball. You've got to caress it. Persuade it where to go and what to do. You can't do that unless you can feel the "sweet spot" on the ball.'

'But my feet'll get wet! My socks'll get dirty…'

'Don't be such a big girl's blouse! Get 'em off!'

'But it's too cold an' all…'

'How often is a rugby match played in cold and wet conditions?'

'Dunt know. How many?'

'I don't know either!' said James. 'But does a sailor complain about the sea?'

He's talking in riddles, thought Mick, lost his marbles from too many tackles.

'You've got to prepare for the worst conditions imaginable. Right?'

'Okay,' said Mick, reluctantly. 'If you say so.'

Mick looked at James as if he really had lost his marbles and just absconded from the Asylum, the 'loony bin' as it was known locally, on the Sandford Road. But obey him he must because James had already notched up a formidable reputation for standing no nonsense by slippering every boy in a class for being cheeky to a student teacher. Aside from that James had carved a name for himself in local rugby circles with Oxford RFC and Oxfordshire as a wonderful tactical kicker. Of slight build and toothy grin, he was a valley boy from South Wales who'd come to South Oxford via national service in the RAF followed by St Luke's College, Exeter, one of the country's elite training colleges for PE teachers; and latterly as a humble council gravedigger in order to earn a crust. Mick did as he was told and removed his precious boots behind a screen of adolescent surliness.

James tipped the balls from the bag. He selected one and held it out in front him. 'This is the sweet spot,' he said, running a finger along the spine of the ball held flat on his palm and pointing toward the goalposts some 25 yards away. 'Place your right hand along this line, lace upwards, and bring it down to strike the instep of your right foot coming up. And remember to point your toe so the instep is as flat as possible when it connects with the surface of the ball. What we're trying to achieve here is a high kick that lands near the posts where the catcher will either drop it because he's wary of attackers pursuing the kick and taken his eyes off the ball, or he will catch it but immediately be overrun by attackers. Watch this.'

James turned sideways on so that Mick could study theory put into execution at close quarters. Thwack! The ball flew upwards to describe a perfect parabolic arc before landing just in front of the goalposts. 'Now, you try.'

That looked a piece of piss, muttered Mick, but judiciously only to himself. He was sensible enough to know things looking that easy invariably aren't; and James was a master at this kicking lark. Consequently it was a nervy Mick Bernard who gingerly selected a ball and placed his hands as he thought James had instructed.

'Hold on! Lace upwards!' shouted James. 'If the lace is on the side your boot strikes you can easily end up with a miscue, the lace will cause the ball to slice off the side of your boot. In a game you may not have the time to adjust the ball like this but that's what you should be trying to achieve.'

Mick adjusted the position of the ball in his hands which he ordered to stop quivering. He took a deep breath and, hoping he'd not make a complete hash of it, let fly. The kick had the correct arc but not the required distance. He shook his foot; the instep stung like blazes.

James tossed him another ball. 'Try again. Not easy to get the purchase on the ground to generate the power without boots but that wasn't bad.'

'Can I put my boots on then?' said Mick, in an effort to capitalize on what James had said. 'No,' came the reply. Mick tried again: 'But you're wearin' boots…'

James didn't let him finish. 'Stop moaning! We're working on mastering the technique at the moment. You can add the power by practicing in boots on your own.'

Five minutes and ten kicks later James nodded satisfaction. 'Now let's shorten the kick and aim to drop the ball just in front of your forwards near the touch-line as if you've just won possession at a line-out. This is called a box-kick. Useful on a wet day when the ball gets too slippery for the backs to handle at speed. So, turn the point of the ball slightly toward the touch-line and tilt it slightly toward the ground.' James stood beside Mick , the better for his pupil to study the angles. 'Then strike as before. Like this.'

'Woomf!' The ball took a steep trajectory, rising some 60 feet into the air before hurtling to the ground about 15 yards in front of them. Mick was suitably impressed. 'Shorter and steeper, so your forwards can get to the catcher,' said James. He took Mick's boots and put them where the ball had landed. 'There. Aim to drop the ball on top of your boots.' He trotted back to where Mick was standing. 'I'll lob you the ball as if I've just won it at a line-out and then I'll follow up your kick like a forward.'

James positioned himself a yard in front of Mick. He tossed him the ball. Mick made the necessary adjustments as quickly as he could and whacked the ball high into the air. James gave chase and was underneath the ball to catch it a few feet from the target. 'Pretty decent, for a first effort. Do it again.'

Mick did it again. And again. And again. Eventually he struck one to drop slap-bang on his boots. 'Yeeess!' he cried.

James merely smiled. The kid may have some talent, he thought to himself. 'Okay,' he said. 'And the action is the same for kicking with the left. Practice with both feet. Six kicks with each foot. But for now let's think about passing. And, yes, you can put your boots on now!'

Mick couldn't get his boots on quickly enough: his socks looked as if he'd been wading through slurry and his feet were cold and wet enough to give him the trench foot that he'd read soldiers in World War One suffered from. James watched him. 'I know we've finished kicking practice but there's one more thing to add when it comes to finding that sweet spot. Look how you've tied your boots.'

Mick looked down at his boots. He tied the laces with a neat bow that nestled atop the instep. He thought for a second. 'You mean I'm obstructing the "sweet spot" with the bow?'

'Good. That's precisely it. Practice tying your boots with the bow on the inside or outside of the boot so it never spoils your contact with the ball.'

'Okay.'

'Right, let's take a look at scum-half passing,' said James. 'Scrum-halves use the dive pass most of the time. But that leaves you on the ground for a second or two, and you're no use there, are you?' Mick nodded. 'Sometimes it's best to stay on your feet! This gives you the option of throwing a reverse pass if that's your only way of getting the ball to your fly-half and setting your three-quarters in motion.'

Mick scratched his head, as much to dislodge some rain as bafflement at hearing about a pass you throw backwards.

'It's just like it sounds. You're looking one way, say to your right, but you propel the ball in the opposite direction underneath your right armpit. If done properly it gets defenders looking and running in the wrong direction,' James explained. 'Stand a few yards over there.'

Mick took up his position, reluctantly now as the drizzle became heavier. 'Watch closely,' said James. He placed the ball on the ground, picked it up with his left foot leading, anchored firmly and pointing right, but then dipped his right shoulder to rifle the ball under his armpit. The ball speared Mick's midriff. 'Think you can do that?'

'I'll 'ave a bash!' Mick said, eagerly; this pass looked a bit special, he decided; a bit flash, maybe, but the very prospect of performing one in a match filled him with enthusiasm to master the technique. 'Think I've seen that pass in a match, when Mr Clifton took us to watch Stanley's the other year. Brace did one.'

'That's right. Throwing a reverse pass was one of Brace's trademarks. Great Welsh scrum-half! Now, I'll stand close to you, say a couple of yards, for you to see the target easily and, as with the kicking, just concentrate on technique not power to start with.'

'Okay.' Mick tentatively adopted the stance he thought James had used.

'Hold on a second,' said James. 'Put more weight onto your left foot or else you'll fall flat on your face when you pick up the ball.'

Mick struck the ground with his first effort because he'd not dipped his shoulder low enough to get the ball underneath and away. 'Bend your knees more,' said James. 'Then you'll find it easier to get the ball away.'

The second slipped out of Mick's hands. He looked to the sky and brushed the rain from his cheeks, hoping James might call a halt for the day. James's response was to fold his arms. Mick tried again and the ball plopped into James's hands. 'That's better! I'll move out another yard or so. Then have another go.'

The pass hit the target. 'Again!' yelled James.

Mick selected another ball and repeated the process. 'That's good. I'm increasing the distance now so you must increase the power. Really get your right hand underneath the ball and try to spin it when you release so it travels through the air like a rifle bullet.'

The instruction sounded easier than the execution: the ball spun out of Mick's hands and rolled along the ground. 'Shit!' he said, quickly adding: 'Sorry, sir, for the swearin'…'

'I've heard worse than that from scrum-halves! The ball's slippery. Try again!'

The next effort did spin from Mick's hands but fell short of James; the third went into orbit to land nowhere near James; but the fourth struck him where it was intended.

'That's good!' shouted James. 'We'd best go in now or you'll be late for registration and I'll get it in the neck from Mr Lander. You can practice both these kicking and passing drills on your own. It's better if you've someone to kick to and pass to. But all you need is a ball and some space. And one last thing to remember, the golden rule when you're practicing skills: always finish with a good kick or pass, never finish on bad ones. Always finish on a high note not a low note!'

'Thanks, sir,' said Mick. He collected the errant balls and carried the string bag back into the changing room alongside his mentor. 'And every chance you get,' said James, 'go down to Iffley Road and watch the University play. They play many of the best sides in the country so you'll be able to study some of the very best scrum-halves. Watch and learn!'

As a brand new school with few players to choose from, South Oxford's results tended to make grim hearing when Masterson read them out at school assembly every Monday morning. Mick seldom had the ball in his hands to make any kind of ordinary pass let alone something as sophisticated as a reverse pass. But he did have plenty of opportunity to perfect box-kicks from the scrappy possession won by his forwards at line-outs. And he soon made a habit of cycling down the Iffley Road to scrutinize the two scrum-halves on show whenever the University had a home match.

Mick took to rugby as instinctively as a cygnet takes to water. James soon had him playing occasionally for Oxford RFC's Colts, out of position to develop awareness of the game in general; and James believed giving two years away to the other players would also toughen him up for the physical hurly-burly scrum-halves endured. Every chance he got, weekends and holidays, Mick went down to the school pitch with a rugby ball and practiced the drills James had taught him: pretty soon a rugby ball served Mick like a paintbrush served Rembrandt. Even the corridors of South Oxford provided useful practicing opportunities between lessons: to develop his elusiveness Mick began side-stepping his way past fellow pupils he imagined as hulking forwards. His scrum-half play improved so rapidly that James had no qualms entering him for the Oxfordshire Schools Under 19 trials even though he was only 16. Mick surprised even himself in the trial, for he comfortably outplayed the incumbent scrum-half to win selection. The County only played over the Christmas holidays which ensured some matches were lost to frost. But Mick played in four of the five matches during his two years in South Oxford's Sixth Form alongside more experienced players from Public Schools like St Edward's and Magdalen College School and the established Oxford grammar schools like Southfield and City Boys. But for a bad spell of frost that wiped out a game against Berkshire he'd have been watched with a view, James told him, to being nominated for an England trial.

The more games Mick played and the more games he watched at Iffley Road the more a plan crystallized in his brain. He wanted to pull on that dark blue jersey worn by the University side. In order to do that he had to be accepted at an Oxford college. And in order to do that he had to persuade Jack Masterson he merited an application. There was a mountain of work to do, on and off the rugby pitch, if that dream was to be realized. Winning a place at Oxford University was the longest of long shots. Mick needed no teacher at South Oxford to assure him of that fact.

But his dream received an unexpected fillip shortly after his sixteenth birthday when Masterson called him to his office.

***

'Bernard, sit down,' said Masterson in the friendliest voice at his disposal. It still sounded menacing to Mick who was rummaging through scrambled thoughts to unearth what he'd done wrong. 'Have you heard of a place called Atlantic College?' Receiving the negative reply he expected, Masterson continued. 'It's a recently opened Sixth Form College for boarders in South Wales. Housed in St Donat's Castle. It caters, as its name implies, for pupils from either side of the Atlantic. But the Oxfordshire Education Authority is offering one scholarship, one free place, to a suitable pupil. Would you like me to apply on your behalf?'

Mick felt his jaw drop somewhere close to his chest.

'Something you'd wish to discuss with your parents, of course.'

'It's free, sir?' was the best response Mick could come up with.

'Entirely free. Your parents need have no financial concerns,' said Masterson. 'But if you are serious about getting into Oxford, as I've heard from the Careers Advisor with whom you spoke at the beginning of term, a place at a Public School will definitely improve your chances because South Oxford, as yet, lacks any academic reputation. The school's ethos is similar to Gordonstoun, in Scotland. Lots of outdoor activities. Sailing. Rock climbing. Sea rescue. That sort of thing. Right up your street!'

Right up my street, thought Mick, you must be joking! The very mention of rock climbing took Mick back to Slade Camp's conker tree. As far as he was concerned anything higher than a bunk bed was not for climbing. He acknowledged Masterson's aside with a grin nonetheless.

'Here, take the prospectus home with you,' said Masterson, pushing a glossy brochure across his desk. 'Show it to you parents. Explain what I've said. Discuss it. Then come and see me with your answer. I'll need to put things in motion within a few days. So don't dilly-dally. Does that sound reasonable?'

'Yes, sir,' said Mick. 'Thank you, sir.' He reached the door and remembered to add: 'Thank you, sir, for thinkin' of me.'

The Atlantic College prospectus received a cursory and suspicious reception when Mick placed it on the table in front of his mother. He related Masterson's information concerning no parental financial contribution, and stressed the boost to his Oxford aspirations this school would give. Neither Edna nor Roy said anything other than express a willingness to read the prospectus; Mick could read nothing from their expressions. But privately they shared a quizzical expression at their son's latest flight of fancy. After flicking through the pages and tutting at the images of dormitories, dining hall, classrooms and boys scaling cliffs, Edna said they may as well let him apply because there was as much chance of him winning a scholarship to a posh school like this than she had of becoming Miss World.

The following morning Mick saw Masterson and asked him to make the application.

Six

'Do take a seat,' said Jack Masterson, gesturing Roy and Edna Bernard to the pair of easy chairs positioned in front of his desk.

The Bernards had been dreading this moment since breakfast. They were dressed for their midday appointment as if they were going to the pub on a Saturday evening: Roy was wearing his dark green suit with matching tie and Edna had picked out the floral dress she reserved for weddings and christenings. Roy had never been to the school and suggested they might stop for a drink in the Wellington for a spot of Dutch courage; he received a sharp reminder from Edna that she wasn't about to let him meet Mick's Headmaster stinking of beer. Instead Roy had to suffice with a constant supply of Woodbines on their 15-minute walk: Edna wouldn't allow the car to be used in case it was spotted by Mick who'd been kept in the dark about their visit. Edna had been to South Oxford once before: she'd attended a Parents Evening two years ago principally to discuss with Masterson her son's behaviour which had, she maintained, become disobedient, insolent and rude towards her. Masterson confirmed Mick could be a mite cheeky at times but assured her that this was not uncommon in adolescent boys and would surely pass.

'I imagine your visit is prompted by the news from the Local Education Authority concerning Michael's application for the Atlantic College scholarship,' said Masterson with the happy smile he believed the occasion warranted.

'Yes, Mr Masterson,' said Edna. 'Thass roight.'

'You must be very pleased and very proud of him,' said Masterson.

Edna looked at Roy, silently confirming her role as spokesperson. But Roy's attention had drifted to the photographs lining the walls of Masterson's sparsely furnished study.

Masterson sensed the uneasiness separating them. 'Michael won the scholarship…'

'Thass what we wornt to talk 'bout.'

Masterson leant forward to rest his hands on the desk. 'Is there a problem?' he asked, his expression becoming as sombre as if he was about to cane a recalcitrant fifth-former.

'Well, Mr Masterson,' said Edna, holding her head high, 'we're grateful for what you've done for Michael but the truth is we dunt wornt him t'go to this boardin' school in Wales.'

'Really?' said Masterson, scarcely believing what he'd just heard. 'You don't want him to take up this marvellous opportunity?'

'No, me an' his dad,' said Edna, glancing toward Roy, 'have talked it over an' we dunt wornt him to go.'

'Have you talked to Michael about this,' said Masterson, 'before you came to this decision?'

'No. We dunt wornt to get him worked up 'bout it.'

Masterson inhaled deeply and manufactured his next comment with immense care. 'But don't you think he had a right to be involved in the discussion? After all, it's his future.'

'We think he's too young to be makin' big decisions loik this.'

'I'm sorry,' Mrs Bernard, 'but I have to say I disagree strongly with you, and your husband. This is a wonderful opportunity for him…'

'Well, thass 'ow it's gunna be.'

Masterson tried again. 'But you must be aware of Michael's ambition to enter Oxford University?'

'We think he's gettin' ideas above his station, Mr Masterson.'

Masterson's battering ram of a jaw gathered momentum. 'It will be extremely difficult for him to achieve that ambition applying from a new and small school like this one, whereas the cachet, the reputation, of a Public School will give him an enormous leg-up.'

Edna glared at Roy. 'And we'd be grateful if you an' your staff would stop puttin' ideas in 'is head.'

'I consider that remark somewhat unjustified, Mrs Bernard,' said Masterson, between gritted teeth. 'Every member of my staff wants only the very best for every one of our pupils and none of them are encouraged to seek goals beyond their capabilities.'

It was Edna's turn to bridle. Nobody speaks to me like that, she said to herself, not even a headmaster. I know what he's up to. He's trying to take my son away from me and I'm not having it.

'Thass as maybe, Mr Masterson, she said, forcefully. 'But Michael has got farther an' farther away from us since he's bin at this school. He only thinks 'bout 'imself these days.'

'Michael is rather an egoist.'

'A what?' said Edna, eyes narrowing.

'Someone who puts their own interests first,' replied Masterson. 'Rather selfish, self-centred.'

'Then I wish youda said that an' not that fancy word…'

'I'm so sorry,' said Masterson who was beginning to understand why communication between Mick and his mother had degenerated. 'But if he's serious about aiming as high as Oxford, being self-centred will be to his advantage. He'll need to focus all his attention on academic work which may give the impression of him being stand-offish, keeping himself to himself, and ignoring everything, and everyone, else. It's the price he, and you, and your husband, must be prepared to pay.'

Edna heard what Masterson said but wasn't actually listening. 'Any'ow, it'd be worse still if he goes to a boardin' school. We'll lose 'im for good.'

'Your motherly concern is appreciated, Mrs Bernard. But as children grow to adulthood they do tend to drift away from their parents,' said Masterson, looking to Roy for some male endorsement. 'Wouldn't you agree, Mr Bernard?'

Roy Bernard felt the crimson climbing up his cheeks. He shuffled in his seat, not knowing what to say. And, anyhow, Edna had told him before they left home that he was to leave the talking to her.

'As someone once said perceptibly,' continued Masterson. 'children are only on loan to their parents.'

Edna glowered. Now he's giving me a lecture on how to be a mother, she muttered under her breath; I'm not putting up with that.

'Well, thass our d'cision,' she said, rising from her chair and beckoning Roy to follow suit. 'We'll tell Michael he didn't get the schola'ship an' you must tell 'im the same. T'day, before he comes home. Goodbye.'

The Bernards left Masterson shaking his head in bewilderment. Their homeward journey was considerably faster than that made an hour earlier in the opposite direction. 'You wuz a lotta bloomin' 'elp!' said Edna, lighting up a Woodbine to calm her nerves.

'But you said…'

'You wuz 'bout as much use as a choc'lut soljer!'

It was the same old story, Edna decided. I shall be painted as the villain of the piece, the one Mick will hate if he learns the truth of the matter. That Masterson had better keep his mouth shut or I'll be back down at that school sharpish. And I shan't take any prisoners. 'Jus' you make sure you dunt let slip to Mick,' she muttered to Roy, 'as 'ow he got this bloody schola'ship!'

Roy kept staring straight ahead as the the effort of putting one foot after the other became harder the nearer they got to the house where his every move and remark would now be under constant surveillance. Even if his wife was in denial he knew this decision had been taken in their best interests and not Mick's. They had let him down; they had betrayed him. More to the point, he had betrayed him by keeping schtum. What kind of father did that make him, putting himself first? How was he going to look his son in the eye? If Mick was the class traitor the Jaykes clan insisted he was, it was only fair to accuse him and Edna of being traitors for betraying their son. But it was done now. He'd have to cope somehow or other.

***

When Mick was called to Masterson's office the following morning he went in two minds. One voice hoped he'd got the scholarship because it would be a means to an end, a helpful route to Oxford; a second hoped he'd not won the place because he didn't fancy the outdoor activities involved, especially scaling cliffs, the very thought of which instantly brought a gale of fear to his innards.

'Sit down, Bernard,' said Masterson, in business-like manner. 'Bad news, I'm afraid. You didn't win the scholarship to Atlantic College.'

'Oh,' said Mick, wondering if he should act disappointed or relieved.

'It went to a boy whose siblings all attended public schools but whose parents no longer had the finances to send him to one,'

Masterson explained. 'I hope you're not too disappointed. It was, after all, rather a long shot.'

'It's okay, sir.'

Masterson's eyes found Mick's and locked in. 'Do you still wish to go up to Oxford?'

'I'd like to try, sir, if that's possible,' Mick replied cautiously.

'In that case,' said Masterson, 'I think you might find it helpful to have a word with Peter Clifton. He lives in Iffley village, not far from you. Why don't I telephone him and ask when might be suitable for you to drop in? Would that be agreeable to you?'

'Yes, sir,' said Mick. 'That would be very good of you.' He hadn't the nerve to say otherwise even though instinct suggested nothing might come of it and he'd be putting Clifton to unnecessary trouble.

'That's settled then. I'll get a message to you, hopefully before the end of today.'

***

So it came about that Mick was knocking on the door of Clifton's whitewashed cottage one fine June Saturday. Recognizing the significance of this visit he was determined to create the kind of impression he believed was essential for a budding Oxford undergraduate. He'd made a mental note to speak the Queen's English rather than rustic Oxfordshire. And he'd broken out his best clothes, his 'Number One' kit reserved for special occasions: black-striped shirt; purple 'V'- necked Shetland wool jumper from Marks & Spencer (the black version was worn for school); grey tapered trousers from Lane's, the only shop in town pandering to the fashion fads of teenage boys; and black suede desert boots.

Mrs Clifton answered his knock. 'Good morning, Michael. Do call me Susan. Peter's waiting for you in the sitting room,' she said cheerfully while pointing him in the right direction.'

The first thing that struck Mick about the Clifton house was the smell. It was not the smell he normally associated with a house, either his own or those of his relatives. His sense of domestic smell was so conditioned by the presence of cigarette smoke that he was hypersensitive to any other household aroma; the Clifton home smelt as fresh as a summer meadow. His eyes were drawn to the gleaming sitting room's wooden floor, the stone hearth and the mat in front of it that he guessed from its design and vivid colours must be Persian in origin; no linoleum and rag-rugs in sight. Clifton was in the process of searching for a book among the shelves that covered the walls either side of the fireplace. Wouldn't I love to have a room like this, my own personal library, thought Mick, his eyes wandering along the lines of volumes standing to attention like so many brightly uniformed guardsmen.

'Ah, good morning, Michael,' said Clifton, on the half-turn. 'No need to stand on ceremony today! Take a seat.'

Mick sank into a well-used armchair in which he instantaneously pictured Clifton frequenting with a book open on his lap and a glass of something alcoholic in his hand. 'You've plenty o' books, sir' he offered, tamely. 'How do you find the time to read 'em all?'

Clifton chuckled as he recommenced his quest. 'I have read them all at some time or other! But I can't bring myself to throw any away or sell them to Dalrymple even if I did find any boring or of no further use.'

'I'm the same, sir,' said Mick, cheered by their common ground. 'I've not got very many but I'd never chuck…'

'Throw or discard,' said Clifton. 'If you're to impress Oxford dons, the tutors, at interview you should develop your spoken English by avoiding the vernacular.'

A sudden silence caused Clifton to realize the ramifications of what he'd said. 'Slang, to you and me,' he said quickly in an apologetic tone. 'Nor, it goes without saying, should we resort to the vernacular in written English, unless one is quoting direct speech.'

'I geddit,' said Mick.

Clifton let the reply pass without comment. 'Mr Masterson will be setting you exercises on the use of English because there is now an examination paper in that subject which all Oxford candidates must pass before they may come into residence,' he informed Mick. 'Think you can manage that?'

'I'll give it a bash...sorry...a try.'

'There,' said Clifton, now beaming. 'You've got the hang of it already!'

It was Mick's turn to smile. 'Wouldn't it be more proper to say "You've got the idea of it already"?'

Before he'd time to realize he'd been impudent to a man who'd invited him into his own castle and was going out of his way to help him Clifton clapped his hands. 'That's precisely it! You may be a cheeky blighter but you're a quick learner! And you'll need to be if you're to persuade an Oxford college to give you a place.'

'Sorry, sir,' said Mick, head bowed. 'That was rude o'me.'

Clifton waved aside the apology. 'Now, let's talk about a strategy. The crux of the matter can be summarized in one word: read. You must read until your eyes glaze over. And then you must read some more. You stop reading when you fall asleep. When you wake, that book is there in front of you, ready and waiting for some more reading. It sounds simple but it demands huge effort. Are you prepared for that? To give absolutely everything?'

Mick was so enthused by Clifton's ebullience that no other response than 'You bet, sir,' was contemplated.

'You must read around your subject. If you're dealing with the French Revolution you should seek biographies of major figures, such as Robespierre or Danton, in order to gain that extra tit-bit of knowledge you can insert not only into essays but that all-important interview with a don. Try to find that tiny snippet of information, the gem, that the don might not even know himself.'

'Righto, sir.'

'Jack Masterson told me how he'd made you read out your extended essay on the Crimean War in General Studies a week or so back. That was mainly to develop your confidence in public speaking, which you'll need at interview. But he was astounded by the number of unusual facts you'd inserted that lifted the piece.'

'Really?' said Mick, cheeks reddening.

Let me put that last point another way,' said Clifton, responding to Mick's expression. 'Being a "Smart Alec" in these circumstances invariably pays off. You may think the look on your interviewer's face states he feels insulted but in reality it means he is inwardly impressed that you've taken him on at his own game. Dons like to be challenged in tutorials. Otherwise they become bored stiff.'

'I understand,' said Mick, confidently.

'Oxford dons, and I'm not gratuitously insulting them by saying this, much prefer undertaking research toward their next book than wasting valuable time teaching undergraduates who are as dull as grey paint. If they discover someone at interview who hints at being an individual thinker, someone who might enliven an hour tutorial by adopting a different slant on an issue or by taking a controversial stance, then they are apt to favour that candidate.'

'Yes, sir. I see what you mean.'

'You are a natural "Smart Alec". Don't be afraid to use it to your advantage.'

'If you say so, sir. I'll def'nitely try.'

'And when it comes to reading,' said Clifton, picking up on his theme. 'I don't mean just history books. Yes, they are essential. But read plenty of fiction. It'll provide light relief and widen your vocabulary.'

'Which books?' asked Mick, picking up his pen ready to write them down.

The answer came quickly. 'Try any of the *Wessex Novels* of Thomas Hardy because they all benefit from a historical setting, contemporary rural life in the 19th century. *Jude the Obscure* might appeal to you because the central character, Jude Fawley, no more than a humble stonemason, also aspires to studying at Oxford, called Christminster in the novel. And see what you think of Michael Henchard in *The Mayor of Casterbridge*. Both stories give you an alternative slant on rural life during the agrarian revolution to the standard historical texts.'

Clifton waited until Mick had recorded both titles before continuing. 'The great thing about fiction is the prospect of finding characters with whom you can relate. The author enables you to read their thoughts: their hopes, their anxieties. Some individuals may draw you in. Once they do, you'll be unable to put the book down.'

'I'll have a look for 'um in the school library.'

'Talking of fiction,' said Clifton, rising from his chair and eyeing the bookshelves, 'Jack Masterson asked me to root out any book on life as an Oxford undergraduate for you to read, something that'll give you a flavour of what you must contend with besides the academic challenges.'

Clifton passed him a smallish book in an unappealing plain white dust wrapper adorned with simple black lettering: the title was *Zuleika Dobson* and the author was Max Beerbohm. Neither name registered with Mick.

'Thanks, sir.'

Clifton recognized the vacant look. 'You won't have heard of this novel,' he said by way of excusing Mick's ignorance of the work. 'It was written back in 1911. It's a comic novel. Yet a savage look at Edwardian Oxford. So, to be honest, it can't give you a totally accurate picture of the life of a student at present day Oxford. But you might enjoy reading it all the same.'

'But it'll be wider reading?' suggested Mick. 'Should improve my use of English?'

'Yes!' replied Clifton clenching a fist. 'It'll widen your vocabulary! Which reminds me.' He ran a finger along a shelf. 'Here it is! You'll need one of these.'

Mick accepted the book: it was a paperback entitled *The Thesaurus of English Words.*

'First compiled by Peter Mark Roget in 1852,' said Clifton. 'It's an educational aid for anyone who wishes to speak better English…'

'Excuse me interruptin', sir, but do you mean my accent or the way I talk?'

'No, not at all,' said Clifton, keen to avoid any misunderstanding or blow to Mick's ego. 'Your accent, your dialect, speaks for you and your heritage; where you come from. You should be as proud of it as any Geordie or Scouser is of their accent and dialect.'

'Exac'ly how does this book 'elp me?' asked Mick.

'It's for anyone who wishes to have a range of words at their command, whether spoken or written. It's simpler to use than you might think. It arranges words according to ideas. You refer to it when you can't find a suitable word, the right word, to express your specific intention. It provides richer alternatives to everyday choices.'

Mick opened the book. Shit, he thought, this looks gobbledegook.

'Pick a word from that page,' said Clifton.

'Existence,' Mick replied.

'Now select another word from the list of nouns that means the same and one you might prefer to use.'

'Actuality.'

'Now choose an adjective.'

'Being.'

'And a verb.'

'Live.'

'Adverb.'

'Really.'

'Exactly so! You've got the gist of it straight away. I knew you would.'

One sentence of praise from Clifton caused Mick's self-esteem to swell, as it always had and always would.

'And if you look toward the back of the book,' Clifton added, 'you'll find an index which tells you in which category to find the alternative words. If you look up "existence", for example?'

Mick thumbed the pages until he found the word: 'Category one.'

'QED!'

'Quod erat demonstrandum…'

Clifton laughed and awarded Mick a thumbs-up.

The sound of footsteps drew their attention to the door. 'How about you two take a breather?' said Mrs Clifton, hands clasped in front of her.

'Good idea!' said Clifton, gesturing Mick to follow his wife. Mick took the opportunity to study her: tall and slender with a fresh face and dark wavy locks tumbling over her shoulders, she was dressed in tweed skirt and twin-set offset with a single string of pearls. She was, thought Mick searching for the best word the *Thesaurus* might recommend, 'elegant' and reminded him of Martha Gibson, which was no bad thing in his view.

'Michael.' she said, on reaching the kitchen, 'Do take a seat over there.'

Mick managed to raise a grin in the act of taking his appointed place next to the two Clifton children, a boy and a girl aged, he guessed, about nine and seven respectively. As he sat down he stole a quick glance at his finger nails to check they were as clean and short as he hoped.

'Beans on toast,' said Mrs Clifton. 'All right for you, Michael?'

'Yes, thanks. That'll be great,' Mick replied cheerfully, safe in the knowledge his nails could pass any scrutiny.

'Tell me, Michael,' said Mrs Clifton, as she put his plate of food in front of him, 'how would you normally spend your Saturdays?'

'In the winter I'd be playin' rugby but this time o'year I'd be watchin' the horseracin' on *Grandstand* with my dad.'

'And what's the attraction of horseracing?'

'Dad puts a bet on for me when he goes to the bettin' shop to put on his bets.'

Susan Clifton covered her surprise with another question: 'How else do you spend your leisure time?'

'I go to the dogs.'

'The dogs?'

'I think Michael is referring to greyhound racing,' said her husband, helpfully.

'My Uncle Bob, well he's not my uncle really but I call him Uncle Bob, has a greyhound an' I help with his trainin' an' always watch him when he races,' explained Mick to his hostess who began showing increasing signs of shock.

'You wager money on this greyhound belonging to your uncle?'

'Yes, I use some of my paper-round money. I put the odd two bob on 'im. But mostly I make do with my cut whenever he wins.'

'Your cut?'

'Yes, I always get ten bob if he wins.'

'Well, Michael,' said Susan Clifton, 'I can safely say there's a world out there about which I know nothing whatsoever!'

Mick felt he ought to smile. 'Goin' to the dogs is an excitin' night out an' it's cheaper than going to horseracing,' he added. 'You should get Mr Clifton to take you over to Cowley one noight.'

The smile left Mick's face and he took a breath. He was gripped by the sudden sense he'd begun lapsing into an Oxfordshire accent as he'd grown more comfortable in his surroundings.

Now it was Susan Clifton's turn to smile. 'Do you like anything else, the theatre perhaps?'

'I've been to a few Shakespeare plays with the school,' said Mick slowly, taking extra care to say 'been' rather than 'bin'.

'Such as?'

'*Richard III* and *Julius Caesar*. But I like going to the pictures more.'

'And what kind of films do you prefer?'

'Westerns, swashbucklers, anythin' historical.'

'So Ingmar Bergman is not for you,' Susan Clifton couldn't resist adding.

Peter Clifton rode to Mick's rescue. 'I imagine you'll be eager to see *Zulu* when it comes to town?'

'Can't wait to see that!' said a relieved Mick. 'It's about the defence of Rorke's Drift in 1879 when 11 Victoria Crosses were awarded, the most ever for one battle.'

Susan Clifton spotted the satisfaction crossing her husband's face. 'Michael, have you seen *Seven Samurai*?'she said.

'No,' replied Mick, wondering how this omission might embarrass him.

'It's a Japanese film, set in the middle ages, about seven samurai, the equivalent of our knights I suppose, who are experiencing hard times and are paid a pittance to defend a village from bandits. It's a Western in everything but name. I'm sure you'd like it. And I'd be interested to hear what you think of it. It's often shown at the Scala in Walton Street.'

'I'll look out for it,' Mick lied. They only show arty-farty pictures at the Scala, he reminded himself, so there's no chance of me wasting my hard earned spondulicks on one of their tickets.

After this burst of enthusiastic conversation Mick returned to his baked beans and safely consumed them without any lapse in table manners while Susan Clifton encouraged her children to do likewise.

Mick then faced a greater problem than explaining his pastimes. 'Please help yourself to some fruit,' said Susan Clifton, pointing to the bowl in the centre of the table containing bananas, oranges and a variety of apples. Mick watched the two Clifton children select apples and then begin peeling and slicing them with knives: why, he thought, don't they just use their gnashers. Having got this far without mishap he wasn't about to risk embarrassing himself with a fruit knife.

'No, thanks, Mrs Clifton. I'm full-up.'

His hostess tried again: 'Will you take a cup of coffee?'

This amounted to the stiffest ordeal – which he'd anticipated because the aroma of coffee had been filling the room for some minutes. He hated everything about coffee: the taste and, especially, the smell; he'd cross Cornmarket rather than walk past the Cadena Café whence the smell of coffee drifted like German mustard gas heading for British trenches. His father occasionally had Camp coffee, a syrup made from coffee and chicory, that came in a bottle and smelt awful. The coffee Susan Clifton brewed, however, had been a fascinating operation to watch out of the corner of his eye: she'd crushed some beans and put the resulting powder into a machine that began to bubble away and eventually squirt liquid through a nozzle into a cup she'd placed underneath. Mick had seen his first espresso machine at work. Although refusing a cup of the despised beverage he did agree to his glass being topped-up with lemonade. And as Susan Clifton cleared the table he realized that throughout the meal no smoking cigarette had polluted the atmosphere.

An hour later, following a brief pep talk from Clifton, Mick began the walk back to Hill Rise. 'If you want it,' Clifton had told him, 'Go for it! No half measures. Concentrate on the prize and give it everything you've got. I believe you can do it, Michael. Others may help you. But, and never forget or underestimate your role, only you can make it happen.'

The Cliftons watched Mick disappear into the distance. 'Is he really up to Oxford standard?' said Susan Clifton. 'He seems very withdrawn and unlikely to impress at interview. Oxford dons are hardly likely to be fascinated by talk of horseracing, greyhound racing and Westerns…'

'Oh, I don't know about that,' replied her husband. 'The unknown may intrigue them. And I'm sure Oxford interviewers are well versed in the art of getting candidates to talk about things they know rather than things they don't. Did you see the way he came alive when military history came up? There's nothing he doesn't know wars, battles, sieges…to which I think we may add the nags and the dogs!'

Susan Clifton shrugged. 'I can understand Jack would like to put South Oxford on the academic map with an Oxford student but don't you think he might've waited for a likelier candidate?'

'Don't be fooled. Michael's quick-witted and is perfectly capable of rising to the occasion. He has tremendous willpower. He loves nothing more than to be challenged. Jack says he doesn't give much away in his schoolwork. If something is of no interest to him he doesn't bother with it. I suspect he deals with people the same way. But once something does interest him he's highly motivated to the point of being pathologically driven. The same with his rugby. He's hardly played the game yet Wyn James says he's come on leaps and bounds. He believes there's no limit on how far he could go.'

'But the social changes alone will cause him untold problems if he does manage to win a place. He's terribly gauche. You saw how he struggled at lunch with small talk. Perhaps his parents are correct and he just won't fit in. You know what Oxford's like.'

'He's well aware the social side will be testing. But he's a watcher and a listener. He'll soon work things out. And, most importantly, he knows that going to Oxford will be a life-changing moment for him and that once Magdalen Bridge has been crossed there may be no turning back.' Clifton paused for effect: 'Susan, take my word for it, this is one committed young man.'

As the Cliftons shut their front door, half a mile up the road Mick was feeling both elated and despondent. With one step he was elated at this new domestic world he'd just encountered, its genteel atmosphere of books and learning and polite discourse; and with the next step he was despondent at the world he was about to re-enter, the harsh reality of dullness, bickering and, above all else, the intellectual and physical loneliness of the Bernard household that frequently left him miserable, frustrated and angry in equal measure.

Suddenly Mick caught a whiff of something on the breeze. It was something he knew and detested. It was the smell of cigarettes. And it was coming from his jumper. Mick sniffed the sleeve: the stench of cigarettes had impregnated every strand of wool. The shame of having introduced this odour into the Clifton home and giving the impression he was a chain smoker made him furious. As soon as he got home the jumper was put out for washing along with every other item of clothing which reeked of cigarettes.

***

Mick had left home toying with dreams but he returned nurturing rebellion.

He was, he had to admit, a reluctant rebel, but a rebel all the same. Mick considered himself a law-abiding individual; he might confess to bending the rules slightly on occasion but he certainly wasn't one who broke the law deliberately, be that of society or his school. But house rules became another matter entirely. And since these rules were laid down by Edna Bernard they led to a declaration of war with his mother. His weapons in their battle of wills were words: words could help realize his dreams, but words could also be twisted to taunt and belittle anyone who earned his displeasure. From being in the direct line of fire from his mother, and her kinfolk, he turned the guns around and began firing back with a deliberate and unadulterated cruelty which would disappoint Peter Clifton and Jack Masterson but gave him enormous pleasure and no little satisfaction.

Mostly Mick waged this guerilla war from his bedroom. It became a cold, lonely barracks in winter and a sweltering, stuffy fort in summer from which to march to war but that was of no consequence to him. These battle lines were tested on a cold Sunday afternoon in the October following Mick's visit to the Clifton home. A seething Edna ascended the stairs intent upon dragging Mick from his lair to fraternize with Uncle Alec, Aunt Peg and their three young daughters who'd arrived for tea and cards: Mick, it was presumed, would occupy the girls while the adults enjoyed themselves. But Mick had other ideas. He'd come to regard Uncle Alec as a man with delusions of grandeur and his wife as graceless as a drunken docker; he'd undertaken this babysitting chore on too many occasions to have any desire to do so yet again. Without looking up from Fisher's *History of Europe* Mick told his mother to 'sod off.' A few short years ago a display of such downright insolence would've been met with 'Dunt you speak to your mother loik that!' and physical chastisement. But no longer. Not since the incident of the blue blazer. Edna was obliged to retreat. Mick read three more chapters of Fisher: the fingers turning the pages were numb but the spirit driving them was vibrant.

Edna couldn't understand why the son whom she fed and clothed, for whom she laundered and ironed, and for whom she'd bought every luxury imaginable (apart from the electric train set – which she thought was too dangerous) could repay her with such ingratitude and such rudeness. The one thing she didn't include in her list of gifts, however, was the gift of love, or more specifically, the gift of expressing that love with a tender hug or a kind word. Edna struggled to appreciate that love was not expressed through material things: love did not come with a price tag. Love was freely given with no strings attached; there was no *quid pro quo*. The only love that satisfied Edna was the unconditional kind: complete adoration, constant genuflection and total subjugation to her will. It was the kind of servile love Mick saw her receiving from Roy after squeezing the masculinity out of him. And Mick vowed it wasn't going to happen to him. When she upbraided him for his coarseness he reminded her with sullen defiance that such words were 'the *lingua franca* in this house'. That he'd offended her and resorted to words she'd not comprehend gave him a buzz of delight that both pleased and appalled him.

Nor was his father spared: Roy became an object of pity if not utter scorn. When Roy struggled to work out, for example, how to cut the battens correctly for a door panel Mick spotted his error but ignored the eyes pleading for advice until Roy was obliged to beg for help. Mick felt becoming more obnoxious informed his family and relatives just how much more fanatical he was about attaining his goal of a place at Oxford. The one fuelled the other: out of negativity, he reasoned, sprang positivity. It never occurred to him that he might be using this obligation to channel all his energies toward his Oxford entry preparation as an excuse to wreak vengeance on his parents by mocking and ridiculing them. In his mind, nice guys didn't win. The more self-obsessed and nastier he became, went his hypothesis, the more likely he was to succeed.

Unfortunately for Mick's inflated ego his recent academic progress convinced him this hypothesis was correct. Following Clifton's departure from South Oxford, his work had deteriorated, and not just in History: his results slumped across the board, causing Masterson to question his resolve in end-of-term reports. But spending those few hours with Clifton and the transformation it triggered at home, however distasteful, saw him rediscover his work ethic and kick-start an academic revival. He sailed through O-levels in seven out of eight subjects: only Latin proved a stumbling block – and a critical stumbling block because an O-level pass was obligatory to study History at Oxford. His subjects in the Sixth Form were the traditional trio of English Literature, History and Geography. One term of the first-named found Mick asking Masterson if he might drop the subject to concentrate on his Oxford preparation: Keats and Jane Austin were tedious, he maintained, and were undermining his commitment to the two other A-levels, passes in which, he politely reminded Masterson, would be enough to satisfy Oxford's entrance requirements – assuming he finally secured Latin O-level. Masterson sat back in his chair, stroked his chin and pondered. Bernard has got a nerve. But he's certainly thought this through. And only has eyes on the prize. 'I'll have a word with the English department and see what they think,' said Masterson. Mick's wish was granted.

***

In the first week of summer term Mick sat down with Bill Lander to complete his Oxford application forms. How much detail Lander knew of Mick's ambitions was quickly tested.

'I daresay as an Oxford boy you should try for Cambridge,' said Lander. 'Best to leave home, get away…'

'It's Oxford I want,' said Mick, guardedly. 'And I won't live at home…'

'Wouldn't it be cheaper and more convenient?'

'No, I want to get away from home,' said Mick firmly while ensuring his reply contained no 'ornt' and dropped aitch. 'I must.'

Lander's head wobbled slightly, as it was apt to do in moments of irritation. 'I see,' he said quietly, but not without a dash of menace. 'Well, St Catherine's would be a wise choice. The Master there is a well-known historian…'

'I don't think Cats would be right for me,' said Mick, hands gripping the side of his chair.

'Really!' said Lander, astonishment written all over his face at this show of impudence. Suddenly Mick thought he was about to receive a detention rather than assistance.

'I've been attending a lot of Blues games at Iffley Road, sir,' Mick said as fast as he could to retrieve the situation in case Lander blew his top, which was not an unknown phenomenon. 'And five or six of the team come from St Frideswide's College, including the captain. It's the college for rugby players, sir. That's my ace card, isn't it?'

'Possibly,' said Lander, stroking the point of his beard. I do so hate, he thought, a boy who thinks he knows it all and then goes about proving he does.

'That's where I think I should apply, sir.'

Lander was unsure whether to laugh or roar. Then he melted into one of his trademark feline smirks. 'All right. St Frideswide's it is. You've clearly given this some thought.'

Mick released his grip on the chair and smiled meekly: it wouldn't be wise to display any triumphalism at his routing of the Deputy Head.

He left Lander feeling on top of the world. He, Mick Bernard, from a humble background, had taken his first step toward an undergraduate career at Oxford University. Two months later he learnt he'd successfully completed the second step by passing O-level Latin. The final year of his time at South Oxford was a maelstrom of success: in the classroom and on the rugby pitch. And even in affairs of the heart. One girl was responsible.

Seven

Mick had been attracted to Sam Owens ever since he'd edited the first school magazine and she'd contributed one of the articles. But what really brought her to Mick's attention was when she played the minor role of maid in the school's production of *She Stoops to Conquer*. Mick couldn't take his eyes off her. Her every entrance didn't come quickly enough; and once she was on stage Mick never wanted her to exit. The magazine review reckoned she 'made a very demure maid', which Mick hoped was a case of art imitating life. He reckoned she was the nearest he'd seen to the goddess of love and a girl he'd love to date. Once he'd entered the Upper Sixth achieving this became a matter of some urgency for time wasn't on his side. He had to find a way of getting close up and personal.

Sam was in the habit of sashaying around school during the lunch break with two of her friends. All three were good looking and bright: God's gifts to lusting teenage boys. Sam, nevertheless, was the stand out and she knew it: she had the exam grades and her reflection in the mirror to prove it. One lunch-time Mick and Pete Livermore were rooted to the spot by the door of the library as the threesome sauntered past. Sam was in the middle and when she looked over at Mick and smiled it was as if someone had introduced him to Helen of Troy. It must be now or never, he told himself.

'Pete,' he murmured, 'who is that girl with the smile?'

'Haven't a clue.'

Mick knew it wouldn't do to reveal the cow eyes of the lovelorn. Better to convey a degree of insouciance rather than confess that he'd been tracking Sam all term. He knew her lunchtime haunts and made a habit of managing to bump into her that struck him as so blatant he became convinced she must regard him as the school stalker.

'I need to find out quick and try to get a date before she's off the market,' Mick continued.

'Good luck with that, mate! Everyone in the Sixth and plenty on the outside must be chasing a bit of skirt like her! Try Keith Collins. He might help. I've seen them chatting once or twice.'

Mick hunted for Collins who was acknowledged as being on speaking terms with every attractive girl in the upper school despite showing no romantic interest in them: he was their 'agony aunt.' Keith smiled at Mick's description of his personal Venus de Milo. 'Not another one chasing Sam Owens! You'll be knocked over in the rush! Give up before you go down with chronic balls ache!'

'You speak with her now and then,' said Mick, conspiratorially. 'Has she ever mentioned me at all?'

'No, mate. Not a whisper of interest…'

'Shit!'

'But she's never included your name among those she wouldn't be seen dead with!' said Collins. 'Now, that can't be bad! That's a good sign, ennit?'

'Thanks for nothing!' said Mick, growing more frustrated by the second. He thought for a moment and decided to go for broke: 'Does she…'

'Put it about?' interjected Collins. 'You know better than that! None of our girls are that sort. If you get a kiss after three trips to the pictures you've got a result!'

'If you were at the speedway of a Thursday you'd not be so sure,' harrumphed Mick. 'There's always a handful of our girls near the pits and they're surrounded by blokes knocking twenty. And ugly buggers too!'

'You know what they say. Good girls do love bad boys!'

'I mean, well, she must be dating blokes out of school,' blurted Mick, 'older, perhaps got a car, a job and money to impress, more experienced in the …'

'Probably you're right about dating boys from outside school from what I've heard but I don't reckon she's a "goer", she's too prim and proper for that. She'll not be givin' it away.'

'Mick groped for the right question. 'But how reliable is your…'

'You muss be well an' truly bitten!' laughed Collins, in the act of walking away.

Mick knew he must be blushing fit to combust. He grabbed Collins's arm 'Don't breathe a word of this to anyone…'

'Not even Sam?'

Collins smiled fast enough to douse the irritation Mick felt coursing through him. 'Your secret is safe with me,' said Collins. 'An' if you believe that you'll believe anything!'

Mick watched Collins saunter down the corridor and wondered whether it would've been wiser to keep his mouth shut. But the damage, if that is what transpired, had been done. Perhaps if Collins did tell Sam of his interest in her she might, just might, give him a positive signal. Thankfully he'd only private study in the library for the afternoon which gave him the opportunity to wrack his brains for a strategy.

But his mind insisted on drifting away. He imagined himself slowly divesting Sam of her clothes until she was stark naked. Sam dressed well and surely undressed just as well. He caressed each part of her luscious body as he revealed it and was in the act of kissing her shoulder when the mood was shattered.

'Bernard! Wake your ideas up!' The distinctive drawl of Simmonds returned Mick to reality. 'You're in here to study! Not daydream!'

If only he knew what I was visualizing, thought Mick, and he'd be asking me for a bedside ticket. 'You'll not get into Oxford wasting valuable time with your head in the clouds.'

Simmonds was a Cambridge graduate. Probably wanted Oxford but was rejected, reasoned Mick. Sour grapes, that's his problem.

Then Mick's eyes lit up at the sudden conception of a plan. He was in the library. Who was the Library Prefect charged with drawing up the lunchtime library rota? He was. He could enlist anyone he wanted from the Lower Sixth as an assistant. Who could he possibly pick? With whom did he want to spend time? Taking next week's rota from his satchel Mick wrote Sam's name beside his for Monday, Wednesday and Friday. Five days a week might seem too obvious, and pushing his luck. Three days was just right.

Sam smiled demurely at Mick when she duly arrived for her first session as his assistant. He explained to Sam how books were issued and returned as though the procedure was nuclear science. Sam showed no sign of grievance for the lack of respect being paid to her intelligence. 'That's all very clear,' she responded, with no trace of sarcasm. 'Good,' said Mick. 'Don't hesitate to ask if there's anything you don't understand.' Sam smiled once again, this time, with justification, far less sweetly.

The pair circled each other like two courting pigeons for the next couple of weeks. Sam was never late and was never less than polite in the face of Mick's tediously sanctimonious advice. Despite tales of Mick's romantic interest trickling through to her, she was starting to think the rumour-mongers were having fun at her expense because Mick never went within a mile of broaching the possibility of a date. Then in the week before the Christmas holidays, as she was clearing up at the end of a session, Mick came up beside her. 'Books are okay,' he ventured. 'But films offer an extra dimension,' he added pompously. 'Do you like the cinema?'

Sam pierced him with her aquamarine eyes. 'Are you asking me out?' she said with musical tonality in her voice.

'Aah…' was all Mick could muster. He was momentarily nonplussed. He'd prepared a line of questioning that built up to asking Sam out and now she'd knocked that into a cocked hat. 'Well, if you'd like to come to the pictures with me one evening that would be great.'

'When?'

This girl takes no prisoners, Mick conceded, hoping Sam hadn't mind-reading among her many attributes. 'How about tomorrow?'

'Fine. Where shall I meet you?'

'Aah…I'll walk down to your house and we can go into town together on the bus.'

Okay,' Sam said, smiling. 'What time?'

Please don't smile at me like that, the tiny voice in Mick's head pleaded, or my knees will give way. 'Seven?' he just about managed to utter.

'Fine. It's a date!' Then she executed a stately about-turn and left Mick standing there attempting to re-attach his lower jaw to the upper. Her face, however, wore the expression of a tease. She knew the effect she had on young men, the spell that attracted their ardour and antagonized other girls. She'd enjoyed playing with Mister High-and-Mighty Bernard. And would do so again if the mood caught her.

Mick's preparations for this special evening out were suitably meticulous: he shaved and splashed on some Tabac after-shave; shampooed his hair; cut his nails; and polished his shoes until their shine rivalled his Elmer Cottons. What to wear was easy: he'd just bought a new pullover from the proceeds of a summer holiday job in the unloading bay at Marks & Spencer which he was saving for the right occasion. This fashion statement had a black corduroy front with plain black sleeves and back; a crisply ironed white shirt and pressed black trousers would complete the ensemble. Roy and Edna couldn't fail to notice such attention to hygienic and sartorial detail. 'Seein' a young lady t'night?' said Roy. 'Dunt do anythin' I wouldn't do!' Edna scowled at her husband's crassness: 'Leave the boy alone!' Mick ignored both of them because his mind was already dreaming of things to come and the attendant pitfalls.

Mick had limited confidence when it came to making small talk – of any kind but more so with the opposite sex. He'd had one girl friend whom he'd met when their two families shared the same holiday hotel in Great Yarmouth. They went on to correspond and spend a week in their respective homes. Paula was pretty; but not the stimulating company Mick craved. Furthermore, he convinced himself when he cruelly abandoned her without explanation, they lived too far apart for anything meaningful to develop.

Nor did Mick have any confidence in his looks as a weapon in the skirmishing for a girl's attention. In mitigation he could offer his athletic build and sporting prowess: and, of course, his singular asset, a ready wit and a sharp sense of humour. What girl wanted to go on a date with a misanthrope (the noun in his *Thesaurus* he thought best described the antisocial creature he frequently became)? If the girl was made to feel happy she might be laughed into bed.

These considerations were just the start. Mick's biggest headache of all revolved around his inability to read the female condition or decipher its signals as astutely as he'd like. The outcome was a degree of bashfulness so acute it could easily be mistaken for indifference or disinterest – neither of which applied when the female in question was Sam Owens. The outcome of all this soul searching was unequivocal: Mick Bernard was one confused young man who was more likely to mess-up tonight than strike it lucky.

Mick was knocking on Sam's front door at 7 o'clock precisely, after loitering five minutes around the corner to ensure he wasn't early. She must've been waiting for him as she answered immediately and was beside him before either of her parents could put a face to the name she'd given them. This opportunity to gaze at Sam without embarrassment filled Mick with joy: at school he couldn't look at her for long without running the risk of being labelled a pervert. Now he had her to himself. They were sharing the same space, sharing the moment and he was grateful for it; he hoped Sam felt the same but appreciated it was she who held the baton. They crossed to the bus stop and the glare from the headlights of an approaching bus offered up Sam's delectable features for Mick's inspection as if he'd ordered them from a menu. The light brown hair cut in something between a pixie cut and a page boy style; the flawless complexion; eyes shining like two blue chips of glacier ice; those kissable lips; the trim figure. She was a knock-out. But Mick was so shell-shocked he omitted to tell her so.

For a classy girl like Sam it was imperative Mick spared no expense. This was no job for a 'flea-pit' like the Electra. Thankfully, Mick was in funds: in fact he was flush. His Post Office savings account was well in the black, despite the outlay on the new pullover, owing to wily investments on the horses – he'd a double come up at Newbury only last Saturday. *The Professionals*, the new Western starring Lee Marvin and Burt Lancaster, was his instinctive choice. But a Western, he reasoned, wouldn't be to Sam's taste. Consequently, it had to be the Ritz in George Street, the plushest cinema in town, to see *My Fair Lady* which surely might be more to her liking. Mick had read *Pygmalion* at school so he knew the story well enough as he did the songs which had been played over and over again on the radio. Just as well he did because his attention was never fixed on the screen but riveted to the girl sitting next to him. The essence rising from the warmth of her neck intoxicated him more than anything Julie Andrews could stimulate.

On the way home Mick suggested they get off the bus a stop early so they might walk the last leg. Sam gave the suggestion a moment of tentative thought; but decided there was nothing sinister involved and agreed. Talk became more sporadic. It didn't help that Mick was so captivated by his partner that he found himself dangerously close to walking into lamp-posts. Their matching steps slowed to a halt by Sam's front gate. He did not know how best to orchestrate their parting; perhaps his best course of action was to abandon all caution and launch himself at her. But he didn't. He just couldn't. What if his advances were spurned?

'Thanks for the evening. I did enjoy our chats,' he said eventually, and pathetically. 'May I take you out again?'

'It'll be embarrassing if you don't! I don't wish to be known as a boring one-date wonder!' she replied.

Then, as Mick turned away, she called out: 'Don't leave me to make all the running! I may get tired quickly!'

Mick walked home with his feet barely touching the pavements with the words of one of the songs from *My Fair Lady* buzzing in his head: 'All at once am I seven stories high.' But he went to school the following morning dreading the reaction from their friends. He knew his pals would be demanding every salacious detail. Sam's friends would, he was certain, be more circumspect, merely wishing to hear what Mick Bernard was really like. Sweet or sour? Did he try it on with you? Did you kiss him? Whether he and Sam told the truth or painted the kind of picture they thought others would prefer was the quandary. Mick just grinned in the face of interrogation; Sam did the same.

Their second date was a riverside walk to the Isis pub to celebrate Mick's offer from St Frideswide's. Alcohol and success loosened Mick's chains and his tongue. They talked and laughed for two hours. 'Talking's fine,' Sam grinned as they left the pub. 'But lips are meant for kissing.' She stood waiting for what seemed an eternity before Mick plucked up the nerve to lean over and kiss her gently on the lips. She returned his kiss with greater expertise, and left him craving more. Mick's lips screamed for more. He'd never grow tired of kisses like Sam's.

A handful of further outings passed in similar fashion. Neither Mick nor Sam recognized any genuine progress in the relationship. But Mick Bernard believed he was on a winning streak and refused to raise the white flag.

PART THREE

Paying the Piper

One

Mick's first day as an Oxford undergraduate would be hectic from breakfast till dinner.

First, he'd to make the short stroll across the High to the Examination Schools where he'd to sit a College Collection, an internal St Frideswide's exam, designed to test his knowledge of the reading list he'd been given on the 'Voyages of Discovery'. This subject was one of the three papers constituting Prelims, the University exam at the end of Hilary (spring) Term, which he must pass in order to progress onto the degree course proper. The other two papers involved the writings of the Venerable Bede (much of it in Latin) and historical texts in his foreign language, German. In the afternoon he was to meet Hammond to arrange tutorials for Bede and then Geoffrey Rumbelow, the senior history don who had been on sabbatical leave when Mick was interviewed, to arrange similar on 'Voyages'. Since Mick's choice of language wasn't the traditional French and was only offered by a dozen Freshmen in the whole University, he was to attend a seminar the following Monday morning to meet a don by the name of Dr Jensch.

What Mick was really looking forward to was a meeting after dinner of all Freshmen wishing to play rugby for the College. Beer was provided while forms were completed with relevant details of position and experience. Mick felt more at ease writing down his rugby qualifications than the previous evening's registration forms because his fortunes had left even him astounded. His senior debut for Oxford RFC the previous Saturday couldn't have gone any better had he scripted the story himself. 'Look at this!' exclaimed Roy Bernard as he'd barged through the kitchen door with the back page of Oxford's Saturday sports paper held out in his hands. 'Look at that headline!' Edna squinted as the page shook in Roy's hands, wondering what all the fuss was about. 'Michael Bernard makes tremendous home debut. Scores three tries.' Roy took the paper through to the living room and dropped into his armchair to read the report in full. 'Says he's a natchrul who finds playin' easy an' has a great future in the game. Thass a better write-up than I ever got!' For the next ten minutes all Edna heard was: 'Well, I never did! Can you believe this! Well, I never…'

Receiving such praise was satisfying but Mick wasn't so conceited as to get above himself. In truth, none of his hat-trick took much scoring: he was left to more or less dot the ball down after the pack had done the hard graft in front of him. But the senior rugby players at St Frideswide's had also seen the report and although Mick was one of three scrum-halves among the Freshmen it was he who was selected to play in the first game of the season against London's Battersea College. Mick was pleased the team was a rugby advertisement for the Public Schools system, containing representatives from Dulwich College, Brighton College, Blundell's, St Paul's, Bedford and Canford from England; Belfast Royal Academy and Campbell College from Ireland; and Scotland's Edinburgh Academy, because it provided his first chance to show his St Fridewide's peers he was more than a match for them.

St Frideswide's scratch team of Freshmen had scant hope of victory. But Mick was keen to gain some insight into his new comrades. All scrum-halves depend on two factors if they are to shine: the quality of their forwards, the pack, who win them the ball; and the quality of the fly-half, to whom they pass it and with whom they must co-operate if the speedier back-line is to prosper through pace and guile.

Mick studied the eight forwards he played behind as if they were rough diamonds: which of them might polish up into gems who'd give him the ball to use without hindrance and which of them might just shovel the ball in his direction along with a few opposition forwards bent on his destruction? Two caught his attention: Garth Dashwood and Jamie Britt.

That Dashwood played in the front row as a prop came as no surprise once Mick saw him rampaging round the pitch like the man-mountain Garth in the *Daily Mirror* strip cartoon or that other Dashwood he'd read about who was one of the wild men of the notorious Hellfire Club. Possessed of thinning hair and a bent nose, Dashwood was loud, pugnacious and not a player happy inclined to take a backward step. He was just the type of rugged, no-nonsense alpha male Mick loved to have in his pack of forwards. Packing down in the second row was 6' 6" lock forward Jamie Britt, long-limbed and maypole thin, whose height and simian arms guaranteed plenty of possession falling into Mick's hands from line-outs – that is unless the ball behaved in transit like a lost coconut, as it initially did. Unlike Dashwood, Britt's features did not epitomize the ruthless brutality of his position: a face, as open and guileless as the simpleton his presence at Oxford clearly disproved, masked a genial, benevolent and generous soul. Dashwood, quick to bestow nicknames, dubbed him 'Jammy'; Mick got away with 'Bernardo'.

Mick's fly-half was Peter Swaby, a star of the public school rugby circuit, who'd represented Richmond Schoolboys versus London Scottish Schoolboys which amounted to an England-Scotland international for public schoolboys; he'd also played senior games for Bedford, one of the country's elite clubs. Short, stocky, heavy-hipped and wearing knee bandages, Swaby didn't give Mick the impression of being anything special for the first 60 minutes. But he was merely lying doggo, assessing the situation. Suddenly, out of nowhere, he executed a slashing line break right through the Battersea defence to set up a try. The knee bandages had been an effective smokescreen.

The match was duly lost. The subsequent visit to the Buttery for ale and songs made a greater impact on Mick. The Buttery was presided over by Mrs Buckley, known as 'Mrs B', who was so Oxonian in accent and demeanour she might have been one of Mick's aunts. Her domain was scarcely bigger than a phone box and jammed with 30 players after a match, plus anyone else who cared to participate in the frolics, it was transformed into a raucous smoke-filled pit of youthful exuberance and coarseness. Star of the cabaret was Reg Brodie, a lanky rubber-lipped senior, whose party piece was to down a pint in two seconds with one swallow. Mick didn't believe this feat was possible until he saw it done – twice! Brodie, Mick learned, was what College termed a 'heavy': low on sporting talent; work-shy; but a prolific boozer and convivial company. Brodie was a geographer, as were many of the College sportsmen – including Dashwood and Swaby.

Monday morning came around too swiftly for Mick's liking. His preparatory work on the German set text hadn't gone well. With the aid of a junior German teacher at South Oxford he'd managed to plod through about half of the book, peppering his copy with crib notes and translations that he hoped to heaven would enable him to survive the coming ordeal. He crossed the High and walked down Merton Street to the University's History Department building where the seminar with Jensch was to begin at 11 o'clock.

Nine others were already on the premises when Mick walked in; a few nods served as the only introductions. No one had the slightest idea who Dr Jensch was. One minute before 11 he entered. Mick thought Dr Strangelove had dropped in by mistake: crew-cut, steel-grey hair; dotted bow tie; red waistcoat. Only the absence of dark glasses and black-gloved stiff right arm distinguished him from the hilariously scary former Nazi scientist created on screen by Peter Sellers in Kubrick's film. As the seconds ticked away Jensch seemed to morph into Sellers's manic creation in front of Mick's eyes; at any moment he envisaged the arm of Strangelove's doppelganger jerking into the perpendicular.

Jensch invited everyone to be seated at a large rectangular table that almost filled the room. Mick chose a seat at the end of the table as far away from Jensch as possible. What ensued made Mick see the room as clinically terrifying as an operating theatre. The seminar was to test 10 months of preparation. Mick trusted his crib notes would enable him to muddle through. The first four victims selected by Jensch rattled through a chapter each in a matter of minutes. None of them received any praise for what Mick viewed as a barely credible performance: Jensch clearly took their competence as the norm. Then he broke off to seek opinions; a chap from Christ Church dared to mutter a platitude or two. Jensch merely thanked him. Then two more victims read out their translations of the next two chapters. It was all over in such a blaze of bravura that Mick felt he must be dreaming. This sextet had completed in 30-odd minutes what had taken him 10 months to translate. There was nothing left Mick could even attempt to translate: his cupboard was bare. Suddenly he knew what a netted rabbit felt like facing the fear of impending doom, in his case the worst kind of fear, intellectual fear, fear of being exposed as an intellectual fraud.

It was an unseasonably warm day for October but Mick's body temperature rose like enraged mercury. He squirmed; he sweated; his mouth quite unable to manufacture one speck of saliva. The walls and ceiling seemed as if they were closing in on him, squeezing the air out of the room so he couldn't breathe. He pleaded with the clock on the wall to move faster. But it wouldn't speed up at all. He prayed it had stopped and in fact there were just a few minutes left to endure. Then the big hand sidled toward the eight. There were all of 20 minutes to go. At this point Mick fervently believed the clock would never reach 12. Nor, he wondered, might he. How was he going to disguise his inevitable ignorance of the text and hide the subsequent embarrassment of being asked to leave, or receive a dressing down from Jensch, in full view of his peers?

Jensch paused once again; and initiated a second spate of social chit-chat. Finally, the clock's hour hand answered Mick's prayer and was about to announce midday. Mick didn't hear one word of what Jensch told them to prepare for the following Monday. He skedaddled as fast as his legs would carry him into Merton Street as if he'd just exited the tunnel in *The Great Escape*.

Mick knew what he had to do. But before he could put his plan into motion there was the not inconsiderable matter of the University Freshmen's Trials at Iffley Road to accommodate. He and Swaby were the half-back partnership for 'C' against 'D' in the first game, very much the junior trial comprised of school-leavers rather than older postgraduates. Dashwood and Britt had made the 'B' team but the two scrum-halves in the 'A' versus 'B' trial were postgraduates from South Africa and New Zealand. Mick came away happy with his performance. He accepted the Blues or Greyhounds, the University's Second XV, were beyond him at present; but there was realistic hope he might get a game for the Freshmen Greyhounds.

Of more immediate significance was the changing-room discussion he had with Dashwood and Swaby. They assured Mick the workload in Geography was less taxing and that Tulloch tended to be sympathetically inclined to all his sportsmen. They urged

Mick to see him straight away. Persuasion was superfluous. Switching subjects was the only way he could retain his place in the University, and the only route open to him if he was to keep alive his quest for a Blue.

Mick returned to his room and smartened himself up before heading for Tulloch's study. His purposeful stride had diminished to a nervous tiptoe by the time he knocked on its door. Tulloch welcomed him with a knowing smile. He'd been visited by many Freshmen at this point in their St Frideswide's career and knew all the sob stories inside out and upside down. He gestured Mick toward a chair, and after the obligatory 'What can I do for you, Mr Bernard', he listened intently as Mick summarized his plight.

'I've always achieved better results in Geography than History,' Mick said with as much bluster as possible. 'I realize Geography Prelims also include a German paper but I believe it's not as arduous as the History component.'

'Quite so,' observed Tulloch. 'You're aware of the other elements of the Geography course?'

'Yes, sir. I had a chat with Dashwood and Swaby earlier this afternoon and they put me straight.'

'Geology and Palaeontology, Cartography and Historical Geography. Do you think you can manage those?'

'I believe so.'

Tulloch rubbed his chin and sat back in his chair. 'I'll see what I can do. I'll have a word with Dr Walters, our Geology man. Work in that area is conducted through University seminars, as is Cartography. The Historical Geography element involves the same "Voyages of Discovery" as History Prelims. The only difference being the tutor: my wife would take responsibility for that. And Mrs Forrestal, the wife of our senior tutor in Languages, would see you for German. You'll be company for Swaby who is also offering German as his language. Partners both on and off the rugby pitch, eh?'

Mick decided he'd better grin at Tulloch's aside.

'Come and see me later this evening, after formal dinner,' continued Tulloch. 'I should have news for you by then.'

'Thank you, sir,' said Mick. 'It's kind of you. Sorry to be such a nuisance.'

'Not at all. A student happy in his work will make for a better scrum-half!'

On this occasion Mick's grin was genuine. And it doubled in size after he'd reported back to Tulloch's study as requested later that evening. His switch had been rubber-stamped. 'You should pop in to see Dr Walters straight away and he'll give you the details of the Geology and Palaeontology seminars. Dr Scott will do likewise regarding Cartography. Mrs Forrestal will see you, along with Swaby, on Thursday morning. And I've had a word with my wife. She will be expecting you at 11 tomorrow morning, in this room.'

Mick high-tailed it to the Buttery to pass the news to Dashwood and Swaby. It barely mattered to him that one of his Oxford dreams had already gone up in smoke. He was never going to become an Oxford historian; never going to be a military historian. But those sacrifices enabled the more important dream to continue. He'd still be an Oxford student who could win the Blue he coveted more than anything in the world.

Two

Mick stumbled through his first week as a geographer without mishap; but without much enthusiasm. Examining fossils to distinguish trilobites from ammonites quickly paled; the laws of stratigraphy proved wearisome; distinguishing choropleth maps from isopleths maps during a Cartography lecture delivered in the driest of forms by an ancient don equally so. The piece of translation ordered by Mrs Forrestal looked achievable but her brusque manner suggested to him and Swaby that her tutorials were never going to touch upon any form of levity. Mrs Tulloch proved a welcome relief. Of olive-skin and crimson lip-sticked mouth, she told Mick how pleased she was to be tutoring him and how promising a student his entry papers suggested he'd become. He didn't know where to look; accepting compliments was not his forte, more so face-to-face with an Oxford tutor. By the Friday he needed consolation. He needed a distraction. He needed Sam Owens; and desperately so. He examined his watch. If he hurried he could catch her in Elliston & Cavell, the department store at the top of George Street, where she worked the late afternoon shift in 'Ladies Lingerie' every Friday after finishing school.

During the summer holidays they'd not met. Maintaining contact posed Mick a problem. Sam had no telephone; a letter was far too weak; and knocking on her door unannounced might result in all manner of awkward situations. If her mother or father answered the door he could hardly ask if Sam's coming out to play. Thinking about his missed opportunities, while others seized theirs, left Mick feeling pathetic. He couldn't get this out of his mind as he raced up the stairs of Elliston & Cavell heading for 'Ladies Lingerie'. The first thing he saw on reaching the department was Sam, standing in serene isolation at a counter specializing in nightwear. She looked even more beautiful and beguiling than ever.

'Hello, stranger!' she said on spying him.

'All the better for seeing you!' he replied. 'What time do you finish tonight?'

'7.30. Why?'

'Would you like to pop into College for a drink? Or must you go straight home?'

'I'd arranged to meet someone later so I'm not expected home till late,' she explained. 'I'd love to…'

'Okay. Great. I'll be back at 7.30 to meet you.'

'My,' she said, 'you're a fast worker these days!'

'We'll see!'

Sam watched him disappear as swiftly as he'd materialized. This could be fun, she thought; the chance to see inside an Oxford college didn't come every day. The offer was irresistible. And she couldn't envisage any danger being alone with an undergraduate in his room - certainly not this particular undergraduate. She felt safe with Mick Bernard. Unlike every other boy she'd dated he'd never made any attempt to fondle her. He was either terribly courteous or terribly shy. She couldn't decide. Perhaps this evening would provide the answer. She used the store's phone to ring her date and tell him she'd developed a terrible headache.

Meanwhile Mick had hot-footed it back to St Frideswide's to locate Cedric, the Principal's scout and keeper of the College cellar.

'Cedric, I need a bottle of wine for this evening,' he said breathlessly.

'Is sir entertaining?'

Cedric smiled the smile of the Cheshire Cat. He was a scout of the old school. Hair slicked down either side of a centre parting, always immaculately turned out in his short white jacket or, if he was disturbed polishing the Principal's silverware or working in the wine cellar, jacketless with elastic sleeve garters to keep his shirt-cuffs free of grime.

'Red or white, sir?' asked Cedric, smoothly adopting his role as part-time sommelier. 'If sir is entertaining a lady may I suggest a white might be preferable. A Muscadet, perhaps? Crisp. Slightly effervescent. Hint of melon.'

Another of Roy Bernard's pearls of wisdom suddenly came to Mick: *Dunt take a horse to water an' do the drinkin' yerself!*

Thus, he did as Cedric suggested and asked him to make sure he put the cost on Battels. 'Oh, Cedric,' he added, 'one more thing, could I borrow a bottle opener?'

Cedric smiled and produced one. 'And, sir, one piece of advice,' he continued, with the tiniest germ of condescension. 'To get the best from the Muscadet, do serve it chilled. I don't suppose you have a fridge in your room, so may I suggest you place the bottle in a jug of cold water for a while beforehand.'

Bottle of Muscadet safely left to cool in a jug of cold water, Mick retraced his steps to Elliston & Cavell for his rendezvous with Sam. She appeared right on time and 15 minutes later Mick led her over the plank bridge to Staircase VIII praying neither of them made the acquaintance of the mud on either side.

'Sorry about this,' he said, which in translation meant 'Please don't think you've come on a wild goose chase to an utter dump.'

'No, it's fine,' Sam confirmed, even though she was starting to think this chase might indeed be of the wild fowl variety. She wasn't accustomed to dates where wellingtons were desirable. But it would provide an amusing tale to spin in the company of young men who treated her as she deserved, like the Queen of Sheba. In any case it was too late to turn back now.

Mick waited for her at the gateway to heaven, as he liked to think it. 'It's just up a couple of flights,' he said as their progress threw up tiny white dust devils from the bare boards. 'Here we are! Chez Bernard!' If walking the plank and negotiating a dust storm hasn't ruined the atmosphere, thought Mick, she's a trooper. He opened the door. 'Pray, enter,' he said, and waited in trepidation for her reaction.

Sam put on a decent act of studying his lair, running a finger over his desk and checking that the curtains closed with an easy glide. 'Very…' she paused, reaching for the kindest word that told no lie, '…cosy.'

'Let me take your coat,' said Mick.

He slid the coat off her back and caught a tantalizing whiff of perfume that would've made any male kiss her neck unless his name happened to be Mick Bernard. 'Take a seat. I'll put the fire on. It gets nippy in here of an evening. Glass of wine?'

Cyril's bottle of Muscadet was standing on the coffee table alongside two glasses. Mick placed one in front of Sam and visualized his lips wandering from her neck to her ear lobes and finally to her mouth. Yet still he did not rise to his imagination.

'So, how's school?' What a corking question, he berated himself as soon as the words left his mouth, straight from the manual entitled *Dull Questions To Ask Your Date.*

Sam was politeness personified and gave a straight answer rather than the flippancy the question deserved. 'Same old routine.

Lots of work. Not much play. Boring, really. Life's rather dull. I'm looking for a spark.'

The bait flew so high over Mick's head he didn't even see it. He merely winced at her discontent instead.

Sam mirrored his expression. Perhaps he'll liven himself up, she thought to herself: he's sweet so I'll give him a chance; it would be rude not to. Most of her dates, she mused, would be trying to get me into that bed over there by now; at least this one's being more chivalrous; but he'd better hurry up.

Mick tried to recover. 'Talking of play, what about this year's school play? You were tremendous in *School for Scandal* as the winsome maid, a perfect example of typecasting in the opinion of the Sixth Form's male contingent,' he waffled. 'Are you in this year's?'

'No,' she replied, pulling a face. 'It's some Flemish morality play. Far too tedious. Didn't bother to audition. No parts in it for me. No fun whatsoever! Why couldn't we have a pantomime!'

'That would be fun,' offered Mick, eager to please, albeit suspecting he was digging himself into a bigger hole.

Sam drank the last drops of her Muscadet. 'Any more wine?' she said, flourishing the empty glass. Another drink struck her as the only way to ease the tension sucking the air out of the conversation. Why is it, she asked herself, that the sweet boys take an age to get physical whereas the bad boys dive in as if there's no tomorrow?

Mick's face creased in what he hoped was not too gormless a fashion and sprang from his chair to do the honours. The prospect of more wine furthering his lust flashed through his brain with lascivious rapidity. Why would an attractive girl come to an undergraduate's room, he reasoned, if she wasn't averse to some love play? Yet an uncoordinated fumble would be a disaster. If only I could read her face or her mind, interpret her body language or pick up any signals. It would be far preferable if she took the lead. Unfortunately, Mick couldn't see how such romantic cowardice invited certain failure.

'Completed your UCCA form yet?' he asked, adopting the serious visage he believed such a question about university application warranted. He winced inwardly as soon as the words left his lips. He'd done it again, made the same mistake. This was no way to woo a beautiful girl into bed, a bed, furthermore, only six feet away.

'Not yet,' sighed Sam. 'Not yet.'

The reply might've applied to her feelings on how this tryst was progressing – or, to be more accurate, not progressing. Not to put too fine a point on it, why hasn't he made a pass at me by now: is it me or is it him?

Mick could've answered that particular question for her. There was no manual for this predicament. And if there were, he'd not read it. He felt sexual inadequacy dampen his collar. He continued with a babbling chain of inane observations. It seemed the harder he sought to kindle a romantic rapport, the more tortuous his manner became.

'Played any rugby?' asked Sam in her desperation to get Mick talking on a subject about which she knew he was definitely passionate. 'It's what you live for isn't it? Everything else is secondary?'

'Well, that's a bit harsh,' he answered before stalling to compose himself. 'It's what I'm good at. If I was an artist or an actor perhaps it wouldn't seem so odd to outsiders. It just so happens I express myself best on a rugby pitch. It probably sounds pretentious to say this about an activity where 30 men run around bashing the daylights out of each other to possess a leather bag full of air but that's the language in which I'm most fluent…'

'You're language is certainly fluent at the moment!' Sam interjected. But Mick failed to read between her lines.

'And to succeed,' Mick continued blissfully now he was on his favourite subject, 'like any aspiring artist or actor, you must be dedicated. Nothing else must get in the way of fulfilling the talent God gifted you. You must be single-minded, selfish and oblivious to any distractions…'

'Like women?' interjected Sam for the second time.

'No, I was thinking about work.'

The passage of a further 30 minutes exhausted the bottle, Mick's blathering and Sam's patience. 'I think I'd best be going,' she said, examining her watch. 'Mum and dad will be wondering where I've got to.'

'Of course,' said Mick. In his own peculiar way he was glad this ordeal was about to end; as was Sam. She couldn't understand why he'd brought her here if it wasn't, as it said in the romantic melodramas, to have his wicked way with her – or at least try to. She'd no intention of offering herself to him like a wanton hussy but had she been wooed tenderly, as a girl like her had the right to expect, it might've been difficult to resist. Clearly Mick Bernard was shy, diffident, bashful and every other adjective describing the intimately inept. But he was sweet. He was likeable. He was, she concluded, just a slow burner. I may give him time.

The pairs of eyes watching them from the Buttery as they passed through the Front Quad reckoned Mick Bernard had just enjoyed 90 minutes, in College parlance, 'getting his end away' with a jaw-droppingly attractive female. That's what he told them later. What he told himself was that he was the biggest chump in Christendom.

Yet there was an even bigger chump lurking inside Mick ready to emerge and announce himself a week later. After dinner in Hall,

Mick had nipped down to the King's Arms, the pub opposite the New Bodleian on the corner of Holywell Street, which Oxford RFC used as its town headquarters. There'd always be a few players there drinking and Mick could catch up on Club gossip. When he walked back into St Frideswide's he bumped into Britt. 'Hello! Where've you been? Thought you'd be getting your oats with that dishy girlfriend we all clocked last week?'

Mick stared at him. 'What? What do you mean?'

'She came through the Front Quad a while back, heading in the direction of your staircase…'

'Sorry, Britt! Gotta dash!'

Mick could feel his heart thumping as he scampered across the plank and ascended the stairs two at a time. As he reached his landing he heard a distinctive laugh coming from the room opposite his that belonged to Rick Watson. Mick ground to a halt, took a deep breath and knocked on the door.

'Ah, look who it is!' said Watson, with a smirk on his face. 'We were hoping you were out for the night!'

Mick didn't wait to be invited in. Sitting cross-legged on a cushion in the middle of the room was Sam, glass of wine in hand, flanked by Watson's two chums from the Jurisprudence clique, Anstruther and Bright, lying on the floor and gazing at Sam as if they were the cats who'd got the cream. To Mick it was a boudoir seduction scene straight from the pages of *Zuleika Dobson*. And he wasn't about to let any of these amateur lounge lizards enjoy any of his cream.

'Mick, where have you been?' said Sam. 'Thank goodness these chivalrous gentlemen spotted my distress and came to my aid!'

'I very much doubt coming to your aid was their motive…'

'Steady on, Mick!' bellowed Anstruther. 'No one forced Sam to come in…'

'That's right, isn't it Sam,' said Bright, full of oily charm.

'Of course it is!'

Well,' said Mick, 'I'm here now. So you can leave these chivalrous gentlemen to their own devices. Come on, Sam. Let's go.'

Mick extended a hand to help Sam to her feet. She ignored it and rebuked him with a glare. 'It looks as if I must go,' she said, in a voice dripping with a sarcasm Mick had never heard her use before. 'Must do as I'm told, mustn't I? Thank you, most chivalrous gentlemen, for your generous hospitality.'

Sam walked past Mick to the door, flashing him a look that, if looks could kill, stated Mick was already on a mortuary slab. Once the two of them were inside his room it became clear he'd already been measured for his coffin.

'How dare you treat me as if I'm your possession!' she said with the speed and venom of a cobra strike. 'You virtually dragged me out of there! Who do you think you are? A caveman with a club?'

'Be reasonable…'

'Be reasonable!' she exclaimed. 'Be bloody reasonable! I'm nobody's possession! And certainly not yours!'

Mick's brain was swimming; swimming, moreover, underwater through seaweed. He never took disapproval well, let alone censure; even being penalized on the rugby pitch might bring him to the boil. But this was different. He'd no experience of being reprimanded by a girl and no clue how best to respond to a Sam he no longer recognized. Rage had transformed the serene face he adored into taut features that would've done justice to his mother when berating his father. One look into Sam's eyes spitting blue fire got Mick to thinking she was going to hit him if he wasn't careful. He went on the defensive. 'Those three are sharks…'

'I don't care if they're sharks or King Kong! I do as I please! I won't behave in a certain bloody way just to please you!'

Sam had barely begun. 'If you think I stay at home every night of the week just to reserve myself for you, think again!' she said, determined to stoke his embarrassment. 'I saw Mark on Monday and I'm seeing Tim tomorrow…'

'Okay,' said Mick, dots of sweat arriving on his forehead. 'I get the picture.'

'Good! I'm not being told what I can and can't do! Have you got that, Mister Michael Bernard?'

Mick took a second in the forlorn hope he might come up with a viable explanation for his infantile jealousy. But none came. Because there was no excuse.

'What can I say…'

'Your behaviour was abominable!'

'I'm sorry…'

'So you should be!'

'Can't we sit down and talk this through?'

'No! I'm leaving,' Sam said, cheeks reddening. 'Just remember this. I have a face, a body, a brain and a voice! Men seem to want just one at a time – and we both know which one they want first! They can't cope with the complete package. But I'll use all of them as I see fit!'

Mick played for time by clearing his throat. But he needn't have bothered because Sam hadn't yet run out of steam. 'I rejected dates from all three of those sharks, as you call them, because I wanted to be with you. But, oh no, you couldn't be patient and allow me to tell you that. You had to act like Mister Big and only wound up playing the spoilt little boy who's had his ice cream knocked out of his hand by a bigger boy.'

The last barb struck home: he had indeed behaved like a small boy having a tantrum after being admonished by his nanny. 'Sam, just let me say…'

'And I've a good mind,' Sam said, 'to go across the landing and invite myself back inside to continue enjoying what was delightful and perfectly harmless company. But I won't. And I won't because I don't want them making snide comments at your expense. And they would because they're likely just as petty as you. I refuse to sink to their level, your level.'

'Thank you…'

'You may be an Oxford undergraduate. You may be cleverer than me. But you've a lot of growing up to do.'

Sam left, without a backward glance. Mick was awestruck. What a girl she was. The only female he'd ever seen in a temper was his mother. If it were possible Sam was even more beguiling in a bate. At that precise second he realized he wanted her on any terms, even on her terms alone. And he knew this gave her a whip in either hand.

Mick went across to the banister and watched her descending. He spotted Sam dabbing her eyes and swore he heard her crying. Her tears were fired by an indignation which even the arrival of her bus failed to quell. Mick Bernard had revealed his true colours and she did not like them one bit. And what annoyed her all the more was the thought that a potentially rewarding relationship had been seriously jeopardized. How could he be so stupid, she asked herself, when I was just starting to warm to his gaucheness that made a welcome change to the smash-and-grab attitude of my usual suitors. Couldn't he notice how the messages I was sending were increasingly positive? She wiped away the last tear as she got off the bus, blew her nose and walked the rest of the short distance home with head held imperiously high.

Mick felt like crying also. He was wrong. Sam was right. He was a jerk. She was gone; possibly forever. And he couldn't blame her.

Three

Mick's acceptance as a St Frideswide's geographer was franked by two invitations for 'drinks' before the first week of term had expired. One involved considerably more danger than the other.

Mick found the Society of Cosmographers to be a thinly disguised excuse for a monumental piss-up from which tutors discreetly departed after a swift sherry so that the main objective of the evening might proceed: namely the senior College geographers abusing the Freshmen with copious amounts of alcohol to render them legless. The weapon of choice was a drinking game called 'Buzz'.

Its rules were simple enough. Once the sherries had begun to work their evil, the assembled company formed a large rectangle around the four walls in the centre of which stood the designated chairman, in this instance Blues' centre, Archie Farrell, armed with a bottle of sherry (or it might be a jug of beer after a match or a bottle of gin prior to some club dinner). The chairman started the game by pointing to a member of the square who had to respond by calling 'one!' The numbering-off continued round the square in the direction called by the nominated drinker. But number seven, any number incorporating a seven or any number formed by a multiple of seven had to be replaced with a cry of 'buzz!', whereupon the direction of the count reversed. Any failure to 'buzz' or reverse direction resulted in the culprit being punished at the chairman's discretion: a sip, a swallow or a whole glass. There was no drinking otherwise unless the chairman called a 'sipper's pause' – which he did often. Anyone caught drinking out of turn, by chairman or snitches, could also expect to be punished. Once someone was seen to be suffering 'under the influence' he could never get off the hook. Numbering off would commence near him and he'd panic into a drunken error, perhaps fooled by the previous caller mumbling his number either looking at the floor or in the opposite direction.

Freshman Bernard, however, was unassailable: he'd served a fierce apprenticeship in the pubs of South Oxfordshire that blessed him with a wonderful tolerance for alcohol. His 'hollow legs' proved invaluable as he watched drinker after drinker slump against the wall or slide to the floor.

The Cosmographers bash was followed three days later by an invitation to the Tulloch's house for pre-luncheon sherry. This soiree would be the polar opposite of the Cosmographers shindig. This was a Sunday lunchtime of sipping and socializing not a bacchanalian evening of quaffing and playing the fool. Dashwood showed Mick how to compose the required RSVP and come Sunday he and Swaby accompanied Mick on the walk to the Tulloch's grand Victorian villa in Norham Gardens, the North Oxford street with some of the most valuable properties in town. Tulloch answered the doorbell and showed them into the front room, where he thrust a schooner of sherry into their hands.

Had a bomb dropped on the Tulloch residence during the ensuing 90 minutes the headlines in the national dailies would've run with something like 'Roomful of Oxford Blues massacred!' Mick's eyes scanned the room and counted the Blues; there were 16 of them encompassing rugby, football, athletics, golf, cricket, hockey, boxing and rowing – a Blue-blazered living testimony to Tulloch's entrance policy. He also studied his fellow Freshmen geographers aside from Swaby and Dashwood. First to catch his eye were Coutts and Cook, who'd sat either side of him on that initial evening in Hall. Beyond them the stocky, bespectacled, hockey-playing Mitchell was chatting with pinch-faced Gordon Ronaldson, whose emaciated frame, suggesting he might profit from patronizing Carlos's mobile fish-and-chips van, belied the fact he was a crack oarsman.. The remaining Freshmen chatting in a corner contained no sportsmen: this foursome was St Frideswide's nod to academic prowess – these were the holders of Scholarships and Exhibitions rather than Blues.

'Come and say "hello" to my wife,' Tulloch said, behind the habitual kind smile. 'Of course, Mr Bernard has already made her acquaintance.'

Mick put on his best grin and sipped his amontillado. 'Yes, sir, I had my first tutorial with Mrs Tulloch on Tuesday…'

'Did you enjoy it?'

Mick had only been an Oxford undergraduate for a week but he'd already learnt one or two valuable rules of etiquette when addressing dons. 'Yes, I did. It was very stimulating and thought provoking', he heard himself saying without a moment's cogitation. A little tilt of the head to the side was also a good move; that and looking deadly interested at whatever the don says in response, gibberish or not.

Tulloch refilled their glasses and ushered them toward his wife. Eva Tulloch unleashed a crimson smile. 'Have you all settled in?' she said, but didn't wait for answers. 'How is the rugby coming along?'

Dashwood instantly declared himself spokesman. 'I'm afraid we were soundly thrashed in the Battersea game…'

'But awfully hard to gel as a team of complete strangers,' replied Mrs Tulloch.

'We were getting there by the end of the match,' added Swaby. 'Bit too late.'

Eva Tulloch turned to Mick. 'I was pleased to read in *The Times* how you and Mr Swaby had combined impressively in the University Freshers Trials.'

'Thank you, Mrs Tulloch. But we were only in the junior trial…'

'Quite so,' she said, before proffering the caveat that had eluded Mick. 'But the senior trial included so many postgraduates who've arrived with considerable experience. Few, if any, of you can cope with them just yet, but I know Randolph is convinced you'll all be competing for a Blue in your third year.'

'Nice of your husband to say so,' said Dashwood, behind tilting head.

'If you will excuse me,' Eva said looking from Dashwood to Swaby, 'I'd like to have a quiet word with Mister Bernard.'

.Swaby and Dashwood edged over to the group containing Coutts and Cook. Mick felt himself quail. Eva saw it and filled his glass. Mick took a long sip. 'I wanted to ask how you've got on, making the adjustment from History to Geography. Can't be easy.'

'I've always coped well with Geography at school,' Mick replied, truthfully. 'But I can't say Geology and Cartography are my cup of tea…'

'I see,' said Eva, with a note of concern.

Mick sensed he was on a retrieval mission already. 'I think I shall enjoy the Historical Geography…'

'Yes,' she interjected brightly. 'And there is a special paper in Historical Geography you may opt for in Finals.'

'Yes, I've seen that and look forward to it, though I'll miss not being able to study the Military History element of the History course.'

'That is a great shame. But I think you'll like the Historical Geography work in due course.'

'I hope so. But I've got to manage Prelims first!'

'I don't think you need worry about that…'

'It's the German paper I worry about.'

Eva didn't respond; but put glass to lips, leaving a pronounced red rim, and then topped up Mick's.

Three schooners inside 30 minutes had loosened Mick's tongue. 'Did I hear you correctly on Tuesday when you said tutors had been impressed by my entry exam papers?'

'Yes, of course,' replied a startled Eva, as if her probity was being questioned.

'You weren't just being kind…'

'Not in the slightest!'

'Then please accept my apologies for bringing it up. I wasn't intending to be rude.'

Eva Tulloch beckoned Mick to come closer. 'Listen, Michael,' she whispered conspiratorially, so close to his cheek he felt sure she'd leave a crimson calling card, 'you mustn't think you're somehow out of place in College. Your work has shown genuine promise. Don't be overawed or fooled by those who bray and boast. That's not showing confidence in their abilities. It's demonstrating a lack of confidence in them.'

'I've never thought of it like that,' observed Mick, downing half of his latest sherry in one gulp. 'Thank you, Mrs Tulloch. That's cheering to know.'

'Just be patient and things will fall into place,' she said, placing a hand on his wrist. 'Remember, patience is not a weakness.'

Mick left Norham Gardens slightly the worse for wear but walked back to St Frideswide's in a more optimistic mood. He managed to get a grip on his work thereafter; and he made his mark in College rugby - he and Swaby were the only Freshmen to be included in the College XV that won Cuppers at the end of

Hilary Term. All that remained before the Easter Vac was the small matter of Prelims. Each paper went as well as Mick could've expected. Except the German paper, that was even more horrendous than he expected. His efforts at two translations were, he was convinced, risible and clearly sub-standard; Swaby was equally downcast. They were certain it was curtains for them and a German re-sit in Trinity Term - when it amounted to pass or be sent down.

At the start of Trinity Term Tulloch assembled them all in his study to receive the results of Prelims. Mick felt the same cold sweat chilling his back as he'd experienced during the Jensch seminar. Tulloch's rheumy gaze travelled from one apprehensive face to another. Then with the theatrical flourish of an Olivier he announced: 'Congratulations! You've all passed! You may enjoy the delights of an Oxford summer without threat of the exam room hanging over your head! Now, be off with the lot of you!'

The relief was audible: muttered congratulations and thanks-be-to-God could be heard circulating within the majority. Swaby and Mick, however, were unable to express anything audible: they were as speechless as a couple of dummies who'd lost their ventriloquist. They exchanged nervous glances that asked whether the old boy had got it all wrong. How could they have passed German?

The pair hung back as the rest left in high humour. 'Excuse me, sir,' said Swaby. 'Myself and Bernard were wondering about the German results…'

Tulloch chuckled. 'I thought you might!'

He sat back in his chair, milking every moment. 'As you know, most candidates offer French. Only a dozen of you out of, what, 100, offered German. Well, the performance of each candidate was so abysmal the examiners decided they must've set far too difficult a task, a decidedly unfair task. Consequently, they either had to fail all of you or pass all of you. They decided, in their wisdom, to pursue the latter course.'

***

Mick knew he'd been lucky: lucky in work, but not lucky in love. He'd tried but could find no substitute for Sam Owens. During the Christmas Vac he'd bumped into a 'blue-stocking' from North Oxford named Alice while working on the post: she was darkly attractive and lively company. Equally vivacious was Helen, a girl from South Oxford days, who'd gone straight from school into a solicitor's office in the town; and one thing had led to another. But something was missing. Mick couldn't put his finger on what it was to start with; not until he realized this very sense of equivocation held the answer. What Sam Owens possessed that captivated Mick Bernard, he concluded, was impossible to indentify or define. She had the yin to his yang.

To Mick's disappointment Sam made herself scarce following the blazing row in his room. His total balls-up, he freely admitted, would've won him the pillock of the year award if there was one going. During the summer Vac he heard worse news: Sam would be even further out of reach because come September she'd begin studying for a degree in French at Ealing Polytechnic. He knew a girl with her charms would be chased rotten on the London scene. If Mick was to set eyes on her again he needed Lady Luck on his side: in the first week of September she shone her light briefly in his direction.

There'd been a cocktail party held by the school's Former Pupils' Association at the Country Club, adjacent to the Thames, on the Henley road. Although they saw each other across the room and smiled politely, the memory of their last meeting prevented either from crossing the floor to fraternize. But when Pete Livermore was giving Mick a lift home afterwards Mick spied Sam walking up the road, swinging her handbag as she went. She was alone. He told Pete to stop the car.

Sam watched the shadowy figure get out of the car and start toward her. She was reaching into her handbag for the pepper spray when she saw who it was. 'You nearly copped an eyeful of this!' she said, brandishing the pepper spray. 'Frightened me to death!'

'Sorry. Put my foot in it again!' replied Mick. 'I didn't want you walking home alone on this dark stretch of road, past the woods, what with no street lamps. Some nasty things have happened around here…'

'Yes. I remember what happened to Sandra Hutchinson from school,' continued Sam. 'Poor thing was attacked and left traumatized.'

'If you get any more alluring you'll drive me so nuts I shall start hosting tea parties for mad hatters!'

'Is that so?' she said, giggling. 'Then why didn't you give me so much as a second glance all evening.'

'I know. But in my defence, neither did you grant one to me!'

Sam laughed. 'Touche!'

'After my childish display on Staircase VIII I didn't think any overtures from me were prudent.'

Mention of their last encounter raised the temperature. 'You were indeed childish and idiotically obsessive…'

'I know.' Mick raised both hands in surrender.

'But life's too short, they do say,' said Sam.

Mick noticed how the moonlight caught the sparkle in her eyes and highlighted her cheekbones. He changed tack. 'You look stunning in that dress. On with the motley?'

'I beg your pardon,' said Sam, quizzically.

'That sort of multi-coloured patchwork is the uniform of a court jester, like Artlecchino, the harlequin, in Italian *Commedia dell'arte*. For some reason it's known as the motley. It's even got bells hanging from the hem, just like yours.'

Mick heard Sam's breathing intensify as he buried himself into a deeper pit of pomposity. 'I've even played for Harlequins in a shirt with that design.'

Sam rolled her eyes. 'I knew rugby would enter the conversation sooner or later! I hope you're not going to be insufferable!'

Mick took the hint: annoying Sam was the last thing he'd in mind. 'Sorry! No more on that subject. I promise!'

'I'll have you know, Mick Bernard, this dress is a fine example of the latest fashion sweeping London.'

'Mary Quant?'

'Oh, so you've actually paid some attention to ladies fashion?'

'That's a secret from my feminine side. Keep it to yourself!'

'In fact it came from Biba, on the King's Road.'

'Is that so?' said Mick. 'Well, you've certainly increased its value.'

'Bought it last week when I went to Ealing to arrange my digs,' she explained, appreciative of the compliment but deciding not to show it. 'Found a nice place in Summerfield Road, close to the campus.'

Mick refused to be diverted and continued his best stab at a charm offensive. 'Some girls can spend pounds on clothes and still look like a scarecrow on a windy day…'

Suddenly he had all Sam's attention.

'...but not you. On you nothing looks out of place. You're a natural model, you see. It's the way you carry yourself. You walk like a ballet dancer, with oodles of grace.'

Her expression relaxed, though she was still unsure how genuine were Mick's blandishments. 'One of the perks studying in London is being near to some great shops in Carnaby Street and the King's Road,' she responded, matter-of-factly. 'By the look of what you're wearing, perhaps you might benefit from shopping there.'

'Touche!' said Mick. He was starting to enjoy this repartee.

And so was Sam. 'Quite so! That makes us even!'

'I see you've let your hair grow,' he said, pausing to give impact to his next word. 'Kissing the shoulders like that suits you.'

Sam stared at him, undecided whether to acknowledge his observation as cheesy or welcome. 'Thank you, kind sir,' she said, at length.'

Mick ran a surreptitious eye over his companion and realized what he'd been missing these last 12 months. 'But, frankly, any style would look good on you. You'd still look a million dollars if you were bald.'

Sam laughed so hard the bells on her dress jingled merrily. 'Have you been practicing these one-liners? On various ladies, perhaps?

'My lips are sealed,' said Mick. 'To protect the innocent!'

'Surely there are some "blue stockings" at Oxford who've fallen for the gauche Bernard persona?' she said, with a knowing wink that betrayed genuine curiosity.

'That would be telling, wouldn't it?' Mick replied, unwilling to reveal his opinion that all the female undergraduates he'd come across were candidates for the 'Ugly Sisters' in any OUDS production of *Cinderella*. Instead, he looked Sam in the eye and told the truth: 'There's no girl in the whole University who can hold a candle to you. Neither brains nor beauty.'

Sam looked away. She didn't like to admit to him, or herself, that she felt she might be blushing. Whether brought about by her own embarrassment at being the recipient of such flattery or whether she felt embarrassed on his part for making a second saccharine sentiment, she did not immediately know.

After passing the railway station and Upton Green they crossed the road at the Wellington and turned into Sam's street, their animated conversation showing no sign of diminishing. If anything it was becoming more intimate, eyes locking when they spoke instead of the blinkered straight-ahead look they'd initially employed. The early evening warmth had been overtaken by a chill in the air that prompted Mick to remove his jacket and slip it round Sam's shoulders. She smiled a thank-you and knew she was now blushing for certain. And she knew Mick had spotted the fact. Moreover, for the first time in their relationship, they both knew Mick was capable of assuming the role of puppeteer.

'How's your love life?' asked Mick, growing bolder.

'How's your love life?' Sam riposted.

Mick grinned. 'Can't get the better of you, can I?'

'At last!' she cried. 'Mick Bernard has seen the light! Praise the Lord!'

Now it was Mick's turn to laugh out loud. 'I'll try again: what about your social life?'

'Well, if you must know,' Sam said, eyes flirting with him from beneath her fringe, 'I met someone at a party who said they could get me a job as a Bunny Girl at the Playboy Club in Park Lane.'

'Really?' said Mick. 'That's a fast and loose crowd you're mixing with.' But quickly appreciating he was straying once more into territory that was none of his business he added: 'Could be fun, though.'

'Don't worry. I'm not as green as I'm cabbage looking!'

'If you were a cabbage I'd become a vegetarian!'

'I turned him down!'

Sam couldn't detect Mick's inward sigh of relief. He read the *News of the World* on a Sunday and was well versed in the sordid repercussions for young girls tempted to indulge in *la dolce vita.*

'Well, here we are,' said Mick. 'Home. Safe and sound.'

'Thank you once again, kind sir,' she said, handing him his jacket.'

'Till the next time,' said Mick, giving Sam a goodbye wave as he closed the garden gate behind him.

He put on his jacket; it still held her smell, and he couldn't resist putting nose to sleeve and inhaling. What a couple we'd make, he decided as he walked back to Hill Rise: we harmonize, we balance, we exchange energy; fire and ice; heart and head. The whole was greater than the sum of the parts. Yet it was hard to shake off the negative: perhaps these qualities clash more than they complement. And perhaps, he conceded, it was merely a matter of fooling himself in the afterglow of an unexpectedly satisfying and enjoyable end to the evening.

Back in the family kitchen Sam put on the kettle to make a cup of tea. She felt a strange breathlessness that couldn't result from a steady walk. It came from an unexpected source, one she knew but did not usually associate with Mick Bernard's company: a sexual arousal sufficient to harden her nipples. She couldn't help thinking how Mick was quite the charmer. She accepted that charm could only go so far: too much decreases its veracity. Yet she couldn't escape the view that Mick was better company this evening than ever before. The 30 minutes she'd spent with him could easily have been multiplied six times over. Perhaps neutral ground had put less pressure on him. But perhaps the reason was very simple: he'd matured. And, to her surprise, she found herself thinking what previously had been the unthinkable: perhaps Mick Bernard might be worth giving another chance if he ever did drum up the courage to ask for one.

Unbeknownst to Sam, she would be asked: their rapprochement, brief as it was, convinced Mick that Sam must be his partner at the next College Summer Ball.

***

Some months after that chance encounter Mick was playing a Saturday morning match in London. The team stayed overnight on the Friday in a hotel a couple of bus rides from Sam's digs. After the team meal and pre-match meeting he was free to do as he wished. Thirty minutes later he was knocking on Sam's door in Summerfield Road. As he reminded himself, he was taking a major liberty by turning up out of the blue and the butterflies conducting a war dance in his stomach caused him to forget all the opening lines he'd prepared during the bus rides. He began to hope Sam was not at home. Then the light came on and the door creaked ajar.

'Good God!' Sam burst out, opening the door wider. 'What are you doing here?'

Mick smiled and spluttered, as much for being gob-smacked by the sight of Sam in a figure-hugging red blouse and black leather skirt as his cack-handed explanation. Sam could only grin as convincingly as the circumstances allowed because Mick's arrival might've just ruined her evening. Her instinct was to turn him away with some lame excuse but her conscience spoke otherwise. 'Come in, come through!'

Mick strode into the lounge with surprising alacrity. Though it was a sportsman's mantra not to indulge in sex the night before a game because it sapped his testosterone and robbed him of vital nervous energy, he was willing to take the risk. However, the spring in his step and every other organ soon vanished.

'Mick,' said Sam, gesturing toward the sofa, 'this is Guy.'

The figure slouching on the sofa gave Mick a look as black as his beard and long hair. Anyone more different in appearance and, quite likely, personality than himself Mick could not imagine. What on earth does Sam see in a prat like this, he thought. Guy grunted; forming the same instant impression of Mick. Mick raised a palm in the interest of cordiality.

'Mick is a friend from Oxford,' Sam informed Guy. 'He's a student at the University, at St Frideswide's.'

Guy shrugged. He couldn't make things any clearer. His body language confirmed his utter disdain for this interloping Oxford bastard who thinks he's going to muscle in and wreck my night.

The aroma of a bolognese sauce cooking next door was enough for Mick to realize that three's a crowd, and he was the unwelcome third person at the feast. There'd be no off the cuff invite for him to stay and eat.

'Okay,' he said, weakly. 'Nice to see you, Sam. Just wanted to see how you'd settled in. Must go. Match tomorrow morning. Come along and watch and we could go for a…'

'Oh!' Sam exclaimed. 'Nice thought. But I'm busy all day. Shopping in…'

'Carnaby Street?'

'Yes…'

'Of course!' said Mick, deciding it was more sensible if he played a straight bat to a possible lie. 'Silly of me to ask at such short notice.'

'Another time, perhaps…'

'Yes, another time.'

Mick waved a hand in Guy's direction that might've been interpreted as either surrender or goodbye. Sam followed him to the front door.

'If only you'd come round last night,' she whispered. 'I was home alone!'

'Just my luck! Never mind, eh? I'm very sorry if I've put a dampener on your evening.'

Sam gave him a wide smile and a mouthed 'Goodbye' as she shut the door.

Mick trudged away uttering every curse in the swear-book. He'd put Sam in an awkward situation as it was by appearing out of the blue; now she'd be on a recovery mission to salvage what was left of her evening. He couldn't complain if Sam gave him the total brush-off and never spoke to him again. But what really niggled him was the thought of what else this bloke intended feasting on after the plates were cleared away. That image flashed on and off in his brain all the way back to the team hotel. Knowing Sam could hardly be expected to live the life of a nun had been endorsed by the evidence of his own eyes. What he didn't know, but would've rejoiced in knowing, was that Sam engineered the swift exit of her black-haired suitor as soon as he'd finished his spaghetti bolognese. On this occasion Mick's arrival had shown him in a good light; and her latest lothario in a bad one. Mick had done her a service rather than a disservice.

Mick went to the hotel's lounge to compose himself. There was no point trying to sleep after an episode like this. In any case it wasn't yet ten. He poured himself a cup of coffee and sat down at the writing desk. Taking a sheet of headed hotel notepaper he began composing an apology to Sam for his surprise visit and disturbing her evening – even though he hoped he'd thrown cold water over the whole shebang. He made no reference to his longing for another date, reasoning it might convey an unseemly eagerness after such a lengthy hiatus. He decided his best chance, his only chance, of seeing Sam on a romantic basis again depended on him denying his feelings and playing the long game instead. So he finished the letter with a postscript, nonchalantly inviting her to the next St Fridewides's Summer Ball. He dropped it in the hotel's post box. But sleep didn't come easy. And nor did Saturday's match. Twice in two days Mick found himself on the losing side.

Four

'That's two-one to me,' crowed Mick. 'Your round!'

He and Britt were sitting in the oldest part of St Frideswide's, in front of the medieval fireplace outside the Buttery. It was that fallow period of the day between tea and dinner when undergraduate thoughts were preoccupied with how the evening was to be spent. While this knotty problem was being subconsciously debated they'd been engrossed in one of the College's traditional pastimes during periods of boredom: shove-halfpenny.

Britt looked up from the board: 'Best of five!'

They both took a swig from the pint glasses resting on the table beside the board.

'Okay,' said Mick reluctantly. 'But if you lose we're not playing best of seven!'

His largesse was provoked by Britt's hangdog demeanour: he'd just broken up with the girl he'd been squiring since arriving in Oxford. Mick had an obvious need to be on good terms with forwards like Britt on the pitch because they had to protect him from the opposition's marauding forwards and give him quality ball with which to launch his backline. But he'd always gravitated toward these amiable piano shifters for friendship off the pitch rather than his fellow piano players who were apt to be prima donnas; in Britt he'd stumbled across a genial giant never slow putting hand in pocket to buy more than his fair share of ale. Mick decided his pal needed cheering up. One of Roy Bernard's stories was in order.

'Did you read about that faith-healer in Alabama?' he asked, straight faced.

Britt shook his head. Mick smiled inwardly and proceeded.

'Well, he's all fire and brimstone, winding-up the congregation to fever pitch in this huge tent. And then he says "Is there anyone here who needs the power of the Lord to be healed?" This chap comes forward. And he's on crutches. So the faith-healer says to him "Your problem is apparent, sir. What is your name?" The chap replies "Arthur." The faith-healer points to a screen and tells Arthur to stand behind it. "Is there anyone else among us who needs the power of the Lord?" Another guy stands up. "I-I-I've g-g-got a sp-sp-speech imp-imp-impediment." The congregation of believers starts clapping.'

Britt's broad face began to crease at Mick acting out the scene complete with Dixieland accent and stutter: Mick sensed his ploy was working and continued with exaggerated gusto.

'The faith-healer says "You surely do possess a speech impediment, my friend" and instructs him to join Arthur behind the screen. "Now, ladies and gentlemen, let's pray to the Lord to heal these two fine people." The congregation shrieks "Amen!" The faith-healer puts his hands together and leads them in prayer for five minutes. "The Lord will have spoken to us and these two brave souls!" he cries, eventually. "The Lord will have sent them a message!" Then he's stopped by tremendous crashing and wailing from behind the screen. And the faith-healer says: "You with the speech impediment, what's going on back there?' And a voice replies "Ar-Ar-Arthur's f-f-fallen over!"

Britt slapped his thighs and rocked with laughter. 'First prize for bad taste!' he said, wiping a tear from his eye. 'But bloody funny!'

A shadow suddenly fell over the board. The heavy scent of Aramis ensured they knew it had to be the one man in College with the wallet to satisfy such an expensive taste in men's aftershave.

'What are you two desperadoes, or should I say loafers, laughing about?' asked Dashwood.

'Bernardo has just relieved the doom and gloom with an outrageous joke!'

'There must be something better for us to do on a lovely evening like this than playing shuvvers and telling jokes!'

'You name it,' said Britt, flipping the tip of his generously proportioned nose with the back of his hand, 'and we'll consider it!'

'Bernardo,' said Dashwood, 'you're the local boy around here. You know what's what. Any ideas?'

'Yes,' added Britt. 'There must be something you Townies get up to in the summer. Something outdoors...'

'And not birds-nesting for blue tit eggs,' interjected Dashwood, stifling a snort. 'Or blackberrying! We don't want to bake a pie! We need a bit of excitement! A thrill!'

'Not the season for blackberries!' said Mick, with authority. He thought for a second. 'There is a dog meeting at Cowley this evening...'

'Greyhound racing?' said Dashwood, suddenly enthused. 'Whadya say, Jammy? Shall we go to the dogs? Have a tiny flutter?'

Britt answered instantly. 'Splendid idea!' he boomed: 'Is your chariot without?'

Assured that Dashwood's ageing brown Ford van was indeed parked outside to provide the necessary transport, the three of them drained their glasses and walked out into a balmy summer's evening with enough sun remaining to send shadows creeping across the manicured green carpet of the Front Quad.

Dashwood's 'chariot' provided only one passenger seat which Britt's height insisted he occupy. Mick was condemned to the rear, along with Dashwood's golf bag: leaning back against one side of the van he stretched out his legs to brace himself for the rocky ride ahead by pressing his feet hard against the other.

'Bernardo,' said Dashwood, 'I recall you telling us once you had something to do with these racing mutts, so you're our expert! How do we go about winning some cash?'

Mick felt an inner glow at this acknowledgement of his prowess in a subject unconnected with rugby. He explained in brief the gospel of 'down-grading' according to Uncle Bob. 'You mean it's one gigantic fiddle?' said Britt after listening to Mick's expose` of the sport's dark arts.

'It can be,' replied Mick. 'Some of the six dogs in each race won't be primed 100%. On the other hand, Cowley is a licensed track, run under NGRC rules. Security is as tight as can be to prevent any skulduggery. Every dog is weighed and kennelled beforehand. The vet will study the dog's weight and bring any discrepancy to the attention of the stewards. They won't allow it to run if it looks under par or is suspiciously heavier than normal...'

'If it looks deliberately fattened-up?' said Britt, eyes widening.

'Given a stopper!' added Dashwood, with eyes even wider.

'Yes, that's the theory,' confirmed Mick. 'But there's always some way of slipping the dog ...'

'A Mickey Finn!' said Britt.

'Yes, pretty much. A chunk of meat lobbed into the kennel when nobody's looking or even the kennel boy slipping a morsel smeared with something detrimental into the dog's mouth while he's pretending to stroke it.'

'But the dogs are muzzled, aren't they?' said Dashwood.

'Yes, but muzzles can be left loose. Clever dogs know exactly how to prise them off with their paws.'

'So,' said Dashwood, taking his eyes disarmingly off the road to turn and face Mick, 'finding the ones that are trying is bloody nigh impossible, let alone which one is the best! Bernardo, I'm starting to think this revealing insight might've been provided before we set off! This smells like a shit-storm in waiting!'

'Treat it as an excuse for an outing and a few ales in unusual surroundings,' said Britt, brightly.

Dashwood grunted. 'I don't suppose you're going to pay me for the wasted petrol, are you?'

'Don't be such a tart!' said two voices.

Twenty minutes later the van trundled into the Cowley Stadium car park. 'Are you sure there's meeting on?' asked Britt, surveying no more than a dozen vehicles spread around its pock-marked and mud-baked surface. 'Looks to me like we've driven into a gigantic cow pat!'

'Definitely a meeting on,' Mick replied, 'but I never said it would be so popular we'd be fighting to get in!'

The clang of opening traps on the other side of the stadium's white perimeter wall confirmed Mick was correct. 'Sounds like we've missed the first race. Let's get inside for the second. We'll need all of the 20 minutes to find the winner of the next.'

The car park did not lie: the stadium was pretty much lifeless, barely 30 or 40 people scattered along the track rail and near the bar entrance on the home straight; the terracing round the remainder of the track, heaving with fans for Thursday's speedway, was completely deserted.

'I'll go and get some ale while you two study the race-card,' said Britt.

'What in God's name gives us any clues among all this mumbo-jumbo?' said an increasingly agitated Dashwood as he thumbed through the card Mick had bought. 'Name and trap number I understand. But what on earth are all these other figures?'

'They're the times from the dog's recent races. The split times are probably the most informative.'

'The what times?'

'It's like lap times in athletics,' said Mick, pointing a finger at the appropriate numbers. 'How long the dog took to run each section of a race. Shows whether he's a good trapper, runs fast early, or whether he's a closer, a dog who does his best running toward the end of his races.'

'I see,' said Dashwood, calmed by Mick's apparent expertise.

'Of course,' Mick continued, 'a closer can be buggered by dogs in front of him tiring and getting in his way when he's trying to get through. He's not a racehorse. He's got no jockey to help him, to steer him clear of trouble. He'll just run and run!'

Britt returned with three pints wedged between his massive paws. Dashwood took one: 'If our expert is right,' he said raising his glass in Mick's direction, 'we've got as much chance of finding a winner as you two have of winning a rugby Blue!'

'Don't be so negative!' said Mick. 'We came for a flutter. Six dogs enter the traps. And there's one winner. We've a one in six chance. The odds are far worse in a horse race when you could have as many as 30 runners. We need a decision.'

Britt looked at Dashwood for a reaction. They nodded in unison.

'Now, would you rather back a dog that breaks well and might hold on to win,' asked Mick. 'Or do you prefer to take a chance on a closer?'

Britt's broad expressive features twisted in bafflement at Mick's terminology: 'Are you speaking in a foreign tongue?'

Mick ignored him and continued with his appraisal. 'The two-dog's initial splits are far superior. He'll be the fastest away...'

'Okay,' said Dashwood. 'Let's trust him to go the whole way! Whadya say, Jammy?'

Britt supped his pint, licked his lips and nodded with the enthusiasm of someone who wasn't bothered one way or the other.

'How much do you want to bet?' asked Mick.

'Two pounds on the nose!' said Dashwood, pointing at Britt's fleshy proboscis.

'And two quid from me too!' said its owner.

'Well, I'm not as flush as you two,' said Mick. 'I'll put in a pound to make the fiver.'

They walked along the line of bookmakers to study their boards. There were only four bookies. The two-dog was on offer at 3 to 1 on three boards and 7 to 2 on the fourth. Mick took the 7 to 2.

'Here's to the two-dog!' said Britt, raising his glass. 'He'd better win or I'm calling the cat-food factory to tell them they've got more raw material coming their way!'

The hissing of the hare trolley induced yelps and howls from the traps. As it shot past, the lids banged open and the blue-jacketed two-dog came out as if someone had stuck a cattle prod up his rear end. His three ardent supporters released yells of encouragement that all too quickly died on the air. Their selection was travelling so fast he couldn't negotiate the first bend, and swung so wide he almost collided with the outside fence. They watched the other five dogs zoom past him on the inside. Half-way down the back straight Mick tore up the betting slip. 'Shit! I might've guessed. He's a chocolate dog!'

'A what?' said Britt.

'A dog that melts on the corners!'

'In other words,' said Dashwood. 'A dog so fucking stupid it doesn't know how to run round a bend properly!'

'That's about the size of it,' said Mick. They sought solace in their beer, standing in silence like three not-so-wise monkeys as the black-jacketed four dog won at odds of 5 to 1.

'Do we have another go?' ventured Mick eventually, putting on an optimistic smile.

'Isn't that what they call chasing your losses?' said Britt, suddenly elevated to the group's sage. 'To be avoided unless you're prepared to lose even more?'

Dashwood swallowed a mouthful of beer and then harrumphed: 'Better to think, recover your losses!'

'What we need is some inside information from a genuine expert,' Britt said, smirking at Mick.

'And I think I know the very man,' said Mick, voice rising enthusiastically. Exiting the bar with a glass of stout in his hand was Uncle Bob.

'Michael!' said Uncle Bob. 'Good to see you. Not lorst the int'rest in the dogs then?'

Mick introduced Britt and Dashwood to the greyhound guru about whom they'd recently been educated. 'We were hoping to win a few bob but failed abysmally in the last race. Backed the two-dog...'

'Oh,' said Uncle Bob behind a chuckle. 'The choc'late dog!'

'Don't rub it in!' said Mick, as his two sidekicks guffawed. 'Do you know of anything special in the next?'

'They say the fav'rite is a cert,' said Uncle Bob. 'He's such a good thing the rest aren't both'rin'. He wunt be much of a price. But fill yer boots!'

'Are you backing it?' asked Britt.

'No, only came to back the winner o'the last race. This one's too short a price for me. I'm off 'ome arter I've drunk this.'

Dashwood, Britt and Mick exchanged looks that stated the same thing: if only they'd met Uncle Bob earlier.

'That does it!' said Dashwood. 'We back the favourite in the next and get our money back!'

'What's the best price?' asked Britt.

'Evens,' said Mick. 'On every board.'

'So, if we put on a fiver we'll recoup the first race losses?' said Dashwood.

Mick sucked his teeth. 'I can't spare another pound...'

'Okay,' said Britt, looking at Dashwood. 'We'll put in two pounds-ten each, and the poverty case here can have his initial pound back from the winnings.'

To the tune of their three hysterical voices the favourite broke as if he were Mick the Miller and looked like imitating greyhound racing's greatest star. That is until the final bend. He was leading by a clear two lengths when the hare seemed to slow up approaching the bend, tricking him into thinking he might actually catch it and eat it. The trio of raucous voices suddenly stilled as if throats had been slit. They watched the leader veer to the outside in a vain lunge for the hare and lose all his momentum. When the hare increased speed once again he resumed his chase. But the damage had been done. The favourite finished the race like he'd started it but failed by a nose to catch the dog in the white jacket.

'I don't fucking believe it!' said Dashwood, looking frighteningly sinister, hands on hips. 'What happened there?'

Mick flung up his hands in surrender. He spotted Uncle Bob heading toward the exit gate and called him over.

Uncle Bob grimaced. 'I think the hare driver wuz bought.'

'What do you mean?' asked Britt.

'Well, the second fav'rite won, didn't it? Wuz the only other dog with any form. So if y'can elim'nate the fav'rite he's gunna win. And at a decent price, coz there wuz a well-backed fav'rite. All you 'ad t'do wuz slip the hare driver somethin' to slow the hare on the last bend so the fav'rite, bound t'be leadin' by then, would be distracted and lose lengths he'd no chance of recoverin' coz it was too near the finish.'

Dashwood was now visibly frothing at the mouth. 'If it's that obvious surely the stewards will hold some kind of inquiry, order a re-run or insist everyone gets their money back.'

Uncle Bob smiled broadly. 'Not if they're in on it and 'ave backed the second fav'rite themselves. Which they prob'ly did!'

'And,' laughed Britt, looking at Mick and then his uncle, 'Bob's yer uncle!'

Mick and Dashwood joined in the hollow laughter. 'I need a stiff drink,' said Dashwood. 'But not here! This place has robbed me of too much cash already! Bernardo, direct us to the nearest watering hole or superior hostelry!'

The Wellington was mere minutes away. That its car park was full might've sounded an alarm bell or two had not the urgent need of restorative alcohol overtaken Dashwood. He parked the van on the side of the road and led them at a trot toward the saloon bar.

Opening the door released a wall of noise. Much of it came from a television set hanging from the ceiling but even more emanated from the animated clientele watching it; groups of young men with slicked-back hair and long sideboards were shaking with as much laughter as the old couples sat at tables and dressed in their Sunday best. The cause of their mirth was *It's a Knockout*, a game show in which teams representing two towns participated in a series of absurdly silly games wearing absurdly silly costumes. Mick looked up at the screen to see a pair of contestants, dressed in huge foam rubber costumes sporting outsized plastic heads, with buckets draped round their shoulders in which they were ferrying water from one large tank to fill their team's smaller version. Mick turned away, but a sudden gale of laughter made him look back at the screen: one of the massive creatures had slipped on the copious amounts of spillage and crashed to the ground, dislodging the plastic head which rolled into the other contestant – who promptly fell over it.

Dashwood stretched out an arm and switched the television off. 'That's enough of that rubbish!'

Mick swallowed hard. And he wasn't the only aghast occupant of the lounge.

'Three pints of your best ale,' said Britt to the barmaid whose middle-aged face had frozen as stiff as her permed hair and crossed arms. Raising himself to his full height so that he towered over her, Britt tried again: 'If you'd be so kind,' he said, archly, like some squire fresh from the hunting field. 'Raging thirst needs quenching!'

Britt's words seemed to reverberate off every surface until a hush soaked in menace overwhelmed the room. It reminded Mick of a scene in a war film where everyone is waiting for a bomb squad to remove a fuse. Visions of that bloody St Scholastica's Day flashed through his brain: this could turn very ugly, he thought, and very rapidly.

'Dunt serve 'um, Gloria!' said a voice from behind Britt. 'Bloody undergrads, I'll be bound! Think they owns the bloody town!'

'D'ya wornt a punch in the mush?' said a younger and more hostile voice. 'We wuz watchin' that programme! Who the fuck d'ya think you are comin' in 'ere all lah-de-dah loik you owns the place!'

Mick watched half a dozen young men rise as one, and noticed several hands going to jacket pockets where he guessed a knuckle-duster, cosh or flick knife was surely lurking

'Bernardo, can you translate?' said Dashwood, with exaggerated haughtiness. 'You're *au fait* with the local lingo! Is this fellow asking for what I think he's asking?'

The panic written across a face rapidly assuming the colour of wallpaper paste suggested Mick believed flight rather than fight might be in order. But Dashwood had recently won a boxing Blue after answering an urgent call to the University's rugby contingent for a heavyweight. One glance at the belligerent set of Dashwood's jaw told Mick all he needed to know: his evening had gone from bad to worse but it could be saved in line with the best traditions of The Hellfire Club founded by his namesake. He was itching for a scrap and putting the plebs in their place. Mick could only see one outcome. And that was Town roughing-up Gown.

Mick watched Dashwood's lip curl. Suddenly he visualized their names in the *Oxford Mail* for creating a disturbance in a public place, and having to explain their conduct to the Dean. He sidled up to Dashwood and, dropping his voice, said: 'Dasher, I know you're reluctant to run from a fight but we're outgunned here. A tactical retreat is in order.'

Before he got an answer a voice piped up: 'I knows you, dunt I?' said an old codger. 'You're Roy Bernard's boy, enchya? The rugby player he's allus bangin' on about. Silly bloody game an' all. Be different if it wuz football!'

Mick manufactured a smile to take his mind off the lump rapidly clogging his airways.

'You should 'ang your head in shame! Behavin' like a nutter!' said the old codger's wife. 'Lookin' down your nose at us! S'all roight for those two buggers with ya but you're one of us, enchya?' Wait till your ol' man comes in 'ere again!'

Dashwood saw the look of humiliation on Mick's face and knew he'd put it there. He was the guilty party; his behaviour that was unconscionable. 'Thank you, Gloria,' he said with as much grace as he could summon while placing a pound note on the bar. 'For your trouble.'

The journey back to St Frideswide's seemed all the slower thanks to the lack of conversation. Britt and Dashwood read each other's mind: they were aware they took the piss out of Mick for his background but they knew, as they hoped did Mick, it was all in jest, only banter. The vitriol they'd just heard Mick publicly suffer, however, was authentic and genuinely toxic: these people, Mick's people, were filled with loathing for him. It brought home to them the ordeal their pal and team-mate faced every time he strayed across Magdalen Bridge and up the Iffley Road.

The van thundered to a halt approaching the Plain. Dashwood wound down his window and stuck out a head; he saw a queue of traffic snaking toward Magdalen Bridge. Seconds passed. No progress. His hands began drumming on the steering wheel. 'Get a move on, you useless peasant!' he shouted at the Morris Minor in front of them. 'Fuck this for a game of soldiers!' He slammed the van into gear and, with foot hard on the accelerator, pulled out from behind the Morris and hurtled down the wrong side of the road, passing one incredulous driver after another. The sudden manoeuvre caught Mick by surprise and sent him spinning around the back of the van as if he were inside a washing machine. On the plus side he'd no time to register what happened next before it was over and done with. Dashwood briefly took his foot off the accelerator; glanced to his right for possible danger; and then sent the van rocking round the Plain in the wrong direction before jumping to the head of the queue waiting to cross Magdalen Bridge – rebuffing the inevitable abuse with a regal wave and nodding smile. That it was nothing short of divine intervention no vehicle had emerged from St Clement's or Cowley Road with fatal repercussions was either swiftly forgotten or never contemplated. Death was never an option. He'd played his 'Joker'. And their bad luck turned to good when it truly counted.

'Bernardo, I'll get you a pint,' said Dashwood as the van drew up outside St Frideswide's. 'You, we, could do with one after this evening's shit-show.'

'You should've gone for a pleasant round of golf instead,' Mick said as cheerfully as he could. 'If you're serious about getting that golf Blue you should've been practising not frittering your time away at a dog track with layabouts like me and Jammy!'

Dashwood's fingers resumed beating their tattoo on the steering wheel. 'Fucking disaster, wasn't it?'

Without waiting for a response he got out of the van and went round to open the back doors for Mick to clamber out. 'Pass me my bag, Bernardo. You may be bang right with that observation! I should be practising!'

They marched into the Front Quad and came to a halt when Dashwood dropped his golf bag on the lawn in front of the Chapel. 'If I can chip a ball from here over the Dining Hall and into the lane, the drinks are on you two. If I don't make the shot, the drinks are on me and...'

'...the Dean will probably rusticate you for ripping turf from the lawn or smashing a window in the Dining Hall,' said Mick.

'Are you nuts!' added Britt, a forefinger tapping his temple.

Dashwood ignored both entreaties, plonked a ball onto the grass, and embarked on a series of practice swings. 'Here goes nothing!' he said, as the fourth swing clipped the ball into the air at a 60-degree angle.

All three of them watched the ball's flight, praying it had sufficient trajectory to miss the Dining Hall windows and clear its roof. The white speck grew fainter and fainter until it disappeared into the black void of the night sky. The silence was broken by a sound akin to ping-pong ball on lino that signified Dashwood's missile had avoided the rough and landed on the fairway.

'Never in doubt!' said Dashwood, casually leaning on his club, oblivious to the beads of anxiety trickling down his forehead.

Two weeks later Dashwood secured his Blue at golf. He lost both his matches.

Five

When no immediate response from Sam was forthcoming to his Ball invitation Mick was left ruing the possibility he and Sam were in the past tense. His only hope was that she, too, was playing the long game. Perhaps she was, because shortly after Christmas a letter arrived accepting his invitation. Her own nonchalant postscript ruled out any prior dates by informing Mick she was going to France for the term on a student exchange to further her spoken French. Mick received one postcard, of a splendid chateau with an 'x' marking Sam's room: 'Wish you were here!' she wrote. Mick doubted that. But it was nice to dream.

Mick delayed writing with the Ball arrangements until Trinity term had started. He wasn't about to put any pressure on Sam. He wanted nothing more than they began where they left off during their walk hom from the Country Club. He suggested meeting at the bus stop by the Regal, just a short stroll from his digs in Warneford Road, on the afternoon of the Ball. Sam agreed: she was looking forward to meeting the new version of Mick Bernard, the one without inhibitions, the relaxed, funny and attentive Mick Bernard whom, she had to confess, she found endearing and not unattractive.

A couple of Number 1 buses came and went with no sign of Sam. Mick looked at his watch for the third time. It was past six now, a good 20 minutes after the time arranged. Was he going to be stood-up? Just as Mick began to pace uneasily, another bus came into view. It stopped and he saw a vision alight from the bus that struck him in the groin with the force of a docker's boot. It spoke: 'Hi there, handsome! Bet you thought I wasn't going to show?'

Sam looked spectacular in a tight black satin blouse and a pair of matching trousers, a simple combination that served to accentuate her natural beauty and bring out the vitality of her azure eyes.

'How do I look?' she said, flashing a toothy smile that dazzled like the sun dawning over a snowy mountain top. 'Will I do?'

Mick puffed out his cheeks. 'You don't need me to say anything, surely? You look ravishing!'

'Thank you, kind sir!'

She sighed dramatically. 'An Oxford Ball doesn't occur often so I wanted to make the most of it.'

Mick held up his hands in capitulation. 'And my word you have done!'

Sam's longer hair framed her face to perfection: the last tiny concessions to puppy fat had gone, spotlighting her remarkable bone structure. She was not a heavy user of cosmetics. She was too much of a natural beauty to need artificial aids. Her cheekbones bore only the slightest traces of rouge, her skin carried only the lightest dusting of powder and her lips shone pink. But it was those eyes, as bright as a blue beacon in a storm, which drew Mick in. Her perfume seemed to inhabit every pore and every strand of hair so that she smelt like Mick thought an angel must smell. And his inner voice was unequivocal: Sam Owens had blossomed from an exceptionally pretty girl into a stunningly beautiful young woman.

'A girl can never get enough compliments,' Sam purred, lowering her eyes.

'Okay! At the risk of repeating myself, you look an absolute knock-out!'

'Aah! That's more like it!''

'And you smell divine. What's that perfume?'

'Kiku,' she informed him. 'It's a new fragrance from Faberge.'

'I shall feel a complete scruff compared to you!'

'Then raise your game, Mr Bernard!'

She laughed at her advice. She seemed genuinely happy to see Mick and grabbed his hand as they negotiated the busy traffic on the Cowley Road. He opened the front door of his digs as quietly as a monk at vespers. There was no sign of his landlady. 'I think Mrs Barnes is out,' he said. 'But she's rather deaf in any case.'

He beckoned Sam to follow. She crossed her lips with a finger in a theatrical 'shush', prompting Mick to put hand to mouth to extinguish a fit of the giggles and hold his breath until they were safely inside his room.

'Shame you're not still in College rooms,' she said, a roving eye scanning the furniture and coming to rest on the bed.

'A lot of the older rooms being demolished in the current rebuilding programme meant we only got the one year in College and had to find digs.'

'Couldn't you have stayed at home and saved money?'

Mick looked at her incredulously. 'You must be joking! I couldn't wait to get away! Even if it was only for eight weeks at a time.'

'Perhaps you should've applied to Cambridge?' she countered. 'After all, they award Blues for rugby, don't they?'

'That's what the school advised, too. An Oxford boy shouldn't go to Oxford. But it was always going to be Oxford for me the moment I watched my first game at Iffley Road. In any case, these digs are far enough away from home whenever I need them to be – which is most of the time.'

Mick invited her to make herself at home while he went to the bathroom across the landing to wash and shave. Sam watched Mick peel off his shirt. The muscular definition of an athlete that met her gaze was in sharp contrast to those of her other suitors and sent a spider of lust tiptoeing up her backbone. 'Don't be long,' she said, moving closer to Mick and stroking the back of his neck. Then her face crinkled with an impish grin.

The face Mick contemplated in the mirror as he shaved also had a grin as wide as the Grand Canyon. His head was bursting with such longing for Sam that he felt it might explode and release the turtle doves billing and cooing inside. He began humming 'Zippidee do-dah, Zippidee-ay. Wonderful feeling. Feeling this way!' He dabbed on some Mennon aftershave lotion recommended by Pete Livermore rather than the Old Spice his mother had given him last Christmas. Only dads and uncles, according to Pete, used that ancient stand-by. And Pete ought to know about matters fashionable: one Saturday a month he caught the train to London specifically to shop in Carnaby Street like all the other hipsters and dudes.

Mick retraced his steps. What he beheld on opening the door to his room made his heart beat fast and loud. Sam was lying on his bed, a sheet clutched up to her chin. 'Phew!' she giggled. 'Just as well it was you coming in and not Mrs Barnes!'

He'd not imagined this scenario in the wildest of wild dreams. The old Mick would've panicked and messed up: the new Mick decided to play the cards Sam had dealt and see what kind of hand they amounted to. It turned out to be a full house.

'Voila!' trilled Sam, throwing back the sheet. 'Do you like what you see?'

'My God, Sam,' he said, edging closer to the bed, 'you are so incredibly beautiful.' At that moment Mick wished he was Mister Jinks so that he could lick every square inch of her. But he made do by devouring her with his eyes.

Sam Owens was accustomed to hearing admirers say she possessed the kind of aura that drove cavemen to chisel on rock walls and, however reluctant she was to believe in their sincerity, she'd been obliged to acknowledge their accuracy. Mick had long since seared her beautiful face into his brain. Now he got to see her body and worship its perfection. The breasts were full, firm and generously nippled; the belly as flat as made no difference; the legs long and toned. Sam knew she was an object of desire. And Mick's first glimpse of her naked body ensured the sensual pull she exerted over Mick Bernard would register 10 on the Richter scale.

Mick kissed her. Sam cupped his face in her hands. 'Come to bed, Mick.' It was an order not an invitation, issued softly, and activating every libidinous nerve-end in Mick's body.

'I don't know why it's taken us so long,' she cooed. 'I was starting to think I was just arm candy…'

'What?'

'Just for show! An ego-booster in front of your pals…'

Mick blew a raspberry.

'Honestly,' said Sam, 'I thought you didn't fancy me!'

'Didn't fancy you! God, if you only knew the sleepless nights you've given me in that bed,' Mick confessed. 'But are you sure? I didn't…'

'I know,' she interjected. 'You didn't expect a lay in return for a Ball ticket.'

'No, it's just that I've no protection…'

'Like all us London girls, I'm on the Pill! Dummy!'

Mick tried to conceal the blushes of ignorance behind the act of removing his socks but succeeded only in almost tripping himself up.

'I just don't know why it's taken so long!' she said,

'Because I'm a numbskull!' he offered while removing his trousers. 'Feared rejection. Afraid of making a fool of myself…'

'In other words, a typically repressed Anglo-Saxon male,' she said, index fingers pointing to her temples.

'I can write what I'm thinking but I can't say it! Especially if those thoughts are about you.'

'Faint heart – or is it words,' she said in a melodious voice, 'never won fair lady.'

'Someone once said the appetites of the body were private battles and I can see what they meant,' said Mick as he made to draw the curtains. 'No, leave them open,' said Sam. 'Let's enjoy the sunshine. It'll be nicer.'

The late afternoon sun gave the room brightness and a stillness that Mick could only describe as unworldly. Sam had never looked more enticing. Sensuality oozed from every pore. As a shard of sunlight kissed her cheek on its way to warming a strawberry-tipped breast, she took hold of his hands and drew him toward her. The orange blossom and vanilla of the Kiku dabbed behind her ears made him want to take a plump pink lobe into his mouth, but her mouth moved first, welcoming his as a starving lioness greets a springbok. He felt Sam's breath fan the hairs on his neck while she slowly enveloped him with the vetvet touch of a warm, wet, mitten, knowing his fantasies were being fulfilled.

For what seemed an eternity, yet amounted to nothing more than a fleeting moment, Mick's world was stuck in suspended animation. It was as if Sam had plunged a hand into his chest and squeezed his heart until it stopped. Everything, everything that mattered, suddenly became clearer to him and he felt every nerve ending tingle from his finger tips to his toe nails. All peripheral vision shut down; all he saw was her face. Her physical proximity made him a different person; someone he preferred to the Mick Bernard with whom he was more familiar. She provided for him what he so conspicuously lacked: their two souls formed one magical life force. Wasn't this, he thought, how poets describe love? He was seconds away from making an ass of himself. He was going to blurt out how much she meant to him, the affection he felt for her, the desire he had for her. Christ Almighty, he suddenly realized he might even go so far as to say he loved her. But he didn't.

'Where did that come from?' he asked, cautiously.

Sam hesitated. 'I've been wanting that since the night you walked me home from the Country Club,' she said, deciding to be honest. 'You'd changed...'

'Really?' said Mick, shocked but quietly proud that someone like Sam had noticed the efforts he'd made.

'Yes. For the better. It struck me within a few minutes. It seems to me you'd found a way of behaving and talking and feeling that suited you. Just don't lose it!'

'That's good to know. Not before time, eh?'

'And you handled that evening when you came over to Ealing and found me with Guy far more maturely than the old Mick Bernard would've done. It was obvious to me you took an instant dislike to him...'

'Why waste any time!' Mick chortled.

'Okay, smart arse! Just accept the verdict. You'd grown up.'

'The new model Mick Bernard! Straight off the assembly line!' he joked. 'Hope I didn't spoil your evening...'

'Oh, don't worry about that!' she giggled. 'I got rid of Guy before dessert!'

They laughed as one. Nothing in their relationship had ever hinted at such an outpouring of affection or relief as had surfaced in the last hour. But even at this sublime moment, as he lay with the girl he idolized, just plumbing these emotional depths caused the other woman in Mick's life to appear like some Banquo come to spoil the feast.

'So,' he said, impervious to the mood-destroying words he was in the process of uttering, 'why can't my mother embrace me without giving the impression of being a praying mantis?'

Happiness ebbed from Sam's face on a tide of confusion. She planted a row of kisses on his neck. The seeds failed. He barely noticed them; gave them no chance to flower. He'd retreated into a little world of his own where there was neither happiness nor goodness, only loneliness and bitterness.

'Why can't I give my father a manly bear hug without feeling a fraud?' he said, continuing his theme. 'And if I think of hugging my mother, why is there some kind of invisible shield that keeps me at bay? I know it's showing a different kind of love to what we've just shared but…'

'But what?' said Sam, growing alarmed at the tremor in Mick's voice.

'It's hard to explain, to put into words…'

'Try. I'm here. I'll listen. I'll help,' she said, recovering her poise.

'I've always felt unloved,' Mick said slowly, after a long silence. 'So I've always found it impossible to give love. The only person I can safely say that I loved was my Granny Jaykes. Any love I had for my mother, and I surely had some when I was a child, she has killed off. And as for my father…well Anglo-Saxon fathers don't talk or act like that with their sons, do they?'

'Yes, I think you may be right. My brother Julian has often hinted the same,' said Sam, sensing Mick's pain. 'It's a shame you didn't have a brother or sister. It does help having a sibling whose shoulder is always there to cry on.'

'Of course. Always longed for a brother. I'd even have put up with a sister! But my mother hadn't enough love for me let alone finding some for a second child.'

'She can't be that devoid of feeling?'

Mick gave some thought to what he might say next before saying it. 'Let me give you an example of my sainted mother. When it became that time of a boy's life when he wants to keep his body to himself and away from the prying eyes of his mother, she agreed to let me wash myself. But every time she made some excuse to come and check on me! I used to feel her eyes examining every inch of me like a dried-up school matron. Then puberty began to announce itself down below. She clocked my short-and-curlies, smirked and left. I felt broken by the humiliation and embarrassment of it all. And she never came in again after that.'

Sam felt his heart beating faster against her chest. 'Did you ever mention this to your dad?'

Mick tensed. 'No point. She routinely embarrasses him, it's a form of blood sport, and he lets her get away with it. He just caves in. My father's made of putty as far as she's concerned. He just looks the other way when she applies the pressure or stands there looking as vacant as a scarecrow. He could've shown some backbone and walked out on the woman. Frankly, I've no idea how the marriage has survived.'

'Could it be love?' Sam suggested, with a dip of the head.

Mick blew a raspberry. 'If you want to survive against my mother you need more than love. You must give as good as you get. That means giving no quarter, bearing grudges and settling them! My Old Man hasn't got the balls to tell her when she's talking twaddle.'

'Sounds to me he's being shrewd.'

'No, he's let himself down. He let us both down. Damn it, he let me down!'

'You do make your mother sound like an ogre!'

'I think you've got the message. I reckon her heart only beats twice an hour! Never a caring word or touch for their own sake. Quick to chide and slow to praise. Emotions always locked away. The trick is to pretend everything is fine and dandy, on the surface. Anything festering underneath is to be overlooked. Learn to cope on your own.'

'So you did?'

'Well, I tried. Became emotionally self-reliant. Not altogether a bad thing. I learnt what it was like to stand alone. I built a protective wall around myself, keeping my resentment at this lack of a storybook family inside, and keeping everyone else outside. But the resentment developed into bitterness the size of a giant boil that grew incapable of lancing. It poisoned my emotions.'

Mick suddenly stopped and turned his head away. He'd released too many demons. His bed was an unlikely confessional box and Sam an improbable confessor.

'Carry on, if you want,' she said, empathetically. 'Get it all off your chest. I don't mind.'

He thought for a moment. 'Well, that wall was cemented by anger so pathological I became fearful of it being released. So I turned it inward and became a slave to melancholy. It seemed to me the safer option.'

Sam tried to look into his eyes to see if he was telling the absolute truth: the tears she saw lurking there insisted he was.

'Keeping up appearances, that's all it's been about,' Mick added with a laugh. 'All three of us. Me. My mother. My father. Doing it for the sake of the family. Yet there is no family. Our house is like the bloody Marie Celeste! From a distance people might be fooled into thinking everything's normal but once you get on board and look below deck there's no sign of a damned crew!'

She kissed the top of his head.

'We're just three people who don't appear to get on with each other. Three vessels sailing the same seas without ever hailing one another. Even Freud would scratch his head faced with the Bernards!'

'Mick,' she said, 'why don't you just leave home for good. Get away as far as you can. Cut the strings completely. You'll destroy yourself if you carry on like this.'

He pressed his head into the pillow. 'I tell myself that over and over. And what stops me? Obligation. Filial duty. And do you know what? Those are principles my mother hammered into me.'

'So she gave you something worthwhile…'

'Yes,' he conceded. 'And it's the same set of grand ideals they drummed into us at school. Things we should aspire to. Things that matter.'

Mick shot upright. 'Good grief! Look at the time,' he said. 'The Ball awaits! Your carriage is without, Princess Owens! Although, sadly, I must tell you there isn't one!'

Sam levered herself upward, dropping the sheet and exposing her bosom.

'Don't try tempting me, you little minx!' said Mick, happy to demonstrate his newly acquired machismo.

'Just giving my hormones an airing…' she said, her words trailing away tantalizingly.

'We must walk into town. I'm not having dirty old men leering at you on the bus! So we'd best get a wiggle on.'

While Mick eased himself into his dinner suit Sam took a compact and lip gloss from her bag to repair what their ardour had ruined. Having completed the task to her satisfaction she stood beside Mick in front of his wardrobe mirror. 'Hold still!' she said. 'That hair looks as though you dried it with a threshing machine!'

Mick reached for his comb. 'Here, let me!' she chided. 'Can't have your Greek-god looks spoiled, can we?'

Sam gently stroked the comb through his hair, stood back and nodded behind a smile. 'You'll pass!' she said and meant it: he looked as dashing as she'd hoped. She straightened his bow tie for effect and the chance to plant a kiss on both cheeks. 'There, all done! The perfect penguin! Now you're fit to be seen with me! You may escort me to the Ball!'

They walked down the Cowley Road and across Magdalen Bridge, holding hands in a show of innocent intimacy, laughing and smiling at each other's comments, be they inane or comical, ignoring the jeers from jealous cyclists and their wolf-whistles aimed at Sam. Mick felt happy in his own skin, the first time he could honestly tell himself he was deliriously happy. And he hoped Sam felt the same. But he wasn't going to pressurize her by asking. Sam was indeed happy, and all the happier for not being pressurized.

The Ball took place in the Front Quad. A large marquee had been erected, its precious grass protected by boards. The music blared and the champagne flowed. Everything was superfluous in Mick's eyes. All this gaudiness was mere flummery. This evening would be memorable for one thing only, one special person. And she was here in front of him. Mick never took his eyes off Sam, unless it was to catch the looks on the faces of those who wished Sam was on their arm and not his. He'd been ecstatic when tearing open the letter of acceptance from St Frideswide's. This feeling was even better; it could last forever and a day as far as he was concerned. It was a state foreign to him, one he was given no option but to identify as euphoria. Whatever it was lasted until the sun came up. As he walked Sam home he told her how the air seemed cleaner; the leaves on the trees greener; the tune of birds seeking the early worm more melodious. Then they both gave way to a fit of giggles at such sensitive imagery coming from the mouth of Mick Bernard, the very epitome of an emotional cripple. But just a few hours shared with Sam Owens, this gorgeous, intelligent and feisty girl by his side, got his mind whirling faster than a carousel at St Giles' Fair.

'Thank you for a lovely evening,' Sam said, once they reached her doorstep. Her voice carried a softness that could only be authentice. She kissed Mick on both cheeks. His mouth opened to pour out words of love but all he heard himself say was a pathetically lame: 'The pleasure was mine.'

Mick knew his emotional life was littered with disappointments. Any dream of a lasting, permanent, relationship with Sam had all the ingredients for another. He was a repressed child of post-war austerity while she was a liberated child of the 'Swinging Sixties.' She was a free spirit who could handle anything the future might throw at her; Mick was chained to the past and shackled to the present and apprehensive of what the future might hurl his way. His mates were not wrong: how could he hope to keep a girl like her. It was their destiny to flit in and out of each other's lives, to bring joy whenever possible, offer solace whenever needed and bequeath sweet memories for the ages.

Mick got as far as the gate when he felt her breath on his neck. Sam wrapped her arms around his waist till he turned to face her and then gave him a long, lingering kiss that spoke of the deepest affection, if not love.

'You must get away, and quickly,' Sam whispered. 'Or else the angry young man will become an angry old man.'

Six

A watery November sun shining from the Jackdaw Lane end picked out 30-odd figures wearing an assortment of tracksuits and rugby kit jogging around the perimeter of Oxford University's Iffley Road pitch. Amongst them was Mick Bernard. It had taken him two years to reach this point in his rugby odyssey and get within touching distance of winning his Blue by playing against Cambridge in the Varsity Match a few weeks hence.

Mick's rugby career with OURFC progressed slowly; and understandably so. His was a three-year mission. He'd no chance of featuring in the Blues side as a callow Freshman straight from schoolboy rugby with just one senior appearance for Oxford RFC to his name. Initially he had to be content with representing the Freshmen side linked to the University's second fifteen, the Greyhounds. But then an unexpected boost: 'Town' came calling.

Three weeks into his first term Oxford RFC lost its regular scrum-half to injury. The Club was upwardly mobile: it was packed with players who'd represented Oxfordshire in the County Championship, the only competition in English rugby and its highest grade of representative rugby, just below international level – three County regulars were capped. Oxford RFC was constantly improving its fixture list and was due to play one of the country's crack outfits in Bedford. Mick was asked to step in. Oxford lost to a side containing four internationals and Mick learnt a valuable lesson: it was prudent to avoid the heavyweight confrontations for which he was not equipped. He did nothing outstanding but neither did he show his inexperience at this level by committing crass mistakes. Four days later he was astonished to find a card in his pigeon hole at St Frideswide's informing him he was selected to play for Oxfordshire against Buckinghamshire.

The risk taken by the County selectors was enormous. This game would decide the winner of the Southern Group and thus a guaranteed place in the quarter finals of the competition. Mick was a callow 18-year-old youth who'd only played his first game of organized rugby a little over three years earlier and had experienced just two senior games – yet he was being entrusted with a pivotal role in the team. Mick changed next to Wyn James, who partnered the County captain at centre; his nerves soon evaporated as his pack of forwards proceeded to give him an armchair ride. Oxfordshire won; and the *Oxford Mail* again sang the praises of the 'young newcomer who impressed with his sound reliability which included a good service and intelligent kicking.' Even the chairman of the England selectors, in attendance to watch the Buckinghamshire scrum-half, told Mick how well he'd performed despite being up against a wily scrum-half on the verge of being capped. Mick kept his place for the last Group match versus Berkshire and was again on the winning side. Post match celebrations featured a sing-song and drinking session at the home of the County President. Mick tried to savour every single second of a new experience he hoped would become a feature of his senior career. He was glad there was a low ceiling because otherwise he'd have floated up into the ether so ecstatic did he feel.

The one stumbling block to Mick's progress was his eyesight. During any match played in murky midwinter conditions he tended to lose sight of the ball whenever play suddenly shifted to the far side of the pitch. He needed contact lenses to correct his deteriorating long sight. There was only one possible source of the

£60 necessary to purchase a pair: he tentatively approached Edna. His mother provided the cash without demur. He accepted with mixed feelings: on the one hand grateful his quest for a Blue wouldn't be hampered by something as unfortunate as poor eyesight but on the other hand deeply troubled by the unspoken *quid pro quo* involved. His mother would be expecting demonstrable gratitude at every turn. Mick began by treating Edna to lunch in town. The encounter hummed with tension. How long Mick could maintain this necessarily obsequious tack filled him with apprehension. But he must try.

After a week of torture growing accustomed to the lenses, Mick wore them in a match for the first time in the final of College Cuppers. He and Swaby were the only Freshmen in the victorious St Frideswide's XV alongside 11 others who'd played for the University, of whom eight won their Blue. This was rarified company and Mick found it hard to keep his head out of the clouds. In addition, over Easter, he went on the Oxford RFC tour to South Wales. With every match his confidence grew. Then, toward the end of Hilary Term, he was presented with the opportunity to impress the University captain by playing for the County against the Blues in the annual friendly at Iffley Road. The County was well beaten and Mick was obliged to concede he'd done nothing in the game that would help his cause. Yet he was confident in telling himself that donning the University's dark blue jersey could only be a matter of time.

That time materialized in the Hilary Term of his second year. Called up to play against the Royal Navy he kept his place throughout the term and the two subsequent Easter tours. In a couple of his eight appearances he'd put in a lot of excellent work. Everything was going according to Mick's master plan designed to bear fruit in his third and final year at St Frideswide's.

Sam's absence only served to concentrate mind and body on rugby: she was in France for the entire academic year. He'd begun weight training in the University sport's centre under the guidance of British international discus thrower Denny Randall whom he'd come across doing his own work in the weights room; and during the Vac he'd put this to good use by a few weeks pushing wheelbarrows of concrete on a building site. That took care of strength conditioning. For speed he'd undertaken pyramids of sprints on Bannister's famous track, wearing spikes for better effect, with another British international in St Frideswide's Jerry Butler. Strength and speed were prerequisites for scrum-halves. Mick never clocked his sprints to confirm greater speed but the scales informed him he'd acquired 7lb of muscle around his chest and shoulders that definitely made him harder to manhandle. Lastly, he'd started playing squash to quicken his reactions and make him more nimble. For light relief from gym and track he'd take a ball down to South Oxford's pitch and go through the kicking drills drummed into him by Wyn James. Only the tedium of running for the sake of running was ignored.

Mick was confident playing with Oxford RFC prior to Michaelmas Term and the start of the University's season would deliver him match-hardened and primed to win his Blue in what would be his final year. He'd thought through every aspect of his game. Nothing was being left to chance in the quest for his personal Holy Grail.

***

'Bernardo! Get your arse to the front!'

The bark of Dessie Mulligan, Irish international lock forward and captain of OURFC, rattled Mick's brain like a 3am alarm call. How Mick dreaded the lapping that started every training session and this was a Monday, the worst session of the week: an aerobic slog of 90 minutes full of unrelenting sprints, over short and long distances, interspersed with physical jerks and carrying exercises. Mick favoured lagging at the back of the group and only exerted himself when the skipper was looking his way.

'When Bernardo gives the word we sprint for ten!'

Mick groaned inwardly and dragged himself to the head of the bunch; he waited until he was almost at the corner of the pitch by the pavilion before making the call. He hoped he could cut the corner and poach a decent advantage because it was a cardinal sin, a sign of unfitness, for any of the hounds to overhaul the fox.

'Grand speed!' shouted Mulligan after Mick's ruse had succeeded. 'That was so fuckin' blinding, you can do it again!'

Lungs were ablaze but not enough to prevent communal guffaws at the biter being bit. 'That'll teach you!' Mulligan continued as Mick came alongside, struggling to combat the jelly in his legs. 'You wee Townie shite!' A friendly wallop to the backside as Mick began the next sprint symbolized the kind of crude banter all rugby players were expected to tolerate. Mick grinned. His comrades jeered.

Four days hence the Blues would play Major Stanley's XV, a team of internationals specifically invited to test the Blues before the Varsity Match. It was watching this game some six years ago that had first fired Mick's ambition to play in the dark blue jersey one day. Now others, including boys from South Oxford accompanied by James, would be watching him in the number 9 jersey. Then it would be only two more games to the Varsity Match just over three weeks away.

He slept late and walked into town at 11.30: he'd to purchase the special Stanley's match tie from Castell's in the Broad and decided the occasion warranted a new pair of blue shorts. The team gathered at midday in Vincent's Club, the University's watering hole for sportsmen above Shepherd & Woodward's shop in the

High. All 15 players were among the allotted 150 elected members currently in residence. Alumni included archbishops, judges and prime ministers. But the quality sought from potential members was simple: Vincent's had no place for cads and bounders. Any member of the Club must possess all the qualities characteristic of what once was termed 'a good egg.'

Mick put on his Stanley's tie and selected a ham sandwich and a cup of tea. He left half of each: he preferred playing on an empty stomach. The Stanley's XV was its usual strength, entirely composed of internationals from each of the home nations: 11 from England; two from Wales; and one apiece from Ireland and Scotland; Mick's opposite number was the incumbent England scrum-half. A decent game in this company, he knew, as did 13 of his team-mates, should be enough to clinch his place in Mulligan's side for the Twickenham date with Cambridge. Each man was aware changes of a surprising nature were not exactly unknown in the last week or so: a team had to be selected specifically to beat Cambridge; someone might be brought in for this one all-important match to fulfill a particular role geared to winning it. Mulligan had dispatched spies to analyze Cambridge, to discover their strategy, how they preferred to play, to look for weaknesses – and the 'Tabs' would have spies at Iffley Road intent on a similar mission today.

Once the team had finished lunch they walked en masse the short distance along the High and Iffley Road to the ground. It was now about 1.30, an hour away from kick-off. Mick picked up his number 9 shirt from the table inside the door of the home dressing room. It was brand new and made him thankful to have invested in those new shorts to do it justice. The shirt lacked one all important feature: it bore no silver crown on the left breast: only shirts worn in the Varsity Match bore that honour.

Mick hung the shirt on his usual peg, next to Britt who'd come into the side as a late replacement to partner Mulligan in the second row. To defuse the mounting tension as the pair exchanged student garb for the jock strap, jersey, shorts and socks of an athlete they challenged each other to recite lines from the Western they'd watched at the Regal the previous evening.

'What was the awestruck greenhorn's response on seeing the veteran gunslinger shoot the fleeing bandit out of the saddle?' asked Mick.

'That's the greatest shot I've ever seen!'

'To which the gun-hand replied?'

'The worst!' drawled Britt in his version of a Texan accent. 'I was aiming at the horse!'

They began chuckling, immune to the curiosity of team mates preoccupied with the challenges that awaited them, but neither Mick nor Britt were the sort who prepared for a match by head-butting the nearest wall. Britt's expressive features now illuminated with trademark bonhomie explained why his chances of securing a Blue had been compromized: they spoke of affability rather than thuggery; in the dog-eat-dog world of scrum and maul there just wasn't enough 'dog' in him. Britt was no pushover: but intimidating an opponent with a smack in the mouth amounted to nothing more! than a polite tete-a-tete between friends compared to squeezing his testicles or jabbing a finger up his backside. If gaining a Blue meant resorting to such dark arts it was Britt's misfortune to be a better human being than he was an enforcer.

The pair had developed a telepathic understanding of each other's play while negotiating the transition from College to University XV and appreciated that striving for a Blue was a strain more than physical. The fear of being dropped was as constant and unrelenting as rain in Count Kerry. Match reports in the papers were scrutinized word by word: had a good display been recognized; had a mediocre performance been spotted - or, more embarrassingly, vilified. Every player yearned for the kind of Press comment Britt once received: he'd won line-out ball so easily and prolifically it was, said the reporter, 'as if he was picking apples'. Henceforth known as 'The Apple Picker', Britt dined off this new moniker unashamedly.

Their insecurity ensured the first training session following a match posed a quandary: whether to enter the home dressing room at Iffley Road reserved for the Blues or the away dressing room occupied by the Greyhounds; to risk self-confidence that might herald immediate and ignominious retreat or display the diffidence of a player feeling unworthy of a place at the top table. Mick had reached the point where praise was distrusted: a player couldn't allow himself to be lulled into a false sense of security by Press or team-mate. Paradoxically, he accepted every criticism at face value, as totally justified and 100% true; and an ear to the ground was always alert for gossip to his detriment. In consequence his innards churned for days with bouts of a land-locked *mal de mer* until relieved by the arrival of a selection card in his pigeon hole. As the games and weeks to the Varsity Match were ticked off the ultimate disaster became uppermost in the mind, the one factor over which the player had next to no control: injury. The threat of injury loomed larger as Twickenham came closer because recovery time grew shorter. It escalated to the point where players were prone to carrying that fear into a match despite knowing that trying to protect themselves bred the half-hearted commitment to physical contact likeler to bring about injury.

The mental torment never ceased; it played like a stuck record in Mick's brain. It wouldn't cease until he ran out onto the Twickenham turf in December and his Blue was assured. Until then, the trick, he told himself repeatedly, was to treat triumph and disaster as the twin imposters Kipling insisted. And trust the opinion of the man in the mirror. Look him in the eye for the truth. He never lies.

That man took the Elmer Cottons, cleaned, polished and buffed, from his duffel bag. He would never claim putting on a pair of rugby boots matched the mystique associated with a matador donning his suit of lights before going out to face the bull: to him it was more akin to a boxer taping his hands prior to a fight because boots and gloves were tools of the trade whereas the suit of lights was an adornment. But there was a certain ritual attached nonetheless. First Mick put on the left boot and gently stamped it into the floor to get a snug fit; then he laced it up, with the bow on the outside of the foot so as not to interfere with the sweet spot of his instep. After repeating the process with the right boot he picked up a ball and undertook a series of stretching exercises.

Mick cleared his mind of trivia and for the umpteenth time in the last 24 hours went through his mental preparation. Prowling the room like the proverbial cat on a hot tin roof, he ran match situations and how he'd respond to them through his mind: a lofted box kick from a line-out; a whipped dive-pass from a scrum; a darting run from ruck or maul, jinking past opponents in the manner of his sidestepping progress along the corridors of South Oxford between lessons. All the while he kept the ball constantly in motion, flipped from one hand to the other. His hands had to be as warm and supple as his hamstrings, biceps and triceps because they were as much the tools of his trade as his boots and dare not be anything other than 100% ready.

From the hive of subdued yet meaningful activity surrounding him came a call from Deates, the hooker, to practice a few scrum-feeds. The front-row trio bound-up and leant against the rim of the communal plunge bath so Mick and Deates could synchronize the action of ball leaving Mick's hands and the hooker striking like a cobra to meet the ball on the half-volley and propel it to the

Number 8's feet in one seamless manoeuvre. After repeating the procedure three times Deates grunted satisfaction.

The treatment table was Mick's last stop. He scooped some Vaseline from the open tub to smear into his knees to prevent grass burns; a final finger-tip of Vaseline was rubbed into his boots to leave them glistening like obsidian. He ended his ball-juggling odyssey by stopping to run through half-back signals with his fly-half.

Fifteen minutes before kick-off the teams left the dressing rooms for a group photograph. Mick looked toward the spot where he knew James would be standing, on the small terrace at the Jackdaw Lane end of the Iffley Road stand. Perhaps Clifton was with him. Mick hoped so. He gave a thumbs-up on the off chance they were returning his gaze.

Now the tension in the home dressing room is cranked up. It begins to assume all the conviviality of a holding cell on Death Row. No-one is now allowed through the door. The players, especially the forwards, are finding it impossible to stay still. Deates disappears into the lavatory and a violent bout of retching ensues. The noise building on the far side of the wall is heard by all as Mulligan began his final team talk. The technical stuff had been discussed. What lay ahead was not one of those dubious 'sports', pub games such as darts or snooker where athleticism, fitness and physicality, has no role. Not for them a drag on a cigarette and a quaff of beer as their final preparation. Only blood and thunder would suffice.

Dressing-room oratory laced with inflammatory rhetoric is frequently lampooned by those who have no truck with rugby or the hooligans that play it. But those who do play the game acknowledge a stirring pre match speech stands parity with Henry V's at Agincourt for effectiveness. Fifteen players can train, practice and drill all week as a team. But it's the five minutes before a match when the drawbridge is raised and the portcullis dropped that forges a band of brothers. Mulligan was an old hand at achieving the desired level of intense yet controlled aggression during these final moments. He'd captained his Irish province and led by example: there was no wall he'd not run through on behalf of his team-mates. At 6' 4" and 16 stones he was a fearsome sight in civvies: the sight of him in rugby kit gave the impression of 76 inches of rolled-up barbed wire that would've put the wind up Goliath.

'Hear them? They think they can psych us out with that racket! Bollocks to that! Fuckin' internationals who reckon they're here for an easy ride, and a free dinner and piss-up tonight after they've annihilated us student wankers! That's not gunna happen!'

Mulligan paused then said quietly. 'Just take a look at the man next to you.'

Fourteen pairs of eyes obeyed their leader's command. Muscles started to twitch involuntarily. Adrenalin was being manufactured in bucketfuls. It now had to be channelled.

'You know how good a player he must be to be sitting here in that blue jersey,' the skipper continues 'You know he'd go the extra mile to get you out of trouble. And he knows you'd do the same for him. No one man makes an error in this team. If an error's made we're all responsible.'

Then he yelled: 'We're a fuckin' team! A proper team! Not a bunch of celebrities! I shit 'em! The whole fuckin' lot of 'em!'

Fourteen figures began to clap and stamp studded boots on the floor. The room temperature had risen 10 degrees and the pungent aroma of embrocation is strong enough to make the eyes water. If adrenalin was possessed of a smell this would be it.

Mulligan was hitting his stride with every oath and obscenity. 'It's tunnel vision from all of us,' he says, casting an eye toward his fellow piano shifters in the pack. 'It's us going forward! Us knocking them back! We'll batter 'em up front! They won't have the balls for this! The greedy fuckers will've scoffed a big lunch on expenses! They're bloated! Ready for a fuckin' siesta not a rugby match! They think we're soft! They've no clue a full-on fuckin' blood and shit storm is coming their way! We forwards are going to fuckin' hurt them! Damage them!'

Mulligan's glare caught Britt in its headlights. 'We've got to be meaner, harder! Love the hits! Relish them!' he bellowed, right fist smacking into left palm. 'Make your opposite number wish he'd not had that second helping of pudding! Hit him in the guts so he pukes!'

Britt smacked his chest like a silverback whose harem was being pestered by an interloping lothario. This was steak and ale to the other forwards who did the same.

'It'll be fast and furious! Are we ready for 'em? Are we up for it?'

The roared answer was unequivocal.

'We'll win good ball for Bernardo. No shit sent his way! Goddit?'

The forwards bellowed their understanding of the task ahead.

'And then Bernardo can unleash our backline. Theirs is just a scratch unit. No cohesion. There for the taking!'

The piano players nodded in unison. But there was something about Mick's body language that attracted Mulligan's attention. Mick's stomach was currently hosting a kicking contest for butterflies but no one would've known from his laid-back deportment. Those who knew him best, such as Britt, had grown to accept he wasn't a player whose warm-up ended with the veins in his temples standing up like mountain ranges and his eyes popping out like Belisha beacons. Mick acknowledged the value of tub-thumping oratory pre-match but he also recognized how it could push some temperaments an inch too far. He wanted to be calm when he ran out into the arena instead of looking around for the first opponent to kill. That attitude might suit his forwards itching to expend their pent-up aggression but his role and his skills demanded a cool mind over hot blood if he was to excel.

'Bernardo,' said Mulligan, wagging a finger at Mick to ensure he'd not gone on a mental walkabout, 'take responsibility, put us in the right areas and don't be afraid of taking them on yourself. Run whenever the chance arises. Keep their defenders guessing. Goddit?'

'Yes, skip. Understood.'

'Okay. Let's warm up!'

A thunderous couple of minutes of studs rattling on the floor from a succession of physical jerks, pumping shoulders into each other and sprinting-on-the-spot preceded the knock on the door that called them out onto the pitch. The air inside the dressing room was now heaving with so much testosterone it was a wonder the pressure didn't blow the door off its hinges.

'Are we fuckin' ready for this?' snarled Mulligan.

'Yeeeesss!'

'Let's get out there and fuckin' do it!'

Mulligan led his team through the pavilion and down the steps at a controlled walk dripping with menace: 15 men about to lay their bodies on the line. A band of brothers pledged to fight together, win together or lose together; a collection of individuals they were not. The skipper refused to increase the pace until his boots trod grass. Only then did he release the pent-up energy from his blue crocodile to a tumultuous reception: feet were being stamped in the two grandstands and the schoolboys who enjoyed a close-up view sitting on the duckboards along the touchlines broke into high-pitched cheers. Mick sprinted past Britt and bent low to wipe both hands over the turf, his usual superstition to encourage adhesiveness – even though he knew it probably made not the slightest difference. What it did achieve, however, was to call full time on the butterfly contest in his stomach and preface one last mental reminder before everything became instinctive: a slick pass to his fly-half and a pinpoint box kick early on were paramount. Get in the groove and stay there.

Stanley's won the toss and chose to kick off. The Blues defended the Jackdaw Lane end with the low sun at their backs; apart from that it was a perfect afternoon for rugby, fresh and just the lightest breeze. Mick's mind was made up: at the first suitable opportunity from a line-out he'd put up a high kick into the sun blinding Stanley's defenders but landing close enough in front of his forwards for them to rough-up the catcher. Mulligan called the first throw to himself at the front of the line-out. He liked a hard and low throw that almost hit him in the chest, whence he could deflect the ball down into Mick's waiting hands. This demanded concentration and accuracy or the ball might ricochet anywhere. It was not the call Mick wanted, for precisely that uncertainty: he'd have called the throw to Britt in the middle of the line-out had the choice been his.

Perhaps because there was still too much of that pre-match adrenaline pumping through their veins Mulligan and Deates weren't quite in sync; the ball rocketed away from Mick and landed to his right, and close to the touchline. Mick instinctively adjusted his feet as he retrieved the ball, dipped his shoulder and fired a bullet of a reverse pass into his fly-half's midriff some 20 yards away infield to his left. As he followed the ball to its target he heard the crowd's collective throat roar in appreciation of his audacious display of individual skill. Wyn James smiled; Mick was now a 'sore-throat player'.

The subsequent kick ahead resulted in another line-out to the Blues. This one was called to Britt; he liked a lofted, hanging throw to capitalize on his height. Mick watched him go through his wind-up, one he'd studied at close quarters for three seasons. Britt rocked back and forth from one foot to the other, ready to co-ordinate his jump with the ball leaving the thrower's hand. Deates lobbed the ball and Britt sprang to meet it perfectly in mid air: his outside arm telescoped, his hand cupped the ball and palmed it perfectly into Mick's clutches. In one and the same movement Mick had put ball to the sweet spot of his right instep and launched a spiralling kick.

For the second time in the opening exchanges Wyn James was purring and eyeing the spectators around him as if to say: *That's my boy! I taught him that!* They watched Mick hare round the front of the line-out to put his forwards onside and saw the charging figure of Mulligan smash the catcher to the ground. While both sets of forwards fought for the ball on the ground the referee's whistle blasted: a scrum to the Blues. Five minutes gone and Mick had achieved his two objectives; any nerves were dispatched; and his confidence swelled.

As the two packs prepared to engage Mick winked at 'Pedro' Dymond, the Number 8 sporting a Mexican moustache that earned him his nickname, who packed down at the back of the scrum. This was the signal for a set move, honed on the training field. Mick wouldn't pass to his fly-half to the right; instead Dymond would pick up the ball and flip it to Mick in the act of running to the left and linking with his left wing. With luck Stanley's disjointed defence would be caught napping.

For the move to succeed the Blues pack had to deliver the ball to Mick crisply and speedily: it must act as one entity not eight forwards in isolation. The subtle distinction between 'forwards' and 'pack' is implied by the terms themselves. One is plural: eight individual forwards had no more impact than eight fingers being poked in the chest one at a time. But the other is singular: if those eight forwards acted as a pack, as one, it yielded the power of a punch to the chest from a mailed fist.

Mick studied his piano shifters as they bound up. Deates took a tight grip on the outside waistbands of his two props and the trio leant backwards awaiting the engagement and weight from the second row. The two locks linked arms and crouched in order to bind through the legs of the props and shove upwards into their buttocks. The flankers on either side of Mulligan and Britt simultaneously bound onto their respective lock in the second row and drove a shoulder in behind him to keep the power going forward. Dymond, meanwhile, had grasped the two locks by the shorts but delayed his engagement between them until he'd scanned the disposition of the opposing defenders. On the referee's command Mick watched more than 240 stones of bone, muscle and sinew collide in front of him. The front rows rippled as they fought to get the upper hand, seeking the optimum feet position to exert maximum leg-drive and forward momentum while striving to thrust a shoulder underneath their opposite number and force him upwards, dissipating his power. If one was a forward the scrum was a thing of beauty, an artful composition of angled limbs and levers sufficient to interest Picasso. To the uninitiated bystander, even one such as Mick, it amounted to a tangled mass of heaving, grunting and farting bodies; the garlic-infused sweat rising from the Stanley's hooker even announcing what he ate for lunch. Stanley's may have the players with international caps, thought Mick, but when he looked at the men in blue he recognized a pack not a rag-tag collection of forwards.

Mick leant against the scrum to straighten it up and ensure there was no chance of him being penalized for a crooked feed. He ordered his forwards to steady. They dropped their knees an inch to gain extra purchase for the surge on Mick's command as he released the ball. In it went with a shout of 'Now!' that was echoed by all eight of Mick's pack. The ball was hooked cleanly and catapulted back through the second row to Dymond's feet. Mick made to pick it up but then dropped off a yard to the left. Collecting the short pass from the Number 8, he made a beeline for the opposing winger, ready to draw his attention before slipping his own winger through the gap along the touchline and toward the unprotected try line some 25 yards away. He braced himself for the anticipated tackle that would take his winger's marker out of the equation. It was the muscle-numbing belter he expected from an international, coming low and hard, hitting him below the right knee and anchoring his foot in the turf; but it didn't prevent him from getting his pass away as he'd kept the ball in both hands, chest high, and free from contact.

Mick saw the ball safely caught when, in the same blink, a covering back-rower struck him under the rib cage with the force of a swinging bag of cement that propelled his upper body through 90 degrees. But his trapped lower leg couldn't follow suit. All the resultant pressure between upper and lower limbs moving in opposite directions went through his knee. He thought he heard a balloon pop followed by the pathetic yelp of a kicked dog. But there was no balloon and no dog. It was his knee and his voice. A gigantic vice seemed to be crushing his knee and demanding he groan. He collapsed.

When the clouds ceased rotating, Mick saw Britt's face peering down at him. Then the referee came for a look. Then someone with a sponge that was rubbed in his face. Then Mulligan arrived. Mick watched the skipper wince: 'Bernardo, you'll have to go off.'

'Not likely! I'll be fine. Just give me a minute. Jammy, help me up.'

Britt and Mulligan sensed this was folly but nonetheless gripped Mick under the armpits and raised him into the perpendicular. He lent into the breeze in a desperate effort to gain additional support.

'Okay, Jammy, let go.'

As soon as Mick's foot touched the ground he thought a red-hot poker had been thrust through his knee. Pain had rapidly overhauled the anaesthesia of adrenalin. He collapsed again.

'Bernardo,' said Brit, solemnly. 'You're fucked!'

Mick didn't hear him. He was writhing like a dying fly. Two St Johns' Ambulance-men appeared with a stretcher. They conveyed him across the pitch amid sympathetic applause and by the time they reached the pavilion steps the agony of the injury had been superseded by the agony of its implications. If his knee was as wrecked as it felt he'd never be fit for the Varsity Match.

Ken Porter, Hon Physiotherapist to the squad, small of stature and kind of face, was there to meet him. 'Okay, Mick, try to relax,' he muttered as he guided him from stretcher to treatment table. 'Let's take a look.'

Porter removed Mick's right boot and rolled down the sock. The hands that invariably healed, gently moved from calf to knee and then from thigh to knee. Mick flinched. Then as Porter slowly ran his fingers over the kneecap the hundred hot needles suddenly pricking the inside of his knee lifted Mick off the table. Nausea swamped him. He knew what Porter was going to say before the words left the physio's mouth.

'Sorry, Mick,' said Porter, softly, cognizant of the blow he was about to deliver, the kind he hated being forced to give a young sportsmen. 'Your medial ligament's gone. May have snapped. Or it might just be pulled off the bone…'

'How long will I be out?'

'You can forget this season. Even with an op you'd need months of rehab. ..'

Mick felt like punching God on the jaw but had to make do with flinging his boot across the room and hammering his head back against the table: 'Shit!'

'Might be best to forget an op and put your faith in an injury's two best friends – Doctor Time and Nurse Patience. Let's take another look when this initial swelling goes down a bit.'

The dressing room door opened and a grim-faced Wyn James entered. One glance at Mick confirmed the worst. 'It's bad, isn't it?'

Mick couldn't speak. Porter nodded.

'This sport can be so cruel,' said James, putting a hand on Mick's shoulder. 'Let's get you into the bath…'

'There's no water in it yet,' mumbled Mick. 'Just get me out of here. I don't want to be here when the lads come back.'

'Okay. My car's parked across the road. Bill Lander brought the boys down on the bus. I'll bring it into the players car park. And get you home…'

'No, not home,' said Mick, urgently. 'My digs in Warneford Road.'

'Okay. I'll be back as soon as I can.'

'Let's get your kit together,' said Porter as James disappeared.

Mick rose unsteadily to his feet, putting all his weight on his one good leg, and peeled off his blue jersey now grubby with mud and sweat. He dropped it onto the treatment table then, pursing his lips, picked it up again. Soiled as it was, he folded it neatly and placed it in the centre of the table with the 9 on display, just as he'd found it an hour or so ago. After one last wistful look round the dressing room Mick Bernard said a quiet goodbye to his OURFC career.

Porter handed Mick his jacket and a shoulder to lean on. 'I've packed everything into your duffel bag, your boots and the rest of you clothes. Get into a bath straight away, not too hot. Then put something cold on the knee. A bag of frozen peas, a cold flannel, anything cold will do.'

Mick hobbled a couple of steps, wincing over each: getting him to the car park wasn't going to be easy. 'I'll see if I can find a walking stick,' said Porter. 'Or there'll be a set of crutches somewhere.'

The image of him hobbling away from Oxford rugby like a cripple cut Mick to the bone. But before he could protest, James was by his side. 'I've got as close as I could. Can you manage 50 yards if me and Ken support a shoulder each?'

Mick nodded. But the pain, mental as well as physical, proved too much. He slumped backwards onto the treatment table.

'Right,' said James. 'I'll carry you. Ken, hold the door open.'

'No, please, I don't want people seeing me like this…'

'They won't. They'll be looking the other way, at the game.'

James gently swept Mick up into his arms and carried him like a baby through the pavilion and out to his car. Mick heard the crowd burst into life with a round of applause and wondered if he'd ever again receive such approval. He stretched out as best he could manage on the back seat without feeling the need to urge his leg be amputated on the spot. Ten minutes later James carried him up the stairs of his digs and oversaw him getting in and out of the bath without further damage. Then he went downstairs, returning, courtesy of Mrs Barnes, with a bucket.

'I'll be back tomorrow morning and take you to Ken's surgery,' said James. 'You've got a flannel and a towel and plenty of cold water. Your landlady knows the situation and says she'll check on you now and then.'

Mick forced an 'Okay.'

'I know things look bleak at this moment,' said James, on the point of leaving. 'But you'll be back. You've overcome greater hurdles than this one. It's a setback, and it'll hurt for a while, probably a long while. But you've got the character to beat this.'

James looked his protégé in the eyes for confirmation. But found what every wounded sportsman carries inside him. He'd dislocated his own shoulder enough times to know precisely what was running through Mick's mind. Would he ever get back to playing; and if he did, would he ever regain the level of performance that had made him into a 'sore throat' player?

No day could get darker than this one. The stark realization that his dream lay in tatters surged up Mick's backbone to emerge as hot tears which scalded his eyeballs. All the years of work wiped out in less than ten seconds. That Stanley's ground down the resistance of their 14 opponents to win courtesy of a flurry of late points barely registered on Mick. Nor did Porter's words on assessing the damage to the knee 24 hours later because he knew in his heart Porter's initial prognosis would be confirmed. Mick was offered the chance to accompany the Blues to Twickenham but he'd no stomach for it. The pain of loss was more than his soul could tolerate. The sight of someone else getting what he'd wanted so badly was always going to be a sight too far.

Cambridge won the match. But Mick Bernard didn't give a hoot.

Seven

Mick's last chance to win his Blue had vanished as quickly as the ensuing seven months brought Finals closer and closer. There was also the little matter of his parents' 25th wedding anniversary that was to be celebrated by a party at the Hill Rise Community Centre. Mick wasn't sure which of the two ordeals was the more horrendous prospect. The latter would place in one room almost every family foe: Mick knew he'd discover how Daniel must've felt. At least he could prepare a mite better for the former, daunting though it was. Finals involved ten papers of three hours duration with barely any respite: two papers per day – Thursday, Friday, Saturday, Monday, Tuesday.

Revision was all the harder for Mick because he'd no love for the material he must spend the first six weeks of Trinity Term absorbing. He planned a daily programme of three sessions: a good 2½ hours every weekday morning in the New Bodleian, packed to the gunnels with anxious, like-minded, undergraduates in the clutch of pre-Schools panic, was his key session; an hour after tea; and finally two hours after dinner. The strategy was to read everything initially with the aim of reducing it by degrees to a sheet or two of key points for each paper that ultimately could be scanned in the hours prior to each one or, since Clifton insisted material studied before sleep tended to stick in the mind, last thing the night before. He was prepared to, and needed to, clutch at any straw. Afternoons were optional. If he did revise after lunch he'd ditch one of the later sessions. This seemed unlikely since he'd never worked during the afternoon in his entire academic life. It was always sport. He couldn't commit to rowing this summer but the occasional game of tennis against other incompetent players on the College court in the Parks would provide a welcome release. Nor had he ever worked on a Saturday, but Saturday morning would be obligatory. Sundays were Sundays: very optional indeed. Whether Mick could stick to this routine for six weeks troubled him. Moreover, there was no Sam Owens to whom he could go for consolation.

On the Sunday preceding the start of Finals Mick ran up the white flag: the pulsating cold sore on his upper lip told him mind and body needed respite. He pushed the books and folders of essays aside. Nor could he face the traditional Norham Gardens soiree designed to lift the spirits of impending Schools where his fellow geographers would be trying, and probably failing, as he knew he would, to mask their dread of 30 hours of imminent inquisition by getting quietly and quickly sloshed on Tulloch's sherry. He decided to ring home, asked if he might come to lunch and, eagerly granted permission, hobbled down Magdalen Road to catch a Number 3 bus to Hill Rise.

His knee had mended sufficiently to walk free of pain but not without a slight limp. Every yard up the hill from the bus stop toward home seemed progressively slower and forced. And the problem wasn't confined to his knee. His heart was saying something to his feet that the brain had yet to ascertain. Instead of heading for the front gate he entered the telephone box on the corner. His mother wasn't best pleased to hear of his sudden heavy cold but her son's acting was proficient. Mick came out of the box and stood for a second with arms akimbo, filling his lungs with the cool air of a summer's day. He hit upon an alternative plan; and continued limping up the hill toward Iffley.

It took Mick twice as long as normal to pass the squat tower of Iffley's Norman church that drew visitors from all over the country to view the elaborate Romanesque carvings decorating its doorways. Peter Clifton's whitewashed cottage was a little farther down Church Way, the end one of three lying under a long dun-coloured thatch on the corner of Mill Lane. Through the familiar forest of crimson hollyhocks and purple delphiniums Mick spied his mentor crouched over the rockery beside the door.

'Need a hand, sir?'

Clifton's mouth broke into that knowing smile he used to allow himself whenever one of his pupils stated the obvious or genuinely touched his funny bone. Mick loved to draw it from him and regarded it as an accolade: it did not really qualify as a smile, thought Mick, more of a nod in the direction of amusement.

'I daresay a beer would suit you better?' said Clifton. 'Fetch a couple from the fridge and we can sit out here, make the most of this beautiful day. Bottle-opener in the first drawer to the left of the sink.'

'Yes, I remember from the last visit,' replied Mick. He was less convinced of the day's beauty but did as he was bid. They clinked bottles and sat down on the doorstep to drink. With each swig their expressions grew more serious.

Clifton was first to break the silence. 'So, Michael, excuse my bluntness but what is it that you want to talk about? Something's worrying you or you wouldn't waste precious revision time with Finals coming up by visiting the likes of me!'

Mick shrugged. Clifton was never a man to be fooled.

'I was so sorry to hear about the severity of your injury.'

'Yes, it was a bugger!'

'I was there…'

'Really?'

'I'd not have missed the match for the world because I knew I'd be unable to get to Twickenham for the Varsity Match and this would be my last opportunity to watch you play in that blue jersey you'd set your heart on wearing.'

Clifton waited for a reaction but none came.

'And missing your Blue in those circumstances…'

'Aah,' Mick said, threatening the delphiniums with the sweep of a hand. 'It's all done with now.'

Clifton's lips pursed. 'But I can see there's something else on your mind.'

Mick started to mouth a reply but knew something more than waffle was necessary when talking with his mentor. He collected his thoughts.

'It's this whole Oxford thing that's got to me. Missing a Blue, which is what the whole exercise was about, brought it all home to me. What was I thinking of? Now, here I am about to sit Finals in a subject I've no love for. At College I'm a token "Townie". And at home I'm the hate figure that spells "Gown." Am I nuts because it feels like it at times?'

'Certainly not…'

'Then I must be one of those poor sods who can't fit in. Who thinks differently, and what he thinks important is different to what other people think is important. But why should I conform to what other people think? My view might be just as right as their view. Perhaps more so! And I'm bloody positive I can't be the only one who thinks they way I do!'

'I can assure you, Michael, you're not alone in feeling this way. Individuals of strong character and opinions can't avoid feeling isolated. Their very strength can act as their Achilles heel.'

Mick sighed. 'All I feel certain about is that I shouldn't have bothered with Oxford.'

'But, Michael, you set yourself a target, one you knew from the outset would be difficult to achieve. You won a place at one of the world's elite universities and you did it on your own terms, with only the minimum of assistance from others.'

'No doubt it might've been easier had I won that place at Atlantic College.'

Clifton pondered what he was minded to say. 'But you did win that place…'

'What?' said Mick, fixing Clifton with eyes that demanded the truth and nothing but the truth. 'Did I hear you right, sir?'

'I've often thought you should've been told at the outset,' Clifton replied, adopting a serious face.

'Then, why wasn't I?'

'Well,' continued Clifton slowly, 'your parents asked to see Jack as soon as they received the letter offering you the place. He saw them straight away and, not to put too fine a point on it, he could sense they never wanted you to go in the first place but had said nothing because they never expected you to be chosen.'

'Why didn't they want me to go,' Mick blurted out. 'They knew how much getting into Oxford meant to me and they knew, because I explained it to them, how a place at Atlantic College would've given me the necessary leg-up.'

Mick clawed the air in front of his face in frustration. The song of a blackbird was all that broke the silence for some seconds. Clifton sipped his beer.

'Your mother told Jack that if you left home for Atlantic College they were afraid they'd lose you…'

'Lose me! Lose me to what?'

'The outside world, an academic and social world of which they knew nothing. And knowing nothing of it, made them frightened of it. And consequently what it might do to you.'

Mick placed his bottle carefully on the doorstep for fear he might smash it to smithereens, 'In other words, they betrayed me.'

'That's maybe a trifle harsh.'

'No, betrayal's the word I'd choose from the *Thesaurus*! They'd done it before, or should I say, my mother had done it before…'

'How so?'

Clifton listened to Mick pulling his demons from the closet one by one. When Mick had finished he patted his troubled visitor's wrist and felt the radial vein pumping against his fingertips. He searched for meaningful words to express his compassion but found only a mouth as dry as an empty bottle of martini.

'I'm having this out with them!' said Mick. 'What I'll say will be ugly but I deserve to say it and they deserve to hear it!'

'Michael, stop chasing the mice in your skull!' Clifton said eventually, tightening his grip on Mick's wrist. 'Think how this would affect them? It would destroy them.'

'They did their best to destroy me, destroy my chances…'

Clifton continued to employ the stern expression of mentor, confessor and surrogate father. 'But, Michael, you're better than this. It would be petty and spiteful. You know neither of your parents is capable of responding to the kind of invective you'd employ. Think of the effect it would have on the future for your family…'

Mick tipped his head back and laughed. 'My family? What family? We're three people who happen to share the same name and the same house. To my mother I'm something to parade before people she calls friends. To my father…'

'He was always so proud of you,' Clifton interjected. 'I saw him at the Stanley's match. Seldom did I see a prouder parent at Iffley Road than your father.'

Mick's mouth fell open. 'Pity he never expressed an opinion on my rugby career. Or, come to that, bothered to tell me he was at Stanley's!'

'He and I discussed that very thing one Saturday afternoon at an earlier match and he explained how he didn't want to risk putting you off your game by telling you he was going to watch.'

'There, see what I mean? There's absolutely no communication in our family! My father will happily sit shuffling in his armchair, staring blankly, willing me to conduct both sides of a conversation, providing answers to my own questions and reading his thoughts to avoid the strain of expressing them himself.'

'But don't ever forget you must've seemed, by your achievements, some superior being from another planet to your father. Perhaps it was up to you to extend the hand, and guide communication between you.'

'I tell myself that, I really do. But, damn it, he is my father. He's the head of the family and should take responsibility, whether he likes it or not. Do you know, he never once physically chastised me, not even when I was a poorly behaved kid.'

'Nothing wrong with that. The belt is no cure…'

'I tend to think it would have done our relationship a power of good had he administered a stroke or two. I've certainly given him plenty of excuses. I'd have respected him far more had he taken the slipper to me when I disrespected him. But he didn't. And so we Bernards just dodder on, existing in our individual boxes! Freud would need a decade to sort us out!'

'If there was some way I could help, I would gladly…'

'You are, sir,' Mick said softly. 'You're listening. I must talk to someone or I fear I'll lose my mind completely.'

Clifton stood up, his lips white with the shock of listening to his disciple spout such irresponsible nonsense. 'Don't talk like that

Michael! Never wish your life away, not on any account. You were not taught to treat life, or yourself, so lightly.'

Mick ran his hands through his hair, feeling as though Clifton had awarded him a detention for impertinence. Why, he asked himself, was he plagued by this destructive knack of lashing out and hurting people? Why was there only black and white on his emotional palette?

Neither he nor Clifton came up with answers to these questions before Mick limped off in the direction of the Cowley Road. His parents' anniversary party might degenerate into a bloodbath. After five weeks of tedious revision topped by Clifton's revelation he knew he was feeling tetchier than a rhino with piles.

***

Despite it being a warm June evening the wooden walls of the Community Centre gave off a suitably cold atmosphere. A motley collection of home-made decorations had been put up in an effort to bring cheer to a cheerless space: some paper chains that hadn't disintegrated over Christmas and a banner stating 'Happy 25th Anniversary' hanging across one corner. Tables lined the walls, leaving a large area for dancing. Glenn Miller was blaring from a record player but no one had as yet accepted the challenge of tripping the light fantastic. Mick's gaze roamed the room with growing alarm. His allies were missing: no Uncle Ern from his mother's side and no Uncle Ben from his father's. But all the enemies were out in force, led by his mother's three brothers Reg, Alec and Gilbert, each with their Gorgons in tow, snakes squirming on their heads in search of a victim. When they spotted him, Mick swore he could hear the serpents hissing.

It needed no stretch of Mick's imagination for him to know what they were saying to each other as he ran the gauntlet. 'We're honoured! Look who's here!' Reg would be telling Alec.

'Slummin' it t'noight, aint he? Alec would be saying to Gilbert. 'To think,' Gilbert would chip in, 'we fought a war fer kids like 'im!'

Mick saw them start to chuckle. 'Woss that on 'is nose, a peg ennit?' Gilbert would be adding. 'The smell of decent workin' folk gets roight up 'is 'ooter otherwise!' would be Reg's next quip, swiftly endorsed by Alec's 'He dunt even talk loik us no more.'

Mick couldn't lip read well enough to know whether his guesses were anywhere near accurate but he shot them a look that would freeze hell all the same. Their very presence reminded him how much he'd changed in three short years. If they considered him an outcast when he was an 18-year-old grammar school boy they must think him a Martian nowadays. The most obvious change, he freely acknowledged, was him no longer speaking like a rustic from the cast of *The Archers*. This change epitomized the raft of social adjustments he was obliged to make to stay afloat at St Frideswide's: drinking claret besides lager; preferring tournedos to sausages and lemon soufflé over rhubarb pie; rowing past Long Bridges in a racing eight instead of swimming there; playing squash instead of drinking it. His introduction to fine dining, cocktail parties and summer balls was summed up by the inevitable purchase of his own dinner suit.

No tuxedo was needed for tonight's party. He was only present by default: a dummy dressed in his clothes would've sufficed – and might've been a better option because his presence was fragile. He was surrounded by living testimony to what he'd left behind: people who were willing and able to heap opprobrium on him if he gave them the slightest opportunity. He decided to banish all thought of the Jaykes and to get through this ordeal by inhabiting a plastic bubble. So he stood there with the liveliness of a skeleton exposing angry bones. He got himself a bottle of Mackeson at the free bar ('Sorry, sir, no lager or wine.') and made for the table occupied by Roy's younger sister Jen and her husband Ted, a decent cricketer and an affable sort – but, of course, Ted was family by marriage and not an authentic Bernard. Mick sat down and began asking Ted his opinion of the current England cricket team. The conversation was soon interrupted.

'There you are!' cried Edna Bernard, wobbling toward her son with a port-and-lemon in her hand that was clearly not her first of the evening. She had clearly made an enormous effort with her appearance for this auspicious occasion. She was, Mick decided, trying desperately to remind everyone how she'd once been quite a beauty. But beautiful old women, in his experience, were rarities and his mother hadn't bucked the trend. The remnants of a beauty that once entranced Roy Bernard might be discerned by detailed study; but the brown eyes that sparkled with life had retreated into their sockets and the porcelain skin was stretched over the cheekbones like so much aged parchment; her hair was neatly coiffed and held in place by plenty of hairspray; and her dress was the green silk sheath with the Chinese adornments that Roy had bought her one Christmas. However, despite the application of Yardley's Lily of the Valley, Mick's overriding sensory perception was of stale cigarette smoke.

'What you doin' hidin' over here? Come an' see your dad. He reckoned you wouldn't show up. I told 'im you wouldn't be so 'oity-toity as t'let your old mother down.'

'I wouldn't dream of ignoring a party like this. Congratulations!' Edna took her son's arm and shepherded him to a table.

'How are you gettin' on? Workin' 'ard, I 'ope. I'll be so proud when you gets that Oxford d'gree. First d'gree in the whole fam'ly!'

'Really?' said Mick, edgily. 'Are you sure my getting into Oxford and getting an Oxford degree means much to you?'

'Wos that s'posed to mean?'

'Tell me,' Mick said, icily, 'about Atlantic College?'

Edna steadied herself and sipped her drink. 'What 'bout it?'

'Tell me about the letter you received from the Oxfordshire Education Authority concerning my application for a place.'

'Well, they said you 'adn't got it, the schol'ship.'

'You're positive about that?' snarled Mick, loudly enough for emphasis but not so as flapping ears nearby might pick up the message. 'Because I'm not so sure. I have it on impeccable authority that I won the place and that you turned it down.'

Edna slumped into the nearest chair. Clifton was correct: she'd no suitable words with which to fight her corner. She looked everywhere other than into her son's eyes now ablaze with nothing less than hatred and felt herself being squeezed to death.

'You knew perfectly well the place at Atlantic College was my best chance of getting into Oxford but…'

'But you did get into Oxford! We knew y'would if y'set your heart on it.'

'Bullshit!' spat Mick. 'And don't try pulling me up for bad language because that cuts no ice with me anymore! Just admit what you did. That's all I ask. Just admit you made a conscious decision to block my ambitions for your own ends.'

'It wornt loik…'

'No excuses!'

Mick saw his father approaching, also on unsteady legs, pint of Double Diamond in hand.

'Wos goin' on?' he said, eyes going from wife to son and back again.

'Congratulations!' Mick said, offering a handshake. 'How on earth have you managed to put up with her for 25 years?'

Roy Bernard laughed. The sly expression on his face suggested he knew his son's question carried sarcastic intent but on a day like this he thought he'd licence to laugh at its veracity and get away with it. 'Sorted a job out yet?'

'He'll 'ave eyes on summat grand, I bet,' ventured Edna, giving her best impression of a contented wife and mother who'd not been crucified by the previous exchanges. 'Well-paid job in town an' no mistake.'

Mick sipped his Mackeson and then inhaled: he'd let Edna tell Roy the cat was out of the bag concerning Atlantic College if she so desired. Common sense rarely laid its finger on her, he mused, but if this was one of those occasions and she kept Roy in the dark so much the better because he certainly wasn't going to make his father's life any more miserable than it already was by accusing him of being complicit in Edna's betrayal.

But this was as good a time as any to reveal his plans. 'I have had some thoughts,' he began haughtily, aware that the truth was going to provoke a reaction out of keeping with a celebration.

'Tell us, then?' said Edna.

'Dunt keep us in suspenders!' said Roy.

'A College pal has got me a job offer…'

'Thass marv'lous!' said Edna.

'In Leicester.'

Edna and Roy looked at each other as though a bonfire had been lit under their feet.

'His parents own an antiquarian bookshop,' explained Mick, 'and they're looking for someone to ease the burden.'

'You're goin' to sell books!' said Edna, voice rising with incredulity.

'Not just selling books. Cataloguing them and travelling around to antique auctions and country-house sales in search of bargains to convert into valuable stock.'

His mother's voice became shrill. 'You dunt need a d'gree for that! Whoever heard of an Oxford graduate wastin' his ed'cation on sellin' books for a livin'!'

'There's another consideration,' Mick continued, looking toward his father. 'Leicester has a top-class rugby club, one of the best in the country. Once my knee has recovered I'm going to join them and see how far up the ladder I can get.'

Roy quaffed his beer, steeling himself for the repercussions of what he was about to say. 'I wish you luck. Can't say I understand the blasted game but you're good at it, thass the main thing. Good luck, son.'

'Thanks,' said Mick. And offered his hand. Roy grasped it enthusiastically. At that instant, father and son enjoyed a millisecond of empathy and bonding each felt ought to have come sooner rather than mark a farewell.

Edna was greeting the news with less generosity. 'All my sacrifices for nuthin'? He might as well do it prop'ly, jus' kick me up the arse an' have done with it!'

'Edna, the boy has to do what he feels roight,' said Roy.

'Too roight!' snapped Edna, brushing aside her husband's consoling arm. 'Only thinks 'bout himself! Always thinkin' o'number one!'

'Look,' said Mick. 'It's not settled yet. It's just a possibility, that's all. Something of a safety net. The job, and the move, has a lot in its favour. But I've not agreed to it yet.'

Edna had heard quite enough. The lump in her throat was nothing compared to the lump threatening to explode from her chest. Her heart was too old for this battering; too exhausted to put it through this degree of anguish again; too shattered to expect yet one more recovery. If she didn't find something to occupy her quickly she knew tears would fall and their burn would simply make matters worse. She marched over to the upright piano next to the bar, plonked her port-and-lemon on its top, and began thumping out *Over the Rainbow*. When it came to fight or flight with her son nowadays there was only one choice.

'She'll get over it,' said Roy, watching his wife's party piece. 'I'd prefer you round the place but if y'gotta go…'

Mick appreciated Roy's comment was the nearest to a declaration of love he'd ever received from him. Like a drowning man seeing his life flash before him he was suddenly assailed by a kaleidoscope of images: he and Roy chuckling at the hapless antics of WC Fields; skimming competitive stones across the Thames; watching Eddy railing like a good 'un to land bets and a tankard; sharing tea and toast in the kitchen of a bitter winter dawn. Mick was surprised to feel a genuine smile creasing his face. Probably for the first time in his life he succumbed to quiet admiration for his father: not only for the pluck he'd shown in the war but also the pluck he'd shown throughout 25 years of marriage. It took a special brand of courage to go to war, to endure combat and live with the horrors of so doing. Roy was no eager volunteer but accepted the burden placed on him by his country without complaint and did his duty. He received three medals for that display of fortitude but received none for displaying similar fortitude during his marriage – for which Mick felt he merited a Victoria Cross.

Son watched father wander across to Uncle Ted, Woodbine cupped in the palm of his hand behind his back, and start an arm-waving conversation that no doubt conveyed the latest news about himself. He tried to catch his mother's eye but she continued hammering the keys as though they were Norma Dowler's ribs and refused to acknowledge him. Mick sank the last of his Mackeson and made for the exit, his mother's version of *Over the Rainbow* assaulting his ears. He shook his head and had to smile.

'There he goes!' muttered Reg as Mick walked past. 'Had 'is fill of the common folk! Surprised he managed to last an hour! Gramma school! Oxford Un'versity! Bugger 'em!'

Mick couldn't resist putting Uncle Reg back in his box. 'At least my grammar school taught me more than Milham Ford taught your Jean,' he said with a grin. 'It should've taught her how to keep her legs together!'

Uncle Reg spluttered so much it gave Mick hope he might be having a heart attack. How he'd grown to hate all these naysayers and saloon-bar critics. The very thought of them and the bile they'd spewed at him over the years fuelled him into a limp-free walk through Cowley until he found refuge in his digs 40 minutes away.

***

Mick flopped down on his bed. He'd decisions to make that had enormous ramifications. He must pick his way through this minefield alone; just like he had back in his Hill Rise bedroom as a teenager. He ordered himself to examine what he'd done, achieved and wrecked; to drag brutally honest judgements from the darkest dungeon of his soul. The task wasn't as hard as he thought. His self-obsessed world was, after all, a small one, its four walls comprised of an Oxford degree in History, a Blue, a future as a military historian, and the affection of Sam Owens. But those walls were tumbling as fast as Jericho's at the sound of Joshua's trumpets.

The positive column was easy to complete. He'd perfected his ability to box-kick a rugby ball to land on a dustbin lid. He'd acquired a taste for coffee, gin-and-tonic, wine of any colour, curry, steak, fish other than cod or pilchards; plus social graces and table manners enabling him to mix in any company. Mick asked himself: did these trivial attainments really amount to much, amount to anything that really mattered in life? Did they bring happiness? At specific moments in time, yes, they had. Being happy, Mick decided, was a transitory emotion: he could be happy one moment having launched a terrific box-kick only to be unhappy a minute later by spilling the ball with the try line at his mercy. It seemed to him dangerous to attach happiness, like sadness, disappointment and every other emotion, to an entire lifespan, even to his relatively short 21 years. To put this conundrum another way: did these attainments bring peace of mind? In his current mood the answer came easily: they did not.

What of the negative column. This list, he confessed, could be as long as Britt's arm. Did he only think about 'Number One', as his mother asserted? He was forced to admit she had a point. He preferred to say he was self-obsessed. The only path to achieving his aims was to adopt tunnel vision, pursue them in blinkers; all else, and everyone else, had to be shut out. He reasoned this was the best way of maximizing the modicum of talent at his disposal. A more cavalier attitude was doomed to failure: spreading his energies more evenly would not have worked for him. Judging how to allocate those precious resources would've driven him to a worse place than he currently inhabited. He'd never have coped.

What of the second charge on the indictment according to kith and kin: class traitor? He had chosen his own path, determined his own experiences and rejected those of his parents. He had not compromised: he believed it was better to please a few individuals a great deal rather than try to please all the people just a little which, he was obliged to admit, was a possible mistake because his highbrow aspirations had come to hover over him like a railway signal waiting to drop. Every move made, expression given or remark uttered had come to be scrutinized for the opportunity to criticize, the chance to scoff. And all three areas yielded enough evidence to prove the charge: Oxford University had forged a character more aloof, more egotistical and more sarcastic than the one who'd left South Oxford three years ago. Those moves, expressions and utterances also came under scrutiny at College. He'd kept the real Mick Bernard under lock and key at St Frideswide's: no talk of Nissen huts and sink council estates to tarnish his image. Survival depended on Mick's alter ego, the rugby player whose talent lifted him above the herd and won respect. The real Mick Bernard was locked away like *The Man in the Iron Mask.* Yet the mask was brittle, and often transparent. They say it's possible to take the boy out of the ghetto. Mick could vouch for that. But it's a tougher proposition excising the ghetto from the man. And he could vouch for that as well. It had been his lot to experience the class system at the closest of quarters, from the top and the bottom, and it brought nothing but anguish. In College he was at the base of the social heap and looked down on by 'Gown', confronted by a social barrier he found impossible to scale. Eight weeks later, at home, he was regarded as atop the heap and castigated for looking down on 'Town', the despised Oxford undergrad who elicited more suspicion and jealousy than familial pride. It struck Mick as if the only things he had in common with each end of this social spectrum were the elements each disliked in the other, which left him at odds with both ends of the social hierarchy, wondering which way to turn. Perhaps, after all, he'd have been better served by a job on the Cowley line and football on a Saturday followed by a bellyful of beer in the pub.

At school Mick had numerous pals and knew he was genuinely popular. In College he made few friends and never felt popular or especially well liked. And of one thing he was adamant: he'd failed lamentably to connect his two lives, the one in 'Gown' and the other in 'Town', to any mutual benefit and as a result he'd been sentenced to wriggle on a pin of his own making. Any guilt he felt from betraying his class, or injustice he suffered from a Killip in College or an Uncle Reg at home, consequently might flare with the speed of a struck match into a self-destructive conflagration over which he had no control. He'd come to realize why it's often said one should beware of what we wish for. Like the Flying Dutchman, Mick was forced to conclude he'd no port to call home.

Hill Rise was definitely no port in a storm. He could see the breakdown in his relationship with his mother ensured that. Where the fault lay was of no consequence anymore. Mick acknowledged Edna's contribution: she came to the rescue with encyclopedias and contact lenses, to name two vital instances. But these were material gifts. What she demanded in return was emotional. He'd long since reached the conclusion his mother believed they'd entered upon some form of Faustian pact wherein his role was to give an infinite display of love, respect and admiration he knew he could never deliver. Yet he acknowledged her to have been the most important woman in his life; more important than Granny Jaykes, Martha Gibson or even Sam Owens. Though not, he pondered, necessarily for all the best reasons. Perhaps the term most befitting her impact on his life was 'significant' rather than 'important'. Her contribution was not always for the good. But there was no scintilla of doubt in his mind that she'd left her mark on him. Tenacity and industry (in areas he enthused about); a hatred of injustice. However, plenty of the marks she inflicted left permanent scars: intolerance; impatience. These wounds wept poison. They festered. Their ugliness was not always visible. But their role in Mick's psyche he acknowledged as undeniable.

Perhaps, he pondered, these judgements were too savage. Edna and Roy were ill-equipped to nurture a son who saw his future at an Oxford college rather than cutting trim or wielding a paint gun on the Cowley assembly lines. They were hostages to their time, their upbringing, and they could only raise a child as they'd been raised. They couldn't be held responsible for their circumstances. Yet nor did they seek alternatives. And they could be held responsible for that. Their way hinged on a blinkered observance of a set of principles owing more to austerity and authority than the individual needs of their child. The raw material was not moulded to maximum benefit. The raw material was crushed to fit the mould. And fear was the bludgeon: one had to be afraid of mother and father as with every other authority figure.

So Mick sought another way to describe his mother's role in his life: she'd coloured his life. Yes, he decided, that had merit. But the colour in question came to him with as much alacrity as its perverse clarity. That colour was black. Mick experienced as many nips from 'black dog' as Churchill. At this very moment of introspection he could smell the beast's hot breath as his thoughts began racing quickly toward the self-destructive. All of a sudden he began to consider man's immortality.

It's often said one should hold no fear of death; Mick saw the logic in that. We return from whence we came: so it's not exactly unknown territory. The endless sleep: nothing horrendously daunting in that. It is the process of dying that's the problem. We can't all be blessed with a speedy departure, from heart attack, stroke or some other whim of God. For the majority, the likes of me, thought Mick, the finger of fate points in another direction. The prospect of a lingering farewell during which one's quality of life deteriorates to the brink of extinction seems agonizing enough without the possible bonus of facing this slow demise in the grip of some painful disease.

Mick knew he was flirting with dangerous subject. But his mind was on a roll, a steeply inclined downward one, and he couldn't halt the snowball. When will that last breath be drawn? When will the last mouthful of food be chewed, the last drink swallowed? The last enjoyment of anything Mick cared to name: pass, kick, kiss, cuddle, fuck? It's the waiting around that hurts. When the final hand of cards has been dealt; when there's hardly anything worth getting out of bed for; when something as simple as eating and drinking what he liked, whenever he liked, is banned utterly. Then he could imagine pleading for death to call. Yet, even then, he imagined a small voice reminding him: don't stop playing until you must. You're a long time retired; keep going until you can't! Sound advice when it comes to playing sport; sounder still when calling time on life. You're a long time retired when you're dead.

The black hole that Mick freely acknowledged was awaiting him wouldn't seem so black if there was someone around to tell him what it's really like. Lacking any such insight left Mick wondering whether death is the feeling he had before he was born. In other words, there is no feeling. The experience of birth and death are the same: neither can be described to others. Of course, that didn't matter so much before he was born because he had no point of reference with which to compare. Life gave him that. Indeed, had he some foresight into what life was going to offer, he argued, quite possibly he'd have preferred not to have been born in the first place.

Mick convinced himself the only way of ensuring death comes where and when one wishes is to arrange it oneself: a country lane; brandy; pills. A few extra days or weeks incarcerated in a hospital or care-home were not worth the struggle. Expiring in one's own sheets surrounded by wife and children seems preferable to us all. But how practicable is it, how selfish is it, to crave such an indulgence from those who have to undertake the death watch? The one thing he did know for certain was that every human must handle death alone. Whether surrounded by loved ones or no-one, each of us dies in our own arms.

This getting of wisdom was painful, decided Mick, and had taken 21 years to acquire. This stranger to outward displays of affection had withdrawn into himself and become emotionally self-reliant. He knew what it was like to stand alone and what inner strength was necessary so to do. The emotional walls he constructed around him were nigh impenetrable. For this mental toughness he could thank she who'd unwittingly instilled it in him: his mother, Edna Bernard.

Mick's gaze came to rest on the two paperbacks he'd lately added to his library. They were the two Hardy novels recommended by Clifton for their depictions of rural life during and after the agrarian revolution. Jude Fawley, the stonemason who aspired to be a scholar at Christminster died without realizing this ambition or any romantic contentment with Sue Bridehead, his beau ideal and personal Sam Owens. Mick stretched out a hand but his fingers bypassed Hardy's last novel and picked out *The Mayor Casterbridge* instead. Michael Henchard, the mayor of the title, and as tragic a figure as Jude Fawley, died alone after writing his own epitaph. Mick went straight to the page and read the baleful passage for the hundreth time. Then he found pad and pen. And following some minutes of cogitation he composed similar lines for himself:

I could be self-reliant yet insecure;
I could be insightful yet intolerant;
I could be humorous yet hateful.
I could be self-obsessed yet thoughtful;
I succeeded and I messed up;
I beat the odds and I self-destructed.
I loved and I lost.
This was me.

He read the lines again, considering each word according to the Clifton law. He decided he'd written a load of pretentious twaddle. It might be okay for Hardy to grant Michael Henchard the privilege of composing his own epitaph but for Michael Bernard to do so was sheer conceit. Hardy gave Henchard a tumultuous life that merited introspection. Michael Bernard was just a stripling of 21 years. He'd neither sold a wife nor betrayed a daughter like the guilt-ridden Henchard. He was just a frustrated young man unable to treat the minor obstacles fate had put in his path with anything other than anger. He screwed up the paper and kicked it across the room.

Then he stood up, rolled his shoulders to ease away the strain from his bones and rubbed his temples to rid them of the emotion swirling beneath. He turned out the light and attempted to turn off his thoughts, longing for sleep. Slumber came but was cruelly and quickly curtailed when he woke in a muck sweat. The more he fought for sleep the more elusive it became and eventually he forsook the sweaty prison of the sheets to pace the room. He was sure he could see Sam Owens reclining on the end of the bed teasing him with her warm smile and her soft body. She reached out a hand to bring him to her but just as cruelly and quickly the siren faded away. He got back into bed, turning the pillow repeatedly in search of a cool spot, and rearranged the tangled sheets. Sleep came in short bursts. Yet peace came there none. And he woke in a semaphore of arms and legs.

Eight

Mick rose early, by his standards, at 8.30 the following Thursday and shook the cobwebs out of his head. After completing his ablutions at a leisurely pace he addressed the not inconsequential matter of his apparel for the day ahead in the Examination Schools. Mick wanted to look the part of an eager 'Schools Man' even if he considered the chances of him acting the part successfully seemed slim. He took the spotlessly clean white shirt that had been hanging in the wardrobe waiting for this day and slipped it on. Then he fastened the white bow tie around his neck. On went the trousers of his grey suit followed by the jacket. The gown and mortar board that completed his *subfusc,* unworn since Prelims two years back, he elected to carry as he didn't wish to have the piss taken out of him when walking down the Cowley Road into town. He slid his pencil case into a jacket pocket and left. He stopped at the corner shop at the end of the road to buy a packet of Jaffa Cakes which he'd consumed by the time he crossed the Plain.

At 9.45 Mick joined Swaby, Dashwood and the other 70-odd geographers jammed into the vestibule of the Examination Schools craning necks and straining eyes to find out which hall they were allocated to and what desk number. The vast 'Jacobethan' pile that was about to become his torture chamber was opened in 1882; as he'd entered Mick had stared frostily at the carved panel over the portico depicting an undergraduate being hit over the head by a book that seemed a unnecessary harbinger of the Armageddon possibly lying in wait. The atmosphere was febrile, a raucous blend of nerves and excitement. The melee would've done justice to a game of British Bulldog in the gym because the building comprised several halls and Finals in the School of Jurisprudence were taking place simultaneously. It seemed perfectly feasible for the unwary examinee to be lifted off his or her feet and carried up the staircase into the examination hall without touching *terra firma.*

Mick found his desk. The ink blots and occasional cries of despair daubed upon it ('For God's sake how many votes lost the first Home Rule Bill') spoke ominously of memory lapses by previous incumbents. The hall's high ceiling was matched by its tall windows flooding the hall with enlightenment that the examiners, Mick pondered, might hope would dispel dimness and promote intellectual illumination. He sat down and unzipped his battered, mock crocodile-skinned, school pencil case containing needle sharp pencils; similarly tipped coloured pencils for diagrams and maps, plus pencil sharpener and rubber essential for repairing bluntness and amending cock-ups; a six-inch ruler; a compass and protractor for drawing perfectly circular pie charts and the division thereof; and spare cartridges for his fountain pen (no biros allowed). Then the waiting for the fateful words: 'Ladies and Gentleman entered in the Honour School of Geography. Paper One will commence as soon as papers are delivered and I start the clock. You will have three hours. Raise your hand should you require further paper and an invigilator will attend to you.' Some candidates, Mick conjectured, might be in urgent need of lavatory paper once they turn over the question paper. He prayed he'd not be one of them.

Three hours passed as Mick had envisaged. His whirring brain and flashing pen were not always in harmony but he completed his four essays on Geomorphology with neither excessive strain nor concern. He'd followed the 'Clifton Plan'. The critical factor in the Plan was discipline. Four essays of 45 minutes apiece; the last five minutes devoted to reading through what you'd written to check for any monumental errors. Four essays ensured four marks. Producing just two essays by spending 90 minutes on each would only yield two marks, no matter how brilliant they were. As for question selection: ignore their numerical order on the question paper. Answer your two best questions second and third when the juices are in full flow to maximise chances of a good mark; answer your third choice first to warm up; and leave your worst nightmare till last, in the hope that, having seen over two hours action, your thought processes should be sufficiently well-oiled by then to make the best of a bad lot (and if you do run out of time losing marks on the poorest essay won't harm your overall percentage so much). It all sounded logical to Mick. And at this stage he wasn't about to ignore the advice of the academic guru who'd done more than most to get him here.

The ritual remained the same Thursday afternoon and on Friday – as did the ordeal. Papers on Britain and France passed in a blizzard of acres and hectares, tons and tonnes. Only Saturday morning's special subject paper in Historical Geography gifted any slight relief. Mick was relieved, positively overjoyed in fact, at the prospect of writing about Britain's agrarian and industrial revolutions following 12 hours testing his knowledge of subjects that meant zilch to him. He was so enthused that on Saturday morning he rose 30 minutes earlier in order to treat himself to a fry-up breakfast of sausage, bacon, fried egg and baked beans at George's Cafe in the Covered Market.

After the last sentence was dotted and the invigilators had collected all the scripts the prisoners were released on bail to re-appear at 2pm. Mick negotiated the wide, sweeping staircase leading to the vestibule as quickly and as nimbly as he could given the pack's urgency to exit this Bastille of a building. He needed some form of escape. He headed straight for the welcoming, alcoholic arms of the Eastgate Hotel next door.

There was no rule against imbibing between exams and Mick elbowed a path through a clientele in which 'Townies' were comfortably outnumbered by ebullient figures clad in *subfusc* smoking restorative cigarettes and alcohol as if there was no examination that year let alone that afternoon. He placed his mortar board on the bar and ordered a pint of Harp lager. As he took a long, satisfying draught he felt a tap on his shoulder. He turned to see the incomparable face of Sam Owens.

'Surprise!' she trilled.

'You can say that again!' His face suddenly changed from dark to light: God had dispatched this angel to say He loved him after all. 'I thought you were in France?'

'I was, but as you can see, not anymore! I spotted you straight away, even from the rear. There's no forgetting those thighs!'

'What on earth are you doing here of a Saturday lunchtime?'

A broad grin almost cleaved her beautiful face in two. 'Get ready for this,' she warned. 'I've just got married!'

Mick didn't know whether, in another of his father's phrases, *to have a shit, shave or a wash-down.*

'I need a seat,' he blustered, and guided Sam toward a corner of the bar where there was an empty table.

'You'd better repeat that because I'm not sure I heard you properly. I think you said you're married!'

'I am! This very morning in the registry office!'

She held up her hand for Mick's inspection and he saw the simple band of gold nestling beside an engagement ring sporting a gemstone matching her eyes.

'To whom?' gulped Mick. 'How?'

'His name's Larry. He's American. And he's a lawyer. We met in France.'

The final wall protecting Mick's world crashed to the ground as surely as Jericho's. He felt as if every cubic inch of smoke in the bar was being drawn his way intent on choking him to death. He took a long draught of Harp as much to steady his nerves as the need to gather his thoughts that presently were scattered throughout the bar. 'How could you do this to me, on this of all days?' was the sentence forming in his brain. But articulating that wouldn't do on a girl's wedding day. Playing party-pooper would be the act of an insensitive cad.

'Well…congratulations!' he garbled.

'Thank you, kind sir!' said Sam, her slight look of apprehension instantly evanescing. 'The reception party is at the far end, in the alcove. Come and meet Larry. You'll love him! He's just over there!

Mick followed her eyes and a slight figure with long, dark curly hair and a day's stubble framing a hawk-like face came into view. He's not much to look at, thought Mick, but he's a Yank which makes him the sort of exotic creature always likely to ensnare Sam Owens. He knew meeting the man who'd nabbed the golden goose, his golden goose, was not someone with whom he wished to swap platitudes. 'I'd best not, I've an exam in a bit,' he said as convincingly as he could.

Sam's hand went to mouth. 'Oh, of course, I should've guessed. You're in *subfusc.* How stupid of me.'

'Yep, half-way through Finals. "Geographical Thought" this afternoon. Quite bizarre! You wouldn't think such a concept existed, would you! And I've somehow to cobble together four essays on the bloody subject!'

'Poor you!'

'Only time in my life I've worked on a Saturday afternoon! It's sacrosanct! Saturday afternoon is for playing sport or watching sport!' he moaned. 'Wait till you have to sit your Finals!'

A smugness came over her that Mick did not recognize. 'I shan't be taking Finals,' she giggled. 'I've left Ealing. We, my husband and I,' she added regally, 'are leaving tomorrow for the States.'

Mick's jaw would've hit the table had it not been wrapped around the rim of his glass in the process of downing another mouthful of lager. 'Good for you,' he heard himself saying, and trying hard to sound like he meant it.

'She snuggled closer to him. 'But what about you? What are your plans?'

'Nothing fixed in stone yet,' he replied with a shrug. 'A few options. Some irons in the fire.'

Sam sensed his uneasiness: she knew him well enough to recognize his discomfort. She sat back as her mood changed. 'I was so sorry to hear about your injury. My dad was watching the game…'

'Well, I never!'

'He is Welsh, after all, he follows rugby and he quite likes telling his drinking mates at the Wellington the Oxford scrum-half is a friend of his daughter.'

Mick manufactured a cheesy grin.

'And he said how well you were playing before you got injured.'

Mick pulled a face. 'Whatever will be, will be…'

'Dad said he was sure you'd have played against Cambridge otherwise.'

'Maybe, maybe not. Funny things happen when it comes to selecting the team for the Varsity Match. A player might feature in every other game but if he didn't suit the tactics the skipper thought were needed to beat Cambridge he could miss out.'

'Oh, I see. But surely if you've played all those games you should be awarded a Blue? It's the equivalent of Colours, isn't it?'

'Yes, it is. But, unfortunately for the likes of me, only the 15 who play in the Varsity Match receive their Blue…'

'That's so unfair!'

'That's reality!'

Sam was momentarily lost for words. She shook her head instead. And then she touched his arm which he took to be a request for him to continue.

'So, it's no Blue for me and a degree in a subject in which I've no interest whatsoever. Oxford's been rather a failure, don't you think?'

'You mustn't…'

'Think like that?'

'Hard not to, I'm afraid,' he said, hanging his head. 'It's been an utter waste of time. Three years flushed down the crapper.'

Sam placed a hand under his chin and tenderly encouraged it upward until their eyes met. A serene expression transformed her face, to Mick's eyes, into something vaguely beatific.

'Getting married doesn't change how I feel about you,' she said. 'I'm very fond of you…'

Mick lowered his eyes at the bland sentiment.

Sam read his mind immediately and sought a stronger word. 'I've so much affection for you,' she said, with emphasis.

'Just no chance of anything greater…'

'Had there been any chance of that, I'd never have married…'

'Of course,' snapped Mick, angry with himself for uttering something so pathetic.

Sam's hands moved to Mick's wrists. 'Get away, Mick' she said, with quiet authority. 'Get right away from Oxford. This place, the town, the University, holds too many bad memories for you, too much pain. It's eaten you up! It's still eating you up! It may be on the inside but I can see it from the outside. Believe me. Leave! Before Town and Gown finally consume every inch of the real you, the Mick Bernard I've come to know. Mark my words, Mick: if you don't, Oxford will chew you up and spit you out.'

Mick sensed his throat tightening: this was the second time she'd tendered this advice. She was dead right, as she invariably was. Sam smiled, and nodded acceptance of her assertion on his behalf. Then she got up. 'I'd better get back to the party. They'll be wondering where I've got to. After all, I am the bride!'

Sam took two steps, and paused. Then she blew Mick a kiss and disappeared from view, and out of his life. He knew it was Sam's destiny to feel the wind beneath her wings and let her blend of brain and beauty cast its spell on a grander scale. She departed with his best wishes. But the voice in his head kept repeating: if only she was leaving with me.

After draining the dregs of his pint, Mick elbowed a path through the crowded bar and out onto the street. He stopped to fill his lungs with clean air; a blast of oxygen blew through the corridors of his brain, dispersing the cobwebs of despair and the strands of regret. Yet he was forced to admit Sam's news had lengthened last Sunday's column of negatives. Too many things were going wrong. *Release Me! Set Me Free!*

Mick looked to the heavens for what seemed an eternity to him but was just a few seconds. He glanced toward the Examination Schools on his left where he was due at his desk in five minutes. He shifted his weight from foot to foot in rhythm with the mental tug of war raging inside his head. Then he turned and walked purposefully in the opposite direction toward Magdalen Bridge.

He got half-way across the bridge and halted. He went to the balustrade, removed his white bow tie and gown, stuffed them inside his mortar board and flung the bundle into the Cherwell. He watched the regalia of an Oxford student sink with a satisfying gurgle. All of a sudden he felt re-energized. And then Mick Bernard marched toward the Plain to the beat of his own drum, singing to the rhythm of his own song.

Printed in Great Britain
by Amazon

49603296R00165